MOONSTONE

Marilee Brothers

Smyrna, Georgia

Bell Bridge Books
PO BOX 67
Smyrna, GA 30081

Bell Bridge Books is an Imprint of BelleBooks, Inc.

ISBN: 978-0-9802453-4-9

Moonstone

Copyright 2008 by Marilee Brothers

Printed and bound in the United States of America.

We at BelleBooks enjoy hearing from readers. You can contact us at the address above or at BelleBooks@BelleBooks.com

Visit our websites,www.BelleBooks.com
and www.BellBridgeBooks.com.

10 9 8 7 6 5 4 3 2 1

Cover design: Debra Dixon

Cover photo:
        Girl - © diego cervo - Fotolia.com
        Moon - © myper - Fotolia.com
        Necklace - © Marie-france Bélanger - iStockphoto.com

Interior design: Linda Kichline

Prologue

I've been wondering . . . is there a normal way to become paranormal? Like, go to Google, type in "Make me magic," click on a website and wait for a list of rules to pop up? I really need a list of rules. How else can an almost fifteen-year-old girl living in Peacock Flats, Washington learn to deal with special powers? Here's how it started . . .

Chapter One

One minute, I was on a ten-foot ladder adjusting the TV antenna on the twenty-four-foot trailer behind Uncle Sid's house, where I lived with my mother, Faye. The next minute, I sailed off the ladder, grazed an electric fence and landed face down in a cow pie.

Swear to God.

Though groggy and hurting, I rolled onto my back. A window in the trailer cranked open and I heard my mother scream. "Allie! Ohmigod! Somebody call 911!"

I was surprised Faye managed to open the window. She'd spent most of the last two years in bed since, at age thirty one, she Retired From Life. But really, call 911? We had no phone and I was the only other person in the area. Who was she talking to? Blaster the bull? I smiled weakly at the thought of Blaster in a phone booth, punching in 911 with one gigantic hoof.

Okay, technically, I landed in a bull pie, not a cow pie. The mess dripping off my face was compliments of my Uncle Sid's prize bull, speaking of which . . .

It was then my wits returned. I felt the ground vibrate, heard the rumble of hooves. I reared up to see a half-ton cranky bull racing toward me, head down, mean little eyes fixed on my prone body.

Faye continued to scream shrilly. I moaned and crawled toward the fence, looking over my shoulder at Blaster who bore down on me like a runaway train. When I tried to stand, I slipped in the wet grass and landed on my belly. Oh God, he was just inches away. I wasn't going to make it! I rolled into a ball and screamed, "No, Blaster! Go back! Go back!"

Laying on the wet grass, trembling with terror, I watched as Blaster stopped on a dime, blew snot out of his flaring, black nostrils and released a thunderous blast of flatulence—that's what my teacher, Mrs. Burke, calls farting—and, of course, is the reason Uncle Sid named him Blaster.

"Back off, Blaster," I said between shallow, panicky breaths. "Good boy."

I hoped the "boy" comment wouldn't tick him off, what with his fully-developed manly-bull parts dangling in full view as I lay curled on the ground looking up. Yuck!

Suddenly my vision narrowed and grew dark around the edges. It was like looking down a long tunnel with Blaster front and center, bathed in light. A loud buzzing filled my head. The next moment, Blaster took a tentative step backward, then another, walking slowly, at first, then gradually picking up speed until he was trotting briskly backwards like a video tape on slow rewind.

Mesmerized by the sight, I sat up and watched Blaster's bizarre retreat back through the tunnel. At that precise moment, I should have known something strange was going on. But hey, I was a little busy trying to save my life.

As I crawled under the fence, my vision returned to normal and the buzzing faded away. I stood and swiped a hand across my sweaty face. At least, I *thought* it was sweat until a trickle of blood dripped off the end of my nose. Surprised because I felt no pain, I touched my face and found the blood was oozing from a puncture wound in the center of my forehead.

I glanced up at Faye, who continued to peer out the trailer window, her pale face framed in a halo of wispy blond curls, her eyes wide with shock. She inhaled sharply, and I knew another scream was on its way. I held up a hand. "Come on, Faye, no more screaming. You're making my head hurt."

"But, but, the bull . . . he, he . . . " Faye began.

I wasn't ready to go there. "I know, I know."

I staggered around the end of the trailer and banged through the door. Two giant steps to the bathroom. I shucked off my clothes and stepped into the tiny shower.

"You okay, Allie?" Faye asked.

She peered through the open doorway, paler than usual. Her right hand clutched the locket that held my baby picture, the one that makes me look like an angry old man. The only time she took it off was to shower.

"I'll live," I muttered.

"Weird, huh? Blaster, I mean. I heard you yell at him. Bulls don't run backward, Allie."

When I didn't answer—what could I say?—she waited a beat. "Use soap on your forehead. Did it stop bleeding?"

"Yes, Mother." I reached over and slid the door shut.

Deep sigh. "You don't have to be snotty. I told you to be careful."

The TV blared suddenly. Oprah. Not that I'm a spiteful person, but I blamed Oprah for my swan dive off the ladder. Late last night, a sudden gust of wind knocked over our TV antenna. When I got home from school today, Faye insisted she had to watch Oprah. Like that was going to change her life. I finally got tired of hearing about it and borrowed Uncle Sid's ladder. Moral of story: Never wear flip flops on an aluminum ladder.

I turned on the water, stood under the weak stream and checked for damage. Other than a slight tingling in my arms and legs and the hole in my head, I seemed okay.

I toweled off my curly, dark-brown hair and pulled it back into a messy ponytail. When I wiped the steam off the mirror, I saw a dark-red, dime-sized circle in the exact center of my forehead. I touched it gingerly, expecting it to hurt. But it didn't. Instead, a weird sensation shot through my head, like my brain was hooked up to Dr. Frankenstein's machine, that thing he used to make his monster come alive. I must have given a little yip of surprise because Faye said again, "You okay, Allie?"

"I'm fine," I said. "Just a little sore."

"Did you check the mail?"

"The first's not until Friday. Today's the twenty-ninth," I said.

"Sometimes it comes early."

The welfare check *never* came early. The state of Washington was very reliable when it came to issuing checks.

"Yeah, okay," I said, not wanting to burst her bubble.

Wrapped in the towel, I took two steps into the living room/kitchen, reached under the table and pulled out the plastic crate containing my clean clothes. I dug around and found clean underwear, a tee shirt and a pair of cut-off shorts.

I slipped into my bra, once again thinking how cool it was I finally needed one. Though I hoped for peaches, I'd managed only to grow a pair of breasts roughly the size and shape of apricots. Oh, well, apricots are better than cherries. Our valley is called "The fruit bowl of the nation," hence, my obsession with naming body parts after produce.

I slipped into my treacherous flip flops, headed out the door and spotted Uncle Sid darting behind the barn. Faye says Uncle Sid is not a people person but I thought he was just trying to avoid Aunt Sandra and her constant nagging. That woman's voice could make a corpse sit up and beg for mercy.

I trotted down the driveway, stopping suddenly when I spotted a pair of denim-clad legs sticking out from under the Jeep Wrangler parked next to Uncle Sid's house. Legs that belonged to Matt, Uncle Sid's son and older brother to spoiled brat, Tiffany.

How can one kid—Tiffany—be so annoying and the other—Matt—so totally hot? I tried to avoid Matt because of the way I got when I'm around him. Though I'm normally loquacious (last Wednesday's vocabulary word that I copied and vowed to use at least three times,) one look at Matt and I lost my power of speech. My jaw dropped and my mouth went dry. There's just something about him—sleepy blue eyes, light brown hair that usually needs combing, a crooked grin and a sculpted, rock-hard body.

It wasn't some creepy, incestuous thing since Matt and I weren't real cousins. Sid was Faye's step brother. Nope, we didn't have the same blood coursing through our veins. Matt's was probably blue, while mine came from the mystery man Faye refused to talk about.

I tiptoed past the Jeep to spare myself further humiliation. I'd almost made it when he rolled out on one of those sled thingies and grabbed my ankle. "Hey, kid, how ya doin'?"

The warmth of his hand against my bare skin turned my normally frisky brain cells to mush. Sure enough, my lower jaw was heading south. "Uh, just great, Matt," I said, averting my eyes and licking my suddenly parched lips.

He released my ankle and stood up. "Good," he said. "Your mom still got that . . . whaddaya call it?"

"Fibromyalgia." As I said the word, I felt my upper lip curl in a sneer. "So she says."

"She getting better?"

"She's trying to get social security benefits, you know, the one for disability."

The words tasted bitter in my mouth.

"Oh yeah," Matt said. "I saw Big Ed's car here the other night. He's her lawyer, right?"

My hands automatically curled into fists. I narrowed my eyes and studied Matt's face, looking for a smirk or maybe a suggestive wink. Even though I didn't want to punch him, I could and I would. I knew how to punch. Faye had made sure.

No problem. He'd moved on. Wonder of wonders, he was looking at me. I mean, really looking at me with those sexy blue eyes. His gaze lingered for a long moment on my chest. Whoa! Was he checking out my 'cots? I was suddenly aware I'd outgrown my shorts and tee shirt. Not knowing what else to do, I shoved my hands into the pocket of my cut-offs and took a step back.

"Well, hey, I gotta go check the mail. See ya, Matt."

His voice followed me as I headed down the driveway. "Hey, kid. If you ever need a ride somewhere, let me know. I got the Jeep running real good."

Because my mouth had fallen open once again, I settled for a casual wave of acknowledgement even though I wanted to pump a fist in the air and scream, "YES!"

As I trotted to the mailbox, the late April sunlight warm on my shoulders, I pondered this strange turn of events. Even though he called me "kid," clearly Matt had noticed a couple of new bulges on my formerly stick-like body. Hmmm. Had my tumble off the ladder, followed by the electric fence zapping, released some sort of male-attracting hormone?

In spite of my mini-triumph, Matt-wise, a dull headache began to throb painfully at the back of my skull. I opened the mailbox and, as predicted, Faye's check had not arrived. There was, however, a familiar tan envelope from the Social Security Office of Adjudication and Review. Probably another form for Faye to fill out asking questions like, "Are you able to push a grocery cart?" And, "Can you walk up a flight of stairs?" Questions Faye had already answered "No" and "No."

When I handed her the envelope, Faye sighed and dropped it, unopened, onto the pile of similar tan envelopes stacked between the bed and wall.

"Big Ed's coming tomorrow. I'll let him deal with it." She looked pointedly at her watch.

I took the hint. It was time for Faye's nightly ritual, two slices of peanut butter toast and two cans of Busch Light. The menu varied only on Thursday night. Big Ed night. He always brought burgers, fries and a fifth of Stoli. Not that I'm around on Thursdays. No way. But, when I come home on Friday, the place smells of grease and vodka.

Let me make this crystal clear. Big Ed was Faye's lawyer, not her boyfriend. That was what Faye said. He'd been working day and night on her case for two years. That was what Big Ed said. Me? I had my doubts.

Later that night, I heard the sound of Faye's rhythmic breathing and tiptoed back to the bedroom. I gathered up the empties and the plate littered with peanut butter-smeared crusts and tossed them in the garbage.

Tomorrow was Thursday, Big Ed night. I'd be staying with Kizzy Lovell, the town witch. That was what a lot of kids called her. Since I wouldn't be home until Friday, I made sure I had clean underwear in my backpack.

As the evening wore on, my headache grew steadily worse. At ten, I turned out the light. I pulled the curtains back so I could see the night sky, a brilliant canopy of far-flung stars and a full-faced moon. I held my hand up to the window. Bathed in moonlight, my palm looked washed in silver, its tell-tale lines carved in dark relief by the unknown maker of my fate. I thought about the times Kizzy studied the lines on my palm and said, "You're a special girl, Alfrieda. Like it or not, you have the Gift."

Every time I'd say, "What gift?" Kizzy would smile mysteriously and say, "You'll see," which really irritated me because, clearly, the only gift I had was the ability to get all-A's on my report card. Even that wasn't a gift, since I hated Algebra and had to work my butt off.

I had no sooner wrapped up in my faded pink quilt and snuggled into the couch bed when I remembered the aspirin and glass of water I'd placed by the bathroom sink before I brushed my teeth. I groaned and switched on the light. The bathroom was only a few steps away. But in my present state—cotton-mouthed and head pounding with pain—the distance seemed as vast as the Sahara Desert. I swung my feet to the floor and turned my head slowly toward the bathroom. I could see the glass of water perched on the counter like it was taunting me, "Come and get me, Allie."

I reached out a hand, thinking, *It would be a whole lot easier if you came to me*, and it happened again. The whole dark-around-the-edges, tunnel-vision, buzzing-in-the-head thing. The glass teetered back and forth, danced a little jig across the counter and shot into the air for a moment before it slammed onto the floor and shattered into about a jillion pieces.

"What the hell's going on, Allie?"

I looked up to see my mother standing in the narrow hallway. My hand, still extended toward the glass that wasn't there, shook violently. "I dropped it. That's all," I said. "Go back to bed. I'll clean it up."

Faye's eyes narrowed in suspicion but finally, she turned and trudged back to the bedroom. When I opened the door and stepped outside to fetch the broom, I was greeted by a symphony of night music. Strangely, the pain in my head was gone. The soft spring air was alive with a chorus of crickets backed by a full orchestra of spring peepers, their mating songs accompanied by the tinkle of wind chimes.

But, hold on. We didn't have wind chimes. We'd never had wind chimes. I walked to the back of the trailer and stared up at the gnarled old apple tree next to Blaster's pasture. Nudged by a gentle breeze, long silver tubes bumped together, creating a melody with subtle variations as the air around them ebbed and flowed. It was stabilized by a dangling iridescent glass ball whose surface caught and held the moonlight.

Must be some prank of Matt's. Vowing I'd figure it out in the morning, I grabbed the broom, opened the door and froze. A woman sat on my couch bed. A woman with flowers in her long, dark hair, wearing a pink-and-yellow, tie-dye dress embellished with a blazing purple sun. A woman, smoking what looked and smelled like weed. I opened my mouth, preparing to scream so loudly and shrilly the shards of glass on the floor would shatter into even smaller pieces.

The woman said, "Hi. I'm Trilby, your spirit guide. Guess what? You just passed your first test. Isn't that groovy?"

Chapter Two

I stepped inside and whisper-screamed, "Are you nuts?" while fanning the air and glancing back toward Faye's bedroom. Thank God, the door was closed. "Out!" I said. "I don't care who you are. Get out!"

All I could think was, *Grounded for Life.* Trust me, it's no picnic being grounded in a twenty-four-foot trailer.

Trilby giggled. "Oh, you're worried about Mom. It's okay. She can't hear me." One of her fingers shot up. "Or see me." A second finger joined the first. She got through "smell" and "taste" then stopped, looking puzzled. "I know there're five senses but I'll be damned if I can remember the last one."

"Who cares?" I jerked my thumb toward the door. "Outside," I ordered. My voice was shrill with panic.

"Allie," my mother called. "Who are you talking to?"

My heart leaped into my throat then settled in my chest, banging so loudly I was sure Faye would hear it and ask who was playing the drums. I flapped my hands at Trilby, frantic to be rid of her. She blew out air in disgust and rolled her eyes but rose from the couch and, in a blur of color and a blast of frigid air, disappeared.

"Nobody's here, Faye," I said. "I have to memorize something for school. I'll go outside." I backed out the door reciting, "We, the people of the United States, in order to form a more perfect union . . . "

"Cool, huh?" Trilby said from directly behind me.

I whirled around. "This isn't happening! I'm sound asleep in the middle of some stupid dream."

But then Trilby fluttered her fingers in my face—and I do mean *inside my face*—and said, "Neato. I didn't know I could do that." She passed her hands through my body. "Wooooo! Are you scared?"

I jumped back, trying to wrap my mind around the fact I wasn't dealing with a flesh-and-blood woman, a living, breathing human being, but an apparition, a spook, a wraith. Swear to God, Trilby was a ghost! Not a particularly scary ghost, but most definitely a ghost.

I said the first thing that popped into my mind. "Scared? I don't think so! Look at you! Your lipstick is on crooked, your eyes are bloodshot, you're higher than a kite. And that 'wooooo' thing? It went out about a hundred years ago."

"That's just mean," Trilby said, pouting. She plopped down in a lawn chair. "I'm trying to help you and you're messing with my groove."

I sat in the other chair and pointed at the wind chimes. "Yours?"

"Yeah, my signature touch. Nice, huh?"

I sucked in a shaky breath. "This is probably a dream, but why are you here? What do you mean, I passed the first test?"

Trilby straightened her shell-and-bead necklace then touched the peace sign painted on her wooden bracelet. She leaned toward me and narrowed her eyes. "You're my ticket out of a bad scene. If we do this right, I get to go up there."

She pointed at the sky.

I sniffed in disapproval. "Smoking weed can't help."

"Listen, little girl. I've been stuck in the SeaTac airport since 1971. Talk about hell!"

My mind swam with confusion. "SeaTac?"

"Yeah. Some of us aren't quite ready for the big crash pad in the sky. So we get to hang out at Concourse A,

watch the planes take off, sleep on the floor, drink coffee
and wait for 'the call.' You're it. So, cooperate, okay?"

"Focus, Trilby. What test did I pass?"

"At journey's end I lie close to her heart, the maid who
is strong of mind," she quoted. "You know, as per the
prophecy. That one."

Trilby had to be in the middle of some sort of drug-
induced hallucination. I wasn't sure how to deal with her
but then, I reasoned, she *was* a ghost, so maybe this was
typical ghostly behavior. I needed more information. "I
have no idea what you're talking about."

"Hmmm," she said, rolling her eyes heavenward. "I'm
trying to remember my instructions. Today's the thirtieth.
Right?"

"No," I said. "It's the twenty-ninth. At least for another
hour."

"Oh, damn, my timing sucks! You don't have it yet,"
Trilby said. "I blew it."

Her lower lip quivered and she blinked hard to hold
back tears.

Chagrined, I thought about poor Trilby, trapped forever
in SeaTac Airport, Concourse A. I'd never been there but
it didn't sound much like paradise.

"Okay, so it's the wrong day," I said. "Maybe that's not
so bad."

She brightened. "Do you really think so?"

"Tell me everything you remember about your
instructions, starting with this thing I'm supposed to have."

Trilby started to answer then pinched her lips together
and shook her head. "No," she said. "If you don't have it,
that part will have to wait."

"Have what?"

She fiddled with her beads. "I said, IT WILL HAVE
TO WAIT!"

"Okay, okay." I cast a nervous glance toward Faye's

window. "You don't have to shout. Just tell me what you can."

"You have the sign on your palm, right?"

I thrust out a hand, palm up, and turned it toward Uncle Sid's yard light. She leaned toward me and traced a finger across my palm. Her feathery touch left a trail of light, and I gasped in surprise.

"Yep, you've got it." She touched the tiny red mark in the middle of my forehead. "And you had an unusual experience today."

I told her about Blaster running backward and the flying glass.

"All right!" She pumped a fist in the air. "I'm not totally screwed. TKP. Telekinetic power. The ability to move things with your mind. You did it. You're 'the maid whose mind is strong.' Oh, this is so groovy!"

I still didn't understand. "What's next?"

"Oh, it gets much better. See ya around, kid. I gotta get back."

"Wait! Wait!" I said as she started to fade away. "Next time write the instructions down. That's what Mrs. Burke makes us do in English class."

Too late. Trilby was gone.

Chapter Three

The next morning I stood out by the road with Mercedes and Manny Trujillo, waiting for the school bus and thinking about Trilby and wondering if I'd dreamed her. The wind chimes were gone. I checked. Maybe she took them with her to wherever . . . SeaTac airport if you can believe a ghost. Or, maybe it didn't happen at all.

I almost told Manny and Mercedes about the night. But they believed in things like vampires, werewolves and wendigos, whatever those were. Manny and Mercedes thought that stuff came from the devil. I was afraid they'd think the devil had paid me a visit, and they'd stop hanging out with me. I didn't have *that* many friends.

I had to talk to Kizzy and find out what the heck was happening to me. Was this the Gift she kept talking about? And, more importantly, could I get rid of it? Maybe there's an exchange counter where a person can go to return special gifts, like I returned the hideous pea-green stocking cap Aunt Sandra gave me for Christmas.

Before I could get answers to my questions, I was faced with a more pressing problem. Namely, protecting Mercedes and Manny from our arch enemy, Cory Philpott. The Trujillos lived on Uncle Sid's property. Their mother, Juanita, cleaned Aunt Sandra's house and Pedro, their dad, ran the Mexican crews that did all the hard work in the orchard.

Manny and Mercedes were way too nice. With seven

kids and two parents sharing a three-bedroom house, it seemed like they'd know how to defend themselves. They didn't. Apparently that was my job. Cory Philpott lived to torment Manny and Mercedes.

At exactly 7:45, the bus rolled to a stop and the doors opened with a groan and hiss. We formed a single-file line. It was always the same. First me, then Mercedes, then Manny.

Patti, our vertically-challenged bus driver, used a booster cushion, had big hair, dagger-like fingernails, and a deep, raspy voice due to the pack of unfiltered Camels tucked in her shirt pocket. She greeted us as she always did, with high fives and our special name.

"Hey, Gorgeous Green-eyed Girl," she said to me. (Sometimes just "G.")

"Sweet Cheeks!" she exclaimed as Mercedes plodded up the steps.

"There's my Stud Muffin," she said to Manny, whose moon face split in a broad grin.

We made our way down the aisle as Patti ground the gears and lurched out onto the road. As usual, the only seats left were next to Cory Philpott, whose evil, troll face brightened as we approached. I gave him a squinty-eyed glare as Mercedes slipped into her spot next to the window.

He looked away from me and hissed at Manny, "Hey, beaner boy. Your backpack full of tacos? Do you share with your big-ass beaner sister?"

Okay, here's the deal. I was fed up with Cory's bullying. More importantly, I had a plan. Last fall, our science teacher trapped a black widow spider in a fruit jar. He passed the jar up and down the rows so we could get a good look at its shiny black body, long, long legs and the red hour glass on its belly. When I turned around to hand the jar to Cory, he levitated about a foot in the air. Beads of sweat popped out on his forehead, and his hands were shaking. He may have even wet his pants. I didn't check, for obvious reasons.

What good is secret information if you don't use it? The time had come. I rose in my seat, my eyes wide with horror as I gazed at the top of Cory's head. "Oh, my God! That's the biggest black widow spider I've ever seen. Cory! *It's in your hair!*"

Ashen-faced, Cory screamed like a little girl and scrambled into the aisle, jumping up and down and clawing at his hair with both hands. "Is it gone? Is it gone?" he yelled.

After a brief flurry of excitement—most of the kids were still half asleep—somebody from the rear of the bus spoke up. "Come on, dude, she's playin' ya. There's no spider."

Patti glanced over her shoulder. "This isn't even black widow season. Get your ass in the seat!"

Hoots of laughter echoed through the bus. Cory collapsed back into his seat then turned to glare at me. He'd pretty much stopped harassing me after I punched him in the face the past January, when he said something gross about Faye and Big Ed.

Mercedes leaned close and murmured, "Cool. I told you he was into you."

She thought Cory had a secret crush on me, that the purpose of his bullying was to get my attention. Mercedes was a total drama queen who saw unrequited love in the strangest of circumstances. She taped every episode of *General Hospital* and watched them on Saturdays.

"As if," I said in Mercedes-speak.

The bus pulled up in front of our pathetic excuse for a high school. John J. Peacock H.S. had exactly eighty-seven students in four grades. The Peacock school district was like a rich family's poor relative—sorta like Faye and me—jammed between two prosperous districts to the north and south.

All the rich kids who lived in Peacock Heights, located on the hills above Peacock Flats, went to Hilltop Christian School. They wore WWJD buttons—What Would Jesus Do—and the teenagers got blitzed every weekend. I don't think Jesus was a big party guy, but then again, he did turn water into wine. Even though Matt and Tiffany lived in the flats, they went to Hilltop. Aunt Sandra wouldn't allow them to go to public school.

After Patti's usual send-off—"You blockheads behave. See ya later, taters—" we poured out of the bus and into the old brick building, down a narrow hallway and through the ancient cafeteria, whose support beams were wrapped in thick insulation to keep the asbestos from seeping out. At least that's what our principal, Mr. Hostetler told us.

I had the perfect opportunity in English class to test out my new super powers. I sat at a perfectly level table with the perfect cylinder, a number two pencil. Could I make it roll horizontally across the desk? I glanced around to make sure nobody was watching before I tried. And tried. And tried. Couldn't do it. All right! Goodbye, super powers. Or maybe my mind was too cluttered with Mrs. Burke's multi-cultural lesson of the week.

Mrs. Burke was big on us learning about other cultures. Each week, we had a foreign phrase to use. This week it was French.

"When I call your name," she announced on Monday, "you will respond by saying, "*C,,est moi, Madame Burke,*" which she told us meant, "It is me."

Sometimes she had to call roll three or four times before everyone cooperated. Today was no exception. Cory Philpott, still surly from our encounter on the bus, kept mumbling, "This is bullshit," under his breath and refused to answer.

Finally, Junior Martinez, who's two years older than the rest us due to his unfortunate incarceration for carving up a rival gang member, turned around and told Cory, "Say it, you little piss pot."

He did.

A lot of the girls at Peacock H.S. had the hots for Junior. He had smooth, olive skin, a deep dimple in his right cheek, and he drove a low rider to school. Rumor had it he was trying to nail every girl in the freshman class and he was right on schedule. Except for me, of course. Faye may not be Mother of the Year, but she told me everything I needed to know about sex. Sometimes more than I wanted to know. Manny saw Junior pushing a kid in a stroller, so apparently he's already reproduced. Extremely uncool.

After I punched Cory—and got kicked out of school for a week—Junior started calling me "Home Girl" and "One Punch." Not that I would ever be part of a gang but it doesn't hurt to have Junior on your side. Mercedes, of course, saw it differently.

"Ohmigod!" she exclaimed. "Junior totally likes you."

After school I stayed on the bus when Manny and Mercedes got off. When Patti stopped in front of Kizzy's house, Cory just had to get in one last shot.

"Oooo, you're staying with the witch tonight. You gonna boil up a couple of little kids?"

I slung my back pack over one shoulder and started down the steps before I answered, "Nope, but we sure could use a big old hunk of white meat. Want to stop over later?"

"Good one, G," Patti said. "That boy never learns."

"Pick me up here tomorrow, okay?"

"Damn straight," she said with a jaunty wave.

The doors slid shut and the big tires spit gravel as Patti tromped on the gas pedal.

As I approached Kizzy's house, I felt my heart beat a little faster. The house could barely be seen from the road. It was hidden behind a humungous hedge that ran all the way around her property. The only way to get in was through the iron gate set in middle of the hedge. I never approached the gate straight on. I cut over to the hedge and sneaked up on it because of the eye. The gate had this spooky eye painted on it. Swear to God, no matter how hard I tried to avoid the eye, it watched me, its glaring black pupil tracking my every move. A falcon's eye, Kizzy told me. A symbol used to ward off evil.

In spite of what Cory said, Kizzy was not a witch. She was a Romany gypsy, and apparently there was a difference. Who knew?

With an involuntary shiver, I averted my gaze from the eye, slipped through the gate and trotted down the walk toward the hulking, two-story house. The porch, with its overhanging roof, wrapped all the way around both sides of the house. A *veranda*, Kizzy called it.

"Alfrieda, you're here!"

Kizzy stood at the top of the stairs and held out her arms. She was the only person who called me by my hideous real name. Thanks to Claude, Faye's dad, I was given the name Alfrieda Carlotta Emerson. Faye ran away from home at seventeen. A year later, stuck in the hospital with a baby she didn't want (me) and no visible means of support, she struck a deal with Claude. In exchange for paying the hospital bill, he got to name me after his beloved, long-dead mother, Alfrieda Carlotta Emerson the First.

"Hey, Kizzy!" I slipped off my back pack and stepped into her embrace. She smelled of incense, lavender and Virginia Slims. Not that I'm a fashion expert but Kizzy always looked like she was dressed for a photo shoot in case a photographer from *Vogue* magazine was hanging around Peacock Flats.

Today, she wore a silk, turquoise dress the same color as her eyes. Her long, dark braid, sprinkled with gray, was draped over one shoulder. Three silver bangle bracelets encircled each wrist. Silver hoops hung from her ears. She'd replaced the rune stone she usually wore around her neck with a pale blue gemstone in an ornate silver setting. The stone was the size of a large marble. A shimmer of light danced on its surface. Strangely, I felt a strong need to reach out, touch it, hold it in my hand and stroke its glistening surface. I clasped my hands together tightly to resist the urge.

Kizzy studied my face then gently touched the mark in the middle of my forehead with a manicured fingernail. "Ah, I see the third eye has awakened. Come. Sit"

She led me to the porch swing.

Okay, sometimes Kizzy creeped me out. Wasn't it bad enough I lived in a travel trailer and wore clothes from a thrift shop? I mean, nothing screamed "Loser," like a third eye popping out in the middle of your forehead. I rolled my eyes in disgust.

"Should I start wearing bangs?"

Kizzy's tinkling laughter reassured me. "It's not a real eye, Alfrieda. The third eye is located deep within the brain. It's called 'the seat of the soul,' the link between the physical and spiritual worlds. Tell me what happened."

I took a deep breath and the words tumbled out. The only thing I held back was my visit from Trilby. When I told her about Blaster and the glass, I watched Kizzy's face carefully, looking for something negative, maybe a flicker of amusement or doubt. Instead, she clapped her hands in delight. Her clear, turquoise eyes danced with excitement.

"Oh, but that's wonderful! Don't you see?" Once again, she reached out and touched the tiny mark in the middle of my forehead. "You hit your head in the exact spot where the third eye is located. And the headache you had? The awakening of the third eye causes pressure at the base of the brain. It's all as it is supposed to be, darling girl."

Impulsively, she drew me in for another hug. Normally, I'm not into touchy-feely stuff, but as Kizzy stroked my hair and patted my back, I felt hot tears stinging my eyes. When there's nobody to talk to, things build up in your mind until you feel like your brain will explode. I mean, what do you do with all that stuff? It bounces around in your head and makes you crazy. In spite of the whole "third eye" thing, at least one person thought I was okay.

"What about the electric fence?" My voice came out muffled, since I was still pressed against the front of Kizzy's silk dress.

She released me and, without thought, I took hold of the gleaming stone that hung around her neck. It felt warm in my hand. "The jolt of electricity in combination with the bump on your head probably gave you a jump-start, so to speak."

I giggled and stroked the smooth blue stone.

She tapped a fingernail against her front tooth, something she did when she was deep in thought. "Hmm, yes, I'm sure of it. The telekinetic power—when you made the bull run backward —was a manifestation of the two phenomena working together. And the buzzing sound and tunnel vision? It's called an *aura*."

"But I can't do it anymore," I said. "I tried in English class. I couldn't even move a pencil." I added hastily, "Not that I want to."

"You weren't motivated," Kizzy said. "The power will return."

The sun slipped beneath the veranda's overhanging roof. I held the pendant to the light and gasped as sunlight sparkled and danced on its opalescent surface. "It's beautiful," I said. "What do you call it?"

"A moonstone," Kizzy said. "It was my mother's. Her name was Magda." She leaned forward and looked deep into my eyes. "What do you see when you look at this house? When you see the way I live?"

Whoa, was there a right answer here? I loved Kizzy for the good person she was. But I was pretty sure her question wasn't about that. I remembered my mother saying, "Look at that house! She has people to drive her around, cook for her, clean for her. Where do you get dough like that?"

"Well," I said, clearing my throat and looking away. "You seem to be pretty rich."

"Exactly!" Kizzy's eyes filled with tears. She dug around in the pocket of her dress and pulled out a tissue. She dabbed at her eyes. "But my mother was the saddest person I've ever known. She said it was because of the moonstone."

I dropped it like it was a burning ember. "Why?"

Kizzy shrugged. "She claimed she was being punished for misusing its power."

Oh great, I thought, looking at the pendant. *More magic B.S.*

"She wanted more children, but my father died when I was four. It was just the two of us in that big house in Seattle, surrounded by riches my mother could not enjoy."

"How did she misuse the moonstone?"

"She said she'd done something shameful, that she'd been greedy. She blamed herself for my father's death. Somehow, in her mind, it was all connected. The moonstone, the money, her loneliness."

"That's all she told you?"

Kizzy nodded. "I didn't know about the moonstone until Mother was dying. She told me to keep it safe until I met the right person."

"But what about your daughter? What about Carmel?"

Kizzy and her husband had adopted Carmel as a baby. The only thing she'd told me was she and her daughter weren't close and that Carmel hung out with a rough crowd. Kizzy always rolled her eyes and murmured, "Bad blood," when I mentioned her daughter. Today was no exception.

"Not Carmel," she said firmly. "She's not the right person."

"Right person for what?"

"Someone with the Gift. Someone pure of heart who would use it for good, not evil."

"Oh," I said. "Somebody like you."

Kizzy took my hand. "No, my dear. I don't have the Gift." She looked at my palm, traced the arc that circled what Kizzy called "the lunar mound," and ended below my little finger. "Mother had a line exactly like this, but you have something she didn't."

I rolled my eyes. Not this again. "Yeah, right," I mumbled and tried to pull my hand away.

Kizzy tightened her grip and pointed at a tiny constellation of whorls and hatch marks in the center of my lunar mound. "Look," she said. "A perfect star."

I jerked my hand away. "Everybody has that."

"No."

Kizzy showed me her palm. No star. No line. I shook my head in denial, suddenly uncomfortable with the whole spooky business.

Kizzy slipped the moonstone pendant from around her neck. Once again, she took my hand and turned it palm up. I knew what was coming and felt powerless to stop it. I watched, hardly daring to breathe. She dropped the moonstone onto my palm, the glistening silver chain pooling around it. She gently closed my fingers.

"And now, it's yours."

Chapter Four

I have a confession to make. The moonstone scared
the crap out of me! Come on, I'm just a kid, and it's not
like it had an owner's manual. What did Kizzy expect me
to do with a big old hunk of costume jewelry that
apparently ruined her mother's life? Rub the stone, twirl
around three times and wait for a genie to appear? Hang it
around my neck and wear it to John J. Peacock High School?
I don't think so!

Such were my thoughts all day Friday. That is, when I
could concentrate, what with visions of Carrie crucifying
her mother with kitchen tools slow-dancing in my head.
Yeah, my overnight stay at Kizzy's concluded with a viewing
of *Carrie*. The old Stephen King horror movie creeped me
out, but Kizzy said it was a crucial part of my education.

"It's important that you remember the consequences
of misusing power," Kizzy insisted when the movie ended.
She said that right before I took "the vow." Really. I know
it sounds hokey, but I placed one hand over my heart, raised
the other to heaven and promised to do no evil deeds. When
I asked her to explain—were the evil deeds I'd sworn not
to do related to my telekinetic power or the moonstone?—
she said, "All will be revealed at the proper time."

As for the moonstone, it wasn't a tough decision. I
needed no more magic in my life. When I got home from
school Friday, I stuffed it in a tube sock and stowed it in
the storage space under my sofa bed. Alongside the photo
of the man I believed to be my father, a photo I'd secretly
lifted from Faye's hiding place.

Since I've been old enough to notice the blank space on my birth certificate, I'd hammered away at Faye with variations on the "Who's my Daddy?" theme. Other than heaving a disgusted sigh and saying, "Give it a rest, Allie," Faye's lips remained sealed.

On Saturday morning, otherwise known as "dump day," Faye and I were chugging along, towing our house behind us, me behind the wheel, Faye in the passenger seat. I drove because Faye thought if anyone saw her driving, she'd be considered fit and healthy and God knows, the last thing she wanted to be was healthy. Her wrong-headed logic was about to bite us in our collective butts.

Since I didn't have a license, I got real uptight during the first part of the journey to Friendly Fred's Trailer Park, where we emptied our tanks every week. In order to access the sparsely-traveled back road, I had to drive the first mile on the two-lane highway that connected Peacock Flats with Peacock Heights.

I was doing fine until we happened upon Lewis and Clark, Uncle Sid's Labrador Retrievers, who love to roam. They turned up in places like the wading pool in the city park or the annual Fruit Bowl Parade. During last year's parade, they'd trotted happily alongside the royal float, a giant fruit bowl with Queen Peach, Princess Plum and Little Miss Maraschino Cherry atop. When the float stopped so the girls could throw candy, Lewis and Clark peed on the giant fake grapes and scarfed up all the candy.

I was almost to the turn-off when I spotted the dogs standing in a driveway barking furiously at some old guy trying to retrieve his newspaper. I couldn't just drive by and leave them. Could I?

I pulled over onto the narrow shoulder which left most of the truck on the highway. Didn't take me long to figure it out the problem. One of dogs had dropped a tennis ball on the driveway and the barking meant, "Aw, come on.

Throw it for us."

But Old Guy didn't get it. He was flapping his robe and yelling, "Shoo! Get out of here you bleep, bleep, bleep'n flea bags." He'd pause occasionally to call over his shoulder, "Vera, call 911! Tell 'em we've got mad dogs in our driveway!"

Fortunately, Vera was nowhere in sight. I climbed out of the truck. "Sir," I yelled. "They just want you to throw the ball. If you throw the ball, you can get your paper."

So he threw the ball. Out in the middle of the highway. Lewis and Clark bounded after it. Before long, they were playing keep-away on the yellow line. Cars from both directions screeched to a halt.

I grabbed Lewis by the collar and yelled at Faye, "I could use a little help here."

Faye slid down in her seat. "I can't. Somebody might see me."

"Oh, right," I muttered. "Government spies."

Faye's convinced the Feds had people lurking around Peacock Flats trying to catch her in the act of behaving like a normal person, so they could deny her application for disability.

With just one dog wrangler on the job, it was a good five minutes before I got them up and over the trailer hitch and loaded in the back of the pickup. Not an easy job, especially with the guy in the Lexus honking his horn, flipping me off and yelling, "MOVE THAT TRAILER!" Who says country folk are nicer than city folk?

Right away I knew I was busted, what with cell phones, Old Guy and very possibly Vera. With "MOVE THAT TRAILER" ringing in my ears, I vaulted into the truck and landed on top of Faye, who had moved to the driver's side during the round-up. She yelped in surprise as I scrambled over her to the passenger side. "Go! Go!" I screamed.

One of my legs was still draped across Faye's lap, the

other wrapped around the stick shift on the floor. From my semi-reclining position I yelled, "Clutch, hit the clutch," as I tried desperately to find first gear. I felt beads of perspiration popping out on my forehead while Faye muttered, "Oh God! Oh God!"

After a series of fits and starts we lurched out onto the highway with a parade of cars following us. We'd just ground into third gear when we heard the siren. Luckily, our turn-off was just ahead. Faye turned too fast then over-corrected. With the trailer fishtailing violently behind us, we skidded to a stop on the gravel road.

Faye and I peered in the oversized side mirrors and saw Deputy Richard Philpott marching toward us, one hand resting on his holstered gun. That's right, none other than evil troll Cory Philpott's father, Peacock Flats' only law enforcement officer. But really, was creating a traffic jam on a rural highway a shooting offense?

Faye pinched her cheeks and fluffed her hair. "Just stay cool, Allie. I'll handle this."

"Go for it," I said.

I felt a wave of relief. Faye, unlike me, knew how to flirt. First, the smile complete with deep dimples in both cheeks, then the sideways glance, her innocent blue eyes peeking shyly through long, fluttering lashes. If she wanted to, Faye could charm the devil himself. But, unlucky for us, we had Deputy Philpott to deal with, not the devil.

He was a little guy trying to look big with his Stetson hat and high-heeled cowboy boots. He wore mirrored sunglasses, which he totally didn't need because his enormous hat blocked the sun as well as most of his face. What with the big hat and sunglasses, the only facial features visible were a pair of dry lips and a pointy chin with a wispy beard.

I fought back a gurgle of inappropriate laughter. "*Baaa*, it's Billy Goat Gruff," I bleated softly in Faye's ear while we untangled our legs.

Through a fit of giggles Faye hissed, "Not a good time to be a smart ass, Allie."

"Morning, ladies. License and registration, please," he blared in a rich, deep voice so filled with authority that Faye and I sobered quickly.

He shifted a toothpick from one corner of his mouth to the other while Faye leaned into the open window and did her thing. While she chatted him up, I retrieved Faye's license from her purse and dug around in the glove compartment for the registration.

Deputy Philpott carefully examined the documents before handing them back to my mother. Then he thrust an arm through the window and pointed at me. "Now yours, missy," he boomed. "I have it on good authority you were behind the wheel when the unfortunate dog incident occurred in front of the mayor's house."

"Mayor's house," Faye repeated. "Great. Just great."

I startled babbling, "Well you see, sir, I usually don't drive but my mother's not feeling well and it's really important that we get to the trailer dump because if we don't, well, you know, things start backing up and . . . "

"Silence!" he barked.

I bit back a hysterical snicker. The Wizard of Oz was alive and well, right there in Peacock Flats.

Philpott stared at me for a long moment. "You're Allie, right? The girl who busted my son's nose?"

Faye spoke up quickly. "She was provoked."

Philpott said, "Yes, I'm aware of that." He paused and stroked his sparse chin whiskers. I held my breath, my heart in my throat. Finally he said, "Young lady, I'm familiar with your situation. You think I've never seen you driving on Saturday morning? I've always looked the other way because of, uh, your situation. But the mayor's really steamed. I'm going to have to write you a ticket."

He reached for the ballpoint pen in his shirt pocket. Faye moaned.

"I'll be fifteen next week. I promise I'll get a learner's permit," I squeaked.

I hated the desperation I heard in my voice. But the fact was, we didn't have the money to pay the fine. Sure, Faye could borrow it from Grandpa Claude. But Faye hated Grandpa Claude—she won't tell me why—and borrowing money from him sent her into a fit of non-stop crying followed by non-stop cursing followed by two days of deep, death-like sleep. I couldn't take it. I had to do something and quickly. I leaned toward the open window and focused on the deputy's pen.

No ticket, I thought, my gaze burning into the pen. *No ticket.*

I heard a faint buzzing noise, punctuated by the painful thudding of my heart. I concentrated harder. The buzzing grew louder while the edges of my vision darkened until I saw only the pen backlit by an eerie, greenish light. *No ticket!*, I thought desperately.

Time seemed to stand still for a moment and then, in slow motion, I saw the deputy's hand move into the glowing light surrounding the pen. When his fingers closed around it, the pen squirted out of his grasp and shot upward like a rocket. The three of us watched as it soared upward in the brilliant morning sun, did a couple of lazy loops and plummeted to the ground.

Faye gasped in surprise. Philpott's jaw dropped and his toothpick fell to the ground.

"What the . . . " he began.

"Wow," I said. "How did *that* happen?"

He lowered his sunglasses and stared at me with pale, suspicious eyes. "Never happened before." He shoved his glasses back up and bent over to pick up the pen. As he reached for it, it skittered away. "Halt!" he ordered, bounding after it. He reached for it again only to have it roll out of reach. And again. Finally, with a roar of rage, he lifted a booted foot and stomped it, one, two, three times. Breathing hard, he unholstered his gun and pointed it at the thin, ink-filled tube and the splintered plastic shell.

"I think it's already dead, sir," I chirped.

Faye, who'd been watching in open-mouthed horror, shot me a warning look.

Philpott walked back to the truck and peered through the open window. He stroked his wispy beard. He looked a little pale. "Young lady," he said. "Let's make a deal. Promise me you'll get your learners' permit, and I'll tell the mayor I threw the book at you."

I nodded my head so hard I probably looked like one of those bobble-head dolls. Thankfully, the aura that accompanied my telekinetic power had vanished.

"Yes sir, I certainly will."

"Are you aware you have to be signed up for drivers' education before the state of Washington will grant you a permit?"

My heart sank. The class cost money we didn't have.

"It just so happens," the deputy continued, "that I'm qualified to teach the class. I know you can drive, Allie. Stop by my office and I'll give you the official letter. But, no driving until you get your permit."

I quickly agreed. After expressing our gratitude—Faye patted his cheek and told him he was a prince among men—we were off to complete our mission. Faye was uncharacteristically silent for the remainder of the trip. In fact she didn't speak again until we parked the trailer next to Blaster's pasture.

She turned off the ignition, folded her arms and gazed at me through narrowed eyes.

"Okay, Allie, what's going on? I know you made that pen move."

Chapter Five

I stared at Faye while my mind searched for an explanation. Something other than the truth. I was pretty sure Faye couldn't handle the truth. But, I'm a lousy liar and Faye could spot a lie before it left my lips.

"Let's trade information," I said.

Faye blinked in surprise. "Trade?"

"Tell me about my father."

Faye's cheeks flooded with color. "Are you trying to make me sick, Allie? I mean, sicker than I already am?" Her eyes flashed with anger.

Faye, the master manipulator. I reached for the door handle. "I'll unhitch."

I hopped out of the truck and unloaded Lewis and Clark who, true to their names, raced off to explore new territory.

I removed the safety chains and unfastened the electrical hook-up, wrapping the cord carefully around the tongue of the trailer. Resentment began to simmer just below the surface and I kicked a tire in disgust. I hated the way we lived. Faye and me. It was totally upside down. Faye was the mom. Right? The one who was supposed to take care of me, the kid. Didn't work that way in my world.

Kizzy told me I needed to cut Faye some slack. She said my mother was trying her best considering what she'd been through. After a series of loser boyfriends, Faye was starting to get it together. That's when boyfriend number eight, Jeremy, delivered the knock-out punch. She'd been working at the Quik Mart and managed to put a little money away so we could get a real roof over our heads. Jeremy, the rat, found the money and took off with it. Goodbye apartment. Shortly after, Faye saw a segment about fibromyalgia on *Oprah* and took to her bed. Now it's me taking care of her.

"Okay, pull it forward," I called. I tried to keep my voice calm even though, by this time, I was furious at Faye for being furious at me. She thought if she copped an attitude I'd back off. Not this time. So what if I found out my dad was a serial killer? I could take it.

Without a glance in my direction, Faye started the engine and pulled the pick-up into its usual spot. I heard the truck door open and close. I ignored her and hooked up the water hose and cranked down the leveling jacks. As I set up the concrete blocks—our front porch—Faye shot me a disgusted look and trudged to a saggy lawn chair. She sat down with a weary sigh. That sigh said it all. I knew I'd won.

Before she could change her mind, I unlocked the trailer and retrieved the photograph hidden next to the moonstone.

I set the snapshot, face up, on the spool table next to Faye. Even though the colors had faded, I could tell the man in the picture had dark, curly hair and green eyes exactly like mine.

Faye glared at me. "You've been in my stuff."

I glared right back at her. "What choice did I have? The only thing you ever told me about my Dad is that he's *swarthy.*" Anger and frustration, my daily companions, boiled over into that single word. At that moment, it signified all that was wrong between us. "You wouldn't even tell me what *swarthy* meant. I had to ask my teacher. Jeez, did it ever occur to you I might want to know where I come from?"

My voice quavered with pent-up emotion. It felt like a big wad of cotton was stuck in my throat. *Do not cry, Allie.*

"I mean, look at the two of us," I said. "It's like we're not even related. You're little and pretty with blond hair and blue eyes. I'm tall, skinny and dark. Yeah, *swarthy!* Maybe I'm not yours at all. Maybe somebody didn't want me and left me in a garbage can. Maybe you found this *swarthy* little baby and, and . . . "

My voice squeaked then faded away altogether. Faye stood up and reached for me. She pulled me into her arms and hugged me, which was kinda awkward because I was way taller than her. I felt her warm breath and hot tears on my neck.

After a long moment she whispered, "Of course you're mine, you silly little girl. Don't ever doubt it." She released me. "Besides, if I'd found you in a garbage can, I'd never have let your grandpa name you 'Alfrieda Carlotta.' Isn't that enough proof?"

She smiled through her tears and I giggled. "I guess so." I swiped at my eyes.

Faye settled into the lawn chair. I gave her the picture and perched on the spool table. Her hand shook slightly as she examined the photo. I stared at her face, trying to read her expression. She bit her lip and blinked hard. Regret? Anger? I couldn't tell.

"It says 'me and Purdy' on the back," I pointed out, hoping to prime the pump. "Is that his name? Purdy?"

I knew the details of the photo by heart because I looked at it every night before I went to sleep. Faye was dressed in jeans and a skimpy top, an explosion of frizzy blond hair cascading over one shoulder. Something about the curve of her cheek, the sweet, trusting look of innocence in her face always clutched at my heart. She smiled up at a tall, dark man who stared straight ahead. His right arm was draped around Faye's shoulders, the left extended toward the camera, palm out. I took the gesture to mean he wasn't pleased about having his picture taken.

Faye sighed and handed the photo back to me. "Mike Purdy. That's your dad's name. Everybody called him Purdy. This was taken before . . . " Her voice trailed off.

"Before what? Before you were pregnant with me?" I heard the urgency in my voice and hoped it wouldn't shut Faye down.

"No," she said. "Before things went to hell. I knew I was pregnant when this picture was taken." She clutched my hand and finally met my eyes. It was like looking into an ocean of pain. "I was happy about the pregnancy, Allie. I want you to know that."

I swallowed hard. "What happened?" Once again, my voice was choked with tears.

"I'm not proud of my past," Faye said. "Things were bad at home. I couldn't take it so I ran away when I was seventeen."

I wanted to know more about Grandpa Claude, who I'm not allowed to visit, but held my tongue.

"I hitched a ride to Seattle and got a job at Denny's, washing dishes. One of the waitresses liked to party. That's how I met Purdy. He had a small apartment in the university district. I moved in with him. He said he was a student, but I never saw him open a book."

She paused, and her face tightened. "He always had plenty of money but he didn't like me asking about it. God, I was such a stupid kid. I loved Purdy. I thought he loved me."

"So he dumped you?"

"Oh, yeah, he dumped me. When his family found out I was pregnant, they threatened to cut him off. He suddenly decided he wasn't ready to be a father. I went into labor the next day."

"You could have asked for child support," I protested.

"Maybe you still can."

She released my hand. "I knew you'd say that. Listen to me, Allie. We're not going to ask him for money. His family tried to pay me off. I told them I'd never take a penny from them."

I stared at my mother, speechless. I'd invested so much time being mad at her and mad at the way we lived, it never occurred to me she had a backbone. Granted, it had crumbled a bit over the years. But at seventeen and pregnant with no money and no hope, she'd kicked my father and his wealthy family to the curb. Pretty impressive.

I swiped at a stray lock of hair and chose my words carefully. "Has he ever tried to contact you?" The rest of the sentence—"and ask about me—?" remained unspoken.

"No." Her lip curled in disgust. "Not once."

I studied the photo again. "Maybe he doesn't know where to find us," I said, still clinging to my dream of a father-daughter reunion.

"You're hopeless, girl." Faye shook her head in mock despair. "Hey, enough about Purdy. Now it's your turn. How did you make that pen move?"

"Oh, that." I stood and stretched as if I didn't have a care in the world then plopped down and sat cross-legged on the spool table. "Promise not to freak out?"

Faye rolled her eyes.

I took a big breath, blew it out and began. "Remember when Blaster ran backward?"

She nodded.

"That's when it started. Kizzy thinks my third eye opened when I hit the electric fence and . . . "

I spilled my guts. The telekinetic power, the flying glass, the incident with Deputy Philpott. The whole thing.

Faye listened intently. "You can really move things with your mind? Show me!"

"I can't do it on command. It has to be a desperate

situation." Something glittered in Faye's eyes. Something crafty and sly. "Come on, Allie, give it a try."

She pointed at the hose lying next to the trailer. "See if you can move that hose. Should be a piece of cake. After all, you made a bull run backward."

I pressed my lips together and acted like I was trying to move the hose, stalling for time while I tried to figure out Faye's agenda. I was pretty sure she had one.

Right on cue, the following scenario popped up in living color and played out in my head like a movie: Faye, fascinated with the prospect of easy money, forcing me into a life of crime. Twenty dollar bills flying out of cash drawers. Faye and I on the run, pulling our house behind us.

Crazy thoughts. Totally illogical. Come on! Would the woman who refused to take one thin dime from my father's family use her daughter for personal gain? No way! But then again, life had smacked Faye right between the eyes. I desperately wanted to trust my mother but couldn't shake the feeling I'd made a terrible mistake.

Thank God the hose didn't budge. Not even a tiny slither.

"Told you I couldn't do it. Super powers are not to be taken lightly." I tried to sound all snotty and superior, like Mrs. Burke when she chews us out for goofing around in class.

"Maybe something smaller," Faye said.

When her gaze fell on the photograph, I began to babble in an effort to distract her. A torrent of words raced down the fast track from my brain straight to my flapping tongue without benefit of thought. Somewhere in that rambling conversation I must have mentioned the moonstone. Faye's eyes widened in surprise.

"Did she give it to you? Where is it?"

"Under the couch," I mumbled.

"Go get it!"

I trudged into the trailer hoping I wouldn't fall into the giant hole I'd just dug. Granted, I had no clue how the moonstone worked. I'd let Faye look it over, get it out of her system then tuck it away again.

I lifted up the couch and retrieved the sock holding the moonstone pendant. My stomach did a strange little flip when I held it in my hand. It was warm to the touch, like it was alive. I could feel it through the sock. Too creepy!

I set it in Faye's lap. She removed the pendant from the sock and set it in the palm of her hand.

"Weird how it feels warm, huh?" I watched her face.

Faye's eyebrows shot up in surprise. "What are you talking about? It's cold as ice."

I shrugged, not wanting to acknowledge the obvious. It only felt warm to *me*.

She rubbed a finger across the moonstone. It caught the sun's reflection and flashed with rainbow sky fire. "Interesting setting." Faye pointed at the strange markings engraved in the heavy sterling silver that encircled the moonstone. "Looks like a pattern. What do you think it means?"

Faye thrust the moonstone toward me. I recoiled slightly but forced myself to look at it. Really look at it. She was right. There was a pattern. Three etched stars followed by three vertical, squiggly lines that looked like tiny serpents. Each set of symbols appeared three times.

"No clue," I said. "Probably doesn't mean anything."

"Sure it does," my mother said. "Otherwise it wouldn't be magic."

She began to fiddle with the moonstone, examining the back, running her finger around the edge.

It bothered me that my mother was so willing to suspend belief and leap into the wonderful world of magic. She needed a reality check. Maybe we both did.

"Kizzy's mother had some bad things happen to her. She had to blame something, so she blamed it on the moonstone. It's just a hunk of rock, Faye, not magic."

Faye looked up at me and grinned. "A hunk of rock that moves."

She held the pendant by its chain and extended her arm. The moonstone swayed back and forth in the space between us.

"What?" My head moved to and fro, following its arc. The strange shimmer of light on the round stone was perfectly aligned with the three stars directly above it.

"Now, watch this." Faye's fingers closed around the stone. She turned it clockwise in its setting. I heard a faint click. "The stone not only moves to a new position, the light moves with it. Weird, huh?"

She was right. The light now pointed at the squiggly lines instead of the stars. My mind searched for a logical explanation. "Maybe it opens," I said. "You know, like a locket."

"It doesn't. I tried."

Before I had time to react, she slipped the pendant over my head. "You should be wearing it."

"Yeah, yeah." I knew it was useless to argue. Besides, how lame was it to be afraid of jewelry? I slipped the pendant inside my shirt and felt its warmth pressing against my heart.

"Time for lunch," I said.

I stood, my mind now focused on my growling stomach. Suddenly, the ground under my feet shifted as if the world decided to change its orbit. I threw out my arms and yelped in surprise. The sensation was like stepping on a board thinking it's solid, but then it moves and a little thrill of fear shoots through your body as you try to regain your balance. Exactly like that.

Faye rose to a half crouch. "Allie! What's wrong?

You're white as a sheet."

"I'm okay," I said. "Just hungry."

On wobbly legs, I moved toward the trailer. I was fairly certain what had caused my Tilt-A-Whirl moment. But I needed to get out from under Faye's curious gaze. I stepped onto the cement blocks and into the trailer, my fingers reaching for the moonstone. I sat on the couch and carefully turned the stone counterclockwise one click. My world returned to normal.

Since I wanted to keep it that way, I knew what I had to do.

Chapter Six

"Allie." Kizzy voice was muffled as she peered through the peephole in her front door. I couldn't blame her for being cautious. After jogging the three miles that separated our homes in record time, I'd charged through the gate, raced up the stairs and pounded on the door with a closed fist.

The door swung open. Kizzy's hand shot out, grabbed my wrist and yanked me into the hallway. I leaned forward and rested my hands on my knees, gulping in air like an oxygen-starved guppy. A sweat-soaked lock of hair fell across my face. Kizzy brushed it back and tucked it behind my ear. "What's happened? Is your mother all right? Do you want some lemonade?"

"No lemonade," I gasped, pulling the pendant out from under my shirt. "I'm giving it back. I'm just a kid, Kizzy. I'm not up for this."

Kizzy glanced nervously over her shoulder toward the kitchen and put a finger to her lips. She led me into the living room and pointed me toward a chair. "My daughter's here. Not a good time to discuss the moonstone."

"Okay, fine," I said, rising. "I'll give you back the moonstone and get out of here."

Kizzy shoved me back into the chair, leaned close and whispered, "Did something happen? With the moonstone, I mean?"

I told her about Faye moving the stone to a new position

and the sickening lurch as my world turned topsy-turvy.

When I finished, she said, "You can't give it back. It says so in the prophecy."

"Prophecy? What prophecy? You mean it comes with instructions, like a magic moonstone manual?"

My voice had risen to a screech. I knew I was being snotty but the words just kept pouring out. "Where is this stupid prophecy? What does it say? Why didn't you tell me about it on Thursday?"

Kizzy gripped my arm. "Keep your voice down, Allie. I don't want Carmel to hear."

"Why?"

Kizzy tucked the moonstone back inside my shirt with shaking hands. "It's complicated. Come back when she's gone and I'll answer your questions."

I folded my arms across my chest. "Tell me now."

Once again Kizzy's gaze darted toward the back of the house. She bit her lip and pointed toward the front door. "Veranda."

I followed her outside and leaned against the railing. Kizzy settled into a wicker chair.

"If Carmel wants the moonstone, she can have it," I said. "After all, she is your daughter."

Kizzy shook her head. Worry lines furrowed her forehead. She plucked at a loose thread in her skirt. "Before my mother died, she was drifting in and out of consciousness. Her last words were, 'The moonstone prophecy . . . you're meant to have it . . . so sorry.'"

I stared at Kizzy, mouth agape, trying to figure out where I fit in this strange scenario.

"At the time, I thought it was nonsense, the babbling of a dying woman," Kizzy said. She pointed up at the tall gabled roof. "I boxed up her things and stored them in the attic. After all, the moonstone was gone."

My fingers flew to the moonstone. I could feel its heat

through my shirt.

"Mother wanted it out of the house. She gave it to Trilby, her housekeeper's daughter."

"Trilby?" I repeated. *Could this be my Trilby?* "What happened to Trilby?"

"She had a string of bad luck. Blamed it on the moonstone. By that time, Mother was dead so Trilby returned it to me. That's when I remembered what Mother said about a prophecy. I found it under the lining of her jewelry box. It's written on paper so old and fragile it's coming apart where it's been folded. The original owner, the man who cut the stone, had a dream, a prophecy, really."

"Can I see it? Where is it?"

"In a safe place. But I know what it says, and I know you're supposed to have it."

I gritted my teeth in frustration. "How do you know that?"

"He wrote it down exactly the way it appeared to him in the dream. The moonstone has passed from person to person exactly as predicted. I'm number five. It ends at six. Clearly, you, not Carmel, are number six."

"Clearly?" I said. "According to who? Is my name on it? Does it say Alfrieda Carlotta Emerson?"

"No."

"Then how do you know it's me?"

Her eyes rolled upward as she thought for a moment. "I know because I'm 'the Guardian.'"

This made absolutely no sense to me. "And the Guardian . . . "

Kizzy smiled. "Seeks the girl whose palm bears the sign of the star. That's you, Allie. Giving it back is not an option. Ignoring the prophecy would create an unbalance in the universe. Terrible things could happen . . . death, disaster."

Whoa! This was getting way too weird. "Death?

Disaster?" My voice was shrill with anxiety. "Wha . . . wha
. . . who . . . who?"

I sounded like a demented owl but couldn't stop
stammering.

The front door burst open and a willowy blond stepped
through, her pale blue eyes flicking back and forth between
Kizzy and me. She wore a sleeveless white tee shirt tucked
into skin tight jeans, black motorcycle boots and moved
with the long, sinuous movements of a beautiful serpent.
She struck a pose, draping her body languorously against
the door frame, hipshot, one arm folded across her body,
the other pointing directly at me.

"You must be Mother's little friend, Allie? Am I right?"
Her voice was high-pitched and breathless, like a little girl
waiting for Santa Claus.

Her eyes did the up and down thing as she assessed my
body, my clothes and possibly what I'd eaten for breakfast.
One corner of her mouth lifted slightly in a brief, insincere
smile.

"Yep, that's me," I said. "Allie. You must be Carmel."
We locked gazes. Remembering my manners, I added, "Um,
it's nice to meet you."

"Likewise."

During this exchange, Kizzy shrunk back into her chair,
her head rotating back and forth between Carmel and me.

In a series of fluid movements, Carmel peeled herself
off the door frame and glided to a chair next to her mother.
She crossed her long, long legs and began to swing one
boot-clad foot.

I suppose Carmel was a beautiful woman if you liked
tall, thin blondes with perfect features and swan-like necks.
But something in her eyes was so cold and calculating, it
sent a shiver of apprehension scampering down my spine.

"Allie was just leaving." Kizzy gave me a significant
look.

Okay, I wasn't totally clueless. I knew Kizzy wanted me out of there but I didn't budge. Not even a tiny twitch. I felt uneasy about leaving her alone with her daughter. How weird is that?

"Oh, darn," Carmel said in her little girl voice. "I was hoping Allie and I could get to know each other. Have a little girl talk."

"Sure. I'm in no hurry. Talk away."

Kizzy frowned at me and jerked her head toward the gate. I ignored her.

Carmel's pale gaze swung over to Kizzy then back to me, coming to rest on my faded, pink *Fighting Pea Hens* tee shirt and my hand covering the lump that was the moonstone tucked inside. I narrowed my eyes and held her gaze, lowered my hand and jammed it into my pocket. Her foot continued to swing back and forth. Back and forth. For a woman who wanted girl talk, she was remarkably silent. Though tempted to fill the dead air with idle chatter, I bit my lip and waited.

Finally, her foot stopped swinging, she unfolded her legs and stood. One long stride brought her into my personal space. I heard Kizzy give a little hiccup of alarm. I braced myself. Was it menace I saw in her face or was she about to engage in the promised "girl talk?" A fashion consultation or a whap upside the noggin? Not knowing the answer, I prepared for the worst. After all, I *had* broken the nose of the biggest bully in Peacock Flats. A tall, skinny blonde should be a piece of cake.

I couldn't have anticipated what happened next. She extended long bony fingers—her nails were bitten down to nubs, not a good look for a glamour chick—and chucked me under the chin. Swear to God.

"Well, aren't you just the cutest thing ever," she said with a winsome smile. It looked like a real one.

I exhaled loudly, relieved I wouldn't have to flatten

her perfect nose. "That's me. The cutest thing ever."

She stared intently into my eyes. "Are you wearing green contact lenses? That color of green isn't natural."

I didn't know how to respond, so I batted my freakishly-colored eyes and shook my head.

Kizzy said, "Green eyes see things other eyes cannot see."

Carmel gave an unladylike snort. "Yeah, right, mother." She leaned closer and whispered, "Magic bullshit. Right?"

I tittered nervously. Hadn't I thought the exact same thing?

"So what *do* your eyes see?" Carmel asked.

"Oh, just the usual stuff." I resisted the urge to tell her about Blaster and Deputy Philpott's pen.

She picked up a lock of my hair and studied it curiously. "Have you ever considered streaking your hair?"

"Uh, no." I looked around for hidden cameras. This had to be a reality show.

'TEDDY!" Carmel yelled.

I started violently. She continued to cling to my hair. "Get out here!"

I heard a raspy baritone answer, "Yeah, babe. Whatcha need?"

I peered around Carmel which wasn't easy considering she had a death grip on my hair. A tall, well-built guy with dark hair pulled back into a pony tail—not unlike my own—strutted through the door, a burning cigarette clutched between the fingers of his right hand. His faded blue jeans clung to muscular thighs and he wore a leather motorcycle vest over his bare chest. He checked out my body with heavy-lidded brown eyes. Frankly, I was getting a little sick of the whole body-assessment thing.

Carmel released my hair and stepped away. "Get the bike. I want to give the kid a lift home."

Teddy smirked. "No way, babe. I'll take her. You can't

handle the bike. Way too big for you." He gave her a crooked grin and added, "Unlike some other things."

Kizzy clucked her disapproval and Carmel bristled while I imagined Teddy and I astride his motorcycle, me clinging to his naked chest, my un-streaked hair whipping violently back and forth across my face as we zipped down Peacock Flats road.

Carmel marched over to Teddy. She didn't stop until they were toe to toe. "Listen, you big jerk! That bike's half mine! You think I can't handle it? Well, handle *this!*"

She extended a middle finger and thrust it in his face. Teddy blinked and took a step back.

I pushed away from the railing. "It's okay. My mom would kill me if I got on a motorcycle. I appreciate the offer, though." I spoke the truth. Faye didn't have many rules but "no motorcycles" was a biggie. "I'll just jog on home. Really."

Squirming under Carmel's withering gaze, Teddy retreated into the house.

Kizzy stood. "I'll walk you to the gate, Allie."

She waited until we reached the hedge before she spoke. "The only time they come here is when they need money."

"Do you give it to them?"

"It's the only way to get rid of them." Kizzy glanced over her shoulder. The porch was now devoid of people. Apparently Carmel had followed Teddy into the house. "I don't have time to tell you the whole story now but be careful. Carmel wants that moonstone. She knows her grandmother used it to accumulate wealth and figures she can do the same thing. I've tried to tell her about the prophecy, that it's dangerous to . . . "

The muffled roar of a Harley Davidson engine stopped Kizzy mid-sentence. Teddy, now wearing mirrored sunglasses, came tearing around the side of the house on a brilliant silver motorcycle, its wheels churning up bits of grass and leaving muddy ruts in its wake. When he reached the front of the house, Carmel popped through the front door and yelled, "Where the hell do you think you're going?"

Kizzy heaved a dispirited sigh. "Allie, don't give up on the moonstone. I think the unpleasant effects will lessen. Please, try. It's important. Now go." She opened the gate, pushed me through and closed it. I thought about the prophecy, the way Kizzy looked when she said, "Death and disaster."

I looked at her through the gate. "If I don't, will something terrible really happen?"

She didn't say, "Maybe." She didn't say, "I don't know." Kizzy looked me straight in the eye and said, "Yes."

So much for giving the moonstone back. When Kizzy started back toward the house I remembered the other reason for my visit. "Kizzy," I called softly. "I found out my dad's name. It's Mike Purdy."

Kizzy loved to surf the internet and had always promised if I gave her a name, she'd locate my father.

She raised a hand in acknowledgement. I murmured my thanks and jogged home.

Later that night, with Faye fast asleep in the bedroom, I sat in the dark, cross-legged on the couch, and tested my resolve. I stared at the moonstone in my palm, its glistening surface lit, not by its namesake moon, but by the dim yard light at the edge of Blaster's pasture. Steeling my mind against the waves of dizziness I knew would follow, my reluctant fingers moved toward the moonstone to grasp it, to move it one simple click. My hand hovered over the stone and stopped when I heard the unmistakable sound of a Harley Davidson motorcycle pull into Uncle Sid's long driveway, idle for a few long moments then roar away, the sound of its engine receding into the night.

Chapter Seven

The next day, Sunday, forced me to focus on more mundane matters, namely grocery shopping. Filling an empty belly took precedence over worrying about silly little details like the possibility of Carmel or Teddy running me down with the Harley, ripping the moonstone off my cold, dead body and using it for some sinister purpose like robbing a bank or overthrowing the government.

Yes, the moonstone still hung around my neck. I'd made a decision during the night. Kizzy said I was meant to have it. Giving it back wasn't an option, so I might as well embrace it. Who was I to challenge fate? Perhaps the moonstone would lead me down the right path. For now, that path led me to Tom's Corner Market, featuring Top Ramen noodles, six packages for a dollar.

I'd just stepped out the door when I saw clouds of dust billowing over the wooden fence behind the parking lot. A terrified whimper and the sounds of a scuffle drew me to the fence.

The battered old fence looked like a gap-toothed smile. A quick peek through a missing slat revealed three members of the PWT gang taking turns bitch-slapping Cory Philpott. The PWT's claimed their initials stood for Proud White Tuffs, which made it pathetically easy for the rest of us to call them Poor White Trash. While the Hispanic gangs limited their violence to rival gang members, the PWT's mugged old ladies and terrorized kids like Cory, who thought he was tough but wasn't.

Okay, part of me was enjoying the fact Cory was getting clobbered. Smart-mouth Cory. Hadn't I punched him in the face for the same reason? But, come on, three guys against one? Sure, Cory had an attitude problem but these punks were batting him around like a beach ball.

A blocky kid with a bright green mohawk clutched Cory by the front of his shirt. He popped him across the face with an open hand then shoved him into the waiting arms of a tall, skinny guy whose pants hung so low I could see a giant pimple on his butt.

Pimple Butt wrapped an arm around Cory's neck and squeezed, "You didn't see nothin', kid. Tell your dad and your dead. Understand?"

Cory grabbed at Pimple Butt's arm and tried to nod, his voice a terrified squeak. "I won't tell. I promise."

The third guy had two nose rings, more hardware in each eyebrow and probably a stud in his tongue. He reached into his back pocket and pulled out a switchblade. He pressed a button and sunlight danced on the blade's gleaming surface.

"Maybe we should teach him a lesson. A little reminder to keep his mouth shut," Nose Ring said, advancing toward Cory.

Cory's eyes rolled in panic. A wet stain blossomed on the front of his jeans.

Without thinking, I kicked the fence then ducked away from the opening. "Hey, Poor White Trash! Tired of picking on old ladies?"

Nose Ring guy whirled toward the fence, trying to get a fix on my position. I scampered around the end of the fence and waved my arms. "Looking for me?"

His lip curled in a sneer and he started toward me. "You're dead meat, little girl. You'd better get the hell out of here while you're still able to walk. We could have some fun with you. Whaddaya think, guys?"

Pimple Butt shoved Cory toward Mohawk and joined his friend. "Yeah, she's kinda skinny but she'll do."

"Run, Cory," I shouted.

He started to run but Mohawk grabbed him before he could get away.

"You're not goin' nowhere, Philpott," Nose Ring said. "Hey, I know, guys. We'll make him watch."

I should have been terrified, but the outrage I felt outweighed the fear a hundred times over. All I wanted to do was teach those creeps a lesson.

Nose Ring was in the lead. I focused the power of my mind on the metal bristling from his face. "Hot," I said. "Ohmigod, so hot. How can you stand it?"

Nose Ring stopped dead in his tracks and gave a shrill yip of pain. He began slapping at his face, hopping up and down and screeching, "Oh, shit! Oh, shit! I'm burning up!"

"What the hell's the matter with you, man?" Pimple Butt was moving toward me.

By this time Nose Ring was rolling around on the ground, pulling various bits of metal out of his face. In my own defense, I could have said "red hot." He probably deserved it.

But Pimple Butt was closing in. I said, "Oops, too bad about your pants!"

I caught him mid-stride. When his pants dropped to his ankles, his feet tangled in the fabric and he plummeted facedown into the dirt.

Mohawk, still holding Cory, stared at me with dull eyes, his mouth hanging open in disbelief.

I pointed at him. "Let him go or I'll make your hair fall out and never grow back."

Honestly, I wasn't sure if I could do that. He must have believed me, though, because he released Cory who, as per my instructions, took off like a gut-shot gazelle.

Pimple Butt got to his feet, turned away from me and pulled up his pants. Nose Ring, his face fiery-red, shiny with sweat and metal-free stood up and started toward me.

I thrust out a hand, palm forward, and lowered my voice an octave. "I wouldn't, if I were you."

Nose Ring stopped. "What the hell are you? Some kind of a witch?"

"Me, a witch? Don't be silly. It's probably karma. You know, past behavior determines your present quality of life. You guys must have done something really bad."

I gave them a one-fingered salute, backed around the fence and walked away, swinging my bag of Top Ramen. Despite the show of bravado, my heart thudded in my chest and I couldn't resist a quick peek over my shoulder to see if I was being followed.

At the edge of the parking lot I broke into a jog, eager to put some distance between the PWT boys and myself. Strangely, the act of jogging created more panic and before long, I was in a full-out, knee-pumping sprint, flying through the shabby neighborhood like a lone goose trying to catch up with the flock. I fixed my gaze on the row of poplars lining a hay field at the edge of town. Farm land and open spaces are not conducive to gang activity. Beating people up requires fences and back alleys.

I was almost to the field when Cory popped out from behind a tree. "Hey, Allie."

I screeched to a halt, dropped the noodles, braced my hands against my knees and gulped air. With a fearful glance down the road, Cory tromped toward me, his over-sized running shoes making a squishing sound. He was soaked to the skin, rivulets of water sluicing off his sandy hair and onto the ground. He gave me a sheepish grin and pointed toward the hay field. "Got in the sprinkler. You know, to clean up."

His clothes were completely sodden, his jeans now a solid dark blue. He swiped at his hair and jutted out his chin—a familiar gesture—one I knew preceded an obnoxious Cory Philpott remark. "You need to keep your mouth shut about what happened back there."

I pressed my lips together in disgust. What did I expect? Gratitude from a jerk like Cody? I stared at the front of his jeans. "Yeah, I'd probably jump in the sprinkler too if I peed my pants."

Cory's face turned ugly. "You start blabbing this around and I'll tell people what you did."

"Oh really?" My words were scorched with anger. "Well, here's what I did, you stupid jerk. I saved your sorry ass because you lipped off to the wrong people!"

Cory shook his head. Water flew. "I didn't lip off. Not to those guys. I saw them steal a carton of cigarettes. I ran out of the store but they caught me."

"Good thing I came along or you'd have PWT carved across your forehead."

Cory blustered, "I saw what you did. You made that guy's pants fall down, and the dude with all the metal in his face? You did something to him too. I'll tell everybody, I'll . . . "

"Listen, Cory. What I did for you I'd do for a dog. I don't give a crap if you pee your pants every day of the week, but don't threaten me!" I picked up my shopping bag and started to walk away. "I should have let them cut you."

I heard Cory's labored breathing behind me. I'd taken only a few steps when I heard him say, "Hold on, Allie."

I stopped.

"I was scared, ya know?" He blinked hard and stared at the ground.

He lifted his head and I saw embarrassment and shame in his face.

I nodded. "Me too."

"And if it got around I got my ass bailed out by a girl, well . . . "

I sighed. "Don't worry about it, Cory. We'll pretend it didn't happen."

His eyes slid away from mine. "Thanks."

"Don't mention it. And, by the way, if I hear you say one mean word to Manny or Mercedes ever again, I'll tell everybody on the bus what happened."

His chin jutted out again, but he said, "Yeah, yeah."

I'd barely passed the hay field when I ran out of steam. I was so tired I could hardly put one foot in front of the other. I leaned against a fence post to rest and saw Matt's Jeep coming toward me. When he spotted me, he jerked the wheel, made a U-turn and pulled up on the shoulder. He wasn't alone. A pouty-faced girl dressed in white shorts and a skimpy pink shirt sat in the passenger seat. She gave me a brief, dismissive glance then looked straight ahead when Matt leaned across her and said, "Hey, Allie. Need a ride somewhere?"

"That's okay. You're going the other way."

"No problem," he said. "Hop in. I'll run you home."

I was about to protest again but when Matt looked at me with those sexy blue eyes, I thought, *Why the hell not? He's cute, I'm tired and to heck with what's-her-name.*

I pushed away from the fence post. At my approach, the girl put her hand on Matt's knee. Her straight brown hair shimmered with streaky, blond highlights. She fingered the tiny silver cross hanging around her neck and turned her head slightly as I climbed into the seat behind her.

Matt hooked an elbow over the seatback. "You know Summer, right?"

He ducked his head toward the girl.

"No." I said. "You go to Hilltop?"

Summer didn't bother to make eye contact. "Uh huh.

Probably why I've never seen you."

"Yeah, well . . . "

Matt squirmed a little. "Summer, this is Allie. She lives by me." He shifted into first gear and pulled out onto the road. Summer's sun-kissed hair blew back away from her face revealing earlobes adorned with tiny diamond studs.

She leaned toward Matt and snickered. "Elfie? Is she one of Santa's little helpers?"

"My name's Alfrieda. Allie, not 'Elfie.'" I wanted to add, "you bitch," but bit my tongue.

"Oh," Summer's fingers moved from the cross. She flipped her hair back then touched the diamond stud in her right ear.

Okay fine. This chick's not the only one with jewelry. Let her get a look at this!

I pulled the moonstone out from beneath my shirt, grateful that Faye made me wear it. As I clutched it with the fingers of my right hand, I felt the outer edge rotate one click.

Oops! I hadn't meant to do that. I shut my eyes, anticipating the dizziness, the blurred vision and nausea. Nothing. I opened my eyes. If anything, my senses were more acute, sharper than the scalpels we used to cut up frogs in science class. The sky was an unnatural shade of blue, the wind whipping across my face felt like warm silk.

The apple orchards lining the road gave off a rich, heady scent even though we were months away from harvest. I felt something bubble up from deep inside me, like I'd captured the beauty and power of the moon and held it in the palm of my hand. Suddenly, I didn't care about Summer or what she thought of me. But I did care about Matt.

I slid over to the middle of the seat so I could focus on him and ignore his snotty girlfriend, if that's what she was. My hand still held the moonstone. Summer murmured something to Matt then glanced over her shoulder at me.

Her gaze flicked over my cut-off jeans and ratty old tank top. Her lips didn't move but clearly, I heard her laugh and the words, "Dollar store. She buys her clothes at the Dollar Store."

Without thinking, I reacted. "Not the Dollar Store, Summer. Value Village, that's where I shop."

Summer's head swiveled around and she stared at me, her eyes wide with surprise. "I didn't say anything about the Dollar Store."

A flush crawled up her neck and flooded her cheeks, a sure sign of guilt, in my opinion. Matt shot me a puzzled look and removed Summer's hand from his leg. Then it hit me. I'd peeked into Summer's shallow little mind and read her thoughts. It had to be the moonstone. What else could it be?

Matt pulled into Uncle Sid's driveway. I sat, motionless, gazing at the moonstone, wondering what I'd done. Summer wouldn't look at me. She gripped the edge of the seat so tightly her knuckles were as white as her French-manicured nails.

Finally Matt turned around, his eyes flicking over my body. The heat in his glance slammed into me and drove me back against the seat. When his invasive thoughts burst into my mind, the ugliness of the words were like a physical blow.

Cute little butt. Bet I'd be the first. Who's going to stop me? Her tramp of a mother?

A yelp of surprise burst from my lips, and I dropped the moonstone. The poisonous brew of anger and betrayal swept through my body like wildfire. I drew back my arm, my hand curled into a fist.

Matt blinked and recoiled. Before I could punch him, the heat in his eyes subsided and the old Matt re-appeared, the one with the *Aw shucks* grin and sleepy blue eyes.

I unclenched my fist and lowered my arm. Shaking with

fury, I leaned forward and whispered, "Not going to happen, mister. Not in your lifetime."

"Huh?" Matt said but his gaze darted away from mine. "You okay, Allie?"

"Yeah, just dandy."

As I stomped down the driveway, I heard the engine idle for a few moments then the spit of gravel as Matt slammed the Jeep into reverse and took off.

Chapter Eight

Later that night, head pounding again—why did a headache always follow these episodes—I heard a familiar sound. Wind chimes. I hurried outside before Trilby could pop in. Faye was a light sleeper. Maybe she couldn't hear, see, smell, etc. Trilby, but she always knew if I was stirring, much less carrying on a conversation with my spirit guide.

I found Trilby in the pasture, astride Blaster, who seemed unaware of her presence. When he saw me, he lowered his head and snorted. Satisfied I'd been duly warned, he went back to grazing, ripping up hunks of grass with his big yellow teeth. The sound of his munching seemed overly-loud in the night air.

"Isn't this cool?" Trilby said. "I always wanted to ride a bull. Hey, why don't you join me?"

"Are you nuts? If I go in the pasture, Blaster will pass gas and toss me into the apple tree."

Right on cue, the bull cut loose with a humongous fart. Trilby levitated upward, hovering over Blaster's back, her lip curled in distaste. "Sounds like one of my old boyfriends," she said, and vanished.

I felt a sudden chill pass through my body, and a split second later, Trilby sat under the apple tree, leaning against its broad trunk. She patted the grass next to her. "Come. Sit."

I sat down beside her taking care to keep my distance. "How's SeaTac?"

"Same old, same old." She shrugged. "But not for much longer. You passed the second test today. One more, and I'm outta there."

"The mind-reading thing? Is that what you're talking about?"

"No, the Cory thing. You know, the kid you saved."

"I should have let those guys beat him up."

"But you didn't," Trilby said. "You put yourself at risk for someone else. Someone you don't give a damn about. That's the second test." She closed her eyes and smiled. "Groovy. Two down, one to go."

"Tell me about the moonstone. I could hear people's thoughts. Did it work that way for you?"

Trilby's eyes flew open. Her smile disappeared. "It ruined my life, that's all. Why do you think I'm here?"

"Ruined your life? How?"

Trilby rolled her eyes. "Come on, pay attention. I'm the Slacker. *The careless woman who defiled its purpose and tarnished its name.* The prophecy, kid. The prophecy." She floated to her feet. "Gotta go. Catch you on the flip side."

She started to fade away.

"No, you can't go yet!" I yelled. Every time I got close to solving another piece of the puzzle, she slipped away like smoke on the wind.

Faye's window cranked open. "What are you yelling about? Go to bed, Allie."

I walked to the trailer shaking my head in disgust. Once again, I had more questions than answers.

Of all the spirit guides hanging around SeaTac, I had to get Trilby.

*

The next day Cory avoided me like I was the Black Hand of Death which suited me fine. Of course, the whole school was talking about the new kid, Didier Ellsworth Thompson the Third. Swear to God, that was his real name. I knew this because his mother, a stern-looking woman dressed in a man suit, marched him into algebra class and introduced him to our teacher, Mr. Boswell. She left after admonishing Mr. Boswell, "I would like you to address him as *Didier*, no matter what he tells you after I leave."

Sure enough, after his mom left, the kid grinned and raked long, bony fingers through his six-inch-tall Afro. "Yo, people. Call me Diddy."

After a stunned silence, the class burst into raucous laughter. Trust me. We weren't being insensitive to racial issues or politically incorrect. No. We laughed because Didier Ellsworth Thompson the Third was a certified Caucasian, a tall, gawky string bean with thick glasses and permed blond hair. One thing we didn't tolerate in Peacock Flats was a phony. Diddy was the real deal.

Between classes, I overheard him tell Sonja Ortegaand her friend, Salome, that he'd just moved from Seattle, where he attended a mostly black high school. It seemed like someone should tell him he'd left that life behind and he should start a new gig. But maybe Diddy was destined to be the only non-black African American in Peacock Flats like I was the only person with paranormal abilities. We all had our crosses to bear.

I took pity on him during lunch. Alone at a table, he left his tray of food untouched and sidled up to a group of boys practicing their hip-hop moves. I watched, aghast, as he flung his gangly body onto the floor and attempted to spin on his back. When he whacked his head against a table leg, I walked over and looked down at him. His face was scrunched in pain. I nudged him with my foot. "Hey, Diddy. Yo. Get your lunch and sit with us."

One pale blue eye opened, then the other. I reached out a hand. He grabbed it like I was pulling him from a watery grave. He shot up to a standing position, lost his balance and stumbled sideways, almost taking both of us down.

"Hey, dude, thanks a lot," he said with a grateful smile.

While we ate, Diddy filled us in on his unusual background. Manny, Mercedes and I gazed at him with wide-eyed wonder. Diddy obviously belonged at our table of misfits.

"My mom hates dudes but wanted a kid so she had me planted, you know, like a seed, in her uterus."

"*In vitro*," I mumbled.

Diddy waved a hand, "Whatever. Of course, I had to be named Didier Ellsworth Thompson the Third because my grandpa's 'Junior.'" His tone was bitter.

I nodded sympathetically. I knew all about bad names. "How come your mom didn't enroll you at Hilltop?" I asked.

"She's real big on me being in multi-cultural settings."

"Oh cool." Mercedes flashed him a flirtatious grin. "Mrs. Burke is going to love him, huh Allie?"

"Absolutely." What I was really thinking was, Oh, great, now I have another one to protect from Cory Philpott, who can spot a victim a mile away.

Still, all in all, it was a pretty fair day, at least until after school. After checking on Faye, I sat under the apple tree with my algebra homework. Blaster was grazing downwind, which meant the air was stink-free.

I heard the crunch of footsteps and looked up to see Aunt Sandra churning up gravel as she stomped down the driveway. A split second later, I caught a glimpse of Uncle Sid's shadow as he darted behind the barn. Swear to God, the man had built-in radar when it came to Aunt Sandra. I knew where he was going: His favorite hidey hole behind the tool shed, a place Aunt Sandra would never set foot because of the cow manure. Every so often, Blaster's best was scooped up and piled behind the shed for "seasoning." Uncle Sid not only sold Blaster's sperm on line, he had a thriving little manure business. Hard to believe, but people pay money for the stuff!

Aunt Sandra wore hot pink slacks and a matching sleeveless top, not a good fashion choice for a woman forty pounds overweight. She spotted me under the tree and abruptly changed course, picking her way through the dirt and weeds.

"Allie! Have you seen your Uncle Sid?"

I shook my head slowly. "Uncle Sid? Nope." Not a total lie, since all I'd seen was Uncle Sid's shadow. But she wasn't buying it. She glared down at me, her eyes narrowed in suspicion. Time for diversionary tactics.

"Oh my gosh." I fanned the air and pointed at her shoes, chunky, three-inch wedgie sandals topped with pink roses. "I think you stepped in something!"

Startled, Aunt Sandra balanced first on one foot, then the other, and examined the soles of her shoes. Lucky for me, the left shoe had something brown and icky clinging to it.

"Dammit!" she swore, her face turning as pink as her outfit. "A decent person can't walk anywhere around here without stepping in shit!"

For a church lady, Aunt Sandra used colorful language. And that "decent person" comment? Guess it was okay if an "indecent" person stepped in something nasty. I coughed to cover up a titter. "Maybe you should check the barn. That's usually where Uncle Sid hangs out this time of day."

"I'll just do that." Aunt Sandra wiped the offending shoe on a clump of weeds and started toward the barn, her chubby little heels oozing over the sides of her too-small shoes.

I watched her disappear into the barn and wondered why she couldn't wait until supper time to talk to Sid.

Something was up. But what? Inquiring minds want to know.

It didn't take long. Aunt Sandra burst from the barn and bellowed, "Dammit, Sid! I know you can hear me. Get your butt over here!"

Uncle Sid must have figured he was busted because he popped around the corner, wiping his greasy hands on a rag. Aunt Sandra said something I couldn't hear, pointed at our trailer and led Uncle Sid into the barn. Whoa! Was this about Faye and me?

I scrambled up and walked casually toward the barn, looking around to make sure nobody was watching. A mountain of hay bales was conveniently stacked next to the barn. I crouched behind them and heard Aunt Sandra say, "You promised! You said they'd only be here until Faye got on her feet. In case you haven't noticed, mister, she's off her feet most of the time!"

Uncle Sid mumbled an answer. I caught only, "no money" and "sister."

"Step sister," Aunt Sandra corrected. Her voice was crystal clear. "You don't owe her a thing. How do you think I feel when my friends come over and see that piece-of-shit trailer in our yard?"

"Mmmph—mmmph—sick," Uncle Sid said.

"Sick, my ass! She's not too sick to entertain Big Ed every Thursday. I suppose you think he's *counseling* her."

Sarcasm dripped from the word "counseling." I shot to my feet, propelled by a towering rage. My body shook violently as I struggled to control myself.

Aunt Sandra was on a roll. "And why does she ship Allie off every Thursday? Huh? Answer that one, Mister Smart Guy."

I heard something heavy slam against the floor and Aunt Sandra's squeal of surprise. Uncle Sid shouted, "Give me a break, Sandra! Faye's got no place to go. You want her in a homeless shelter? Is that what you want?"

When Aunt Sandra spoke, I could tell by her voice she'd changed her approach. Her tone was soft and wheedling and sounded exactly like Tiffany when she wanted something from her dad.

"Okay, Sid, I'll tell you what really worries me. Have you seen the way Matt looks at Allie? He's thinking about her . . . you know . . . like he shouldn't. Mothers know these things. All we need is for Matt to get her pregnant. Then we'll have another brat to look after."

I inhaled sharply. My trembling legs seemed to have their own agenda and took a giant step toward the front of the barn.

"Aw, come on, Sandra. He's seventeen. He looks at all the girls that way."

My sense of reason caught up with my body, and I retreated back behind the hay bales.

Aunt Sandra's voice rose to a screech. I heard her footsteps scrape across the rough floor. "Apparently, you're choosing to ignore my feelings, as usual. Do I need to remind you the farm is in *my* name? Daddy wanted it that way. If I wanted to, I could kick you and your trashy so-called family out on your butts!"

After a long moment of silence, Aunt Sandra stormed out of the barn and headed for the house. I counted to one hundred slowly. When Uncle Sid didn't appear, I slipped away, another worry gnawing at my mind which, by now, probably looked like a moth-eaten sweater.

Tell Faye or don't tell Faye? I sat under the apple tree and pondered the question. Thinking about my mother, the moonstone and the surprise I had in mind, father-wise, I chose "Not."

Chapter Nine

Alfrieda Carlotta Emerson. In the back of a limo drinking a soda and eating little sandwiches with the crusts cut off. On a school day. Happy Birthday to me!

"Fifteen is special," Kizzy told me. She also told Faye, which is why my mother wrote the following note for me to take to school:

To Whom It May Concern: Though it's really none of your business, today is my daughter's fifteenth birthday and she has my permission to do whatever the hell she wants. She'll be back in school tomorrow.

Very truly yours,
Faye Emerson.

Alice, the school secretary, read the note, gave me a wink and said, "Have fun, Allie. See ya tomorrow."

Faye thought Kizzy was taking me on a surprise outing. In a way, I guess she was. We were on our way to Tukwila, WA, home of Mike's Magic Carpets. That's right, my dad, Mike Purdy, sold rugs.

We hit the freeway, flew by Vista Valley and headed for the interstate. Peacock Flats was located in Central Washington, the rain shadow of the Cascade Mountains. No green forests dripping with rain, no Space Needle but plenty of apple orchards, vineyards and tumbleweeds.

Kizzy, sipping bottled water and smoking Virginia Slims, filled me in on the details as we headed west to Snoqualmie Pass.

"I did an Internet search. Your dad's been in business for twelve years and he's doing well. Just built a brand new store, way bigger than the old one."

"Good," I muttered into my Pepsi. "He can afford child support."

"Oh yes," Kizzy said. "He can afford it. And if he doesn't do the right thing, you have another option."

I knew what she was talking about. Washington State Support Enforcement. I also knew that Faye would never go for it. If we were to get any help, it had to be me.

The way I saw it, he owed us thousands of dollars. Why should we be living like Uncle Sid's poor relations parked next to a cow pasture? Even though that's what we were. Of course, if Aunt Sandra had her way, we'd be looking for a new home.

Tukwila turned out to be a dizzying array of shopping malls, mattress factories, fast food restaurants and, of course, carpet stores. Magic Mike's Carpet Heaven filled an entire city block and featured a gaudy sign with a guy in a business suit sitting cross-legged on a flying carpet framed against a background of bright blue sky and puffy white clouds. Above the front door, a huge banner proclaimed, GRAND OPENING! PAY NO INTEREST FOR A YEAR!

When the limo pulled up to the front door, I got cold feet. "What if he's not here? Maybe he's gone somewhere on a buying trip. Maybe we made this trip for nothing. Maybe we should forget about the whole thing."

"He's here," Kizzy said. "I made an appointment. I told his assistant I intend to re-carpet my whole house and that I'd only deal with the owner."

She glanced at her watch. "Our appointment is for eleven. It's ten forty-five. Gives us a little time to snoop around. Right?"

Charlie, the limo driver, opened Kizzy's door. She

stepped out and started for the store. I jumped out and hurried after her. At the very least, I wanted to get a look at the guy responsible for my curly hair and permanent tan.

We stepped through the door and into carpet heaven. Carpet displayed on giant rolls. Carpet hanging from walls. Carpet featured in cozy little rooms complete with furniture. Carpet squares bound together in giant books. An odd chemical smell filled the air. Maybe it was nerves, but the smell made me nauseous.

Other than Kizzy and me, the only other customers were an elderly couple on the receiving end of a lecture by an enthusiastic salesman. In a high, excited voice, he spoke of continuous filament nylon, textured cut, invisible seams and built in stain resistance while running his hands up and down a roll of cream-colored carpet. The woman sank down on a nearby couch and began to rub her temples.

Kizzy swept through the showroom, her bearing as regal as a queen. Was she really going to re-carpet her house just so I could find my father? I trailed behind her, gulping nervously. A cluster of salesmen huddled together at the back of the cavernous room. An attractive young woman sat behind a counter, working at a computer.

A salesman peeled off from the crowd and trotted toward us with a wide grin. His tummy poked out far beyond the gap in his unbuttoned sport coat and jiggled as he made his way through the rolls of carpet. Something about him made me want to run out of the store. As he approached Kizzy, he thrust out a hand. "Hello and welcome to Magic Mike's Carpets. My name's Dick. How may I provide you with extraordinary service today?"

Kizzy hesitated a moment before giving his hand a brief squeeze. "Thank you, Dick, I'm sure your service is extraordinary but we have an appointment with Mike Purdy at eleven."

Dick beamed. "Oh, you're the one who drove all the way over the pass to buy carpet. Ms. Lovell, right?"

Kizzy nodded.

Dick gave me a wink. "We'll take good care of you. Follow me, ladies. I'll take you to Mike's office."

As we approached the counter, the phone chirped. The woman pounced on it. "Magic Mike's Carpet Heaven. This is Brenda. How may I provide you with extraordinary service today?"

After a brief pause, her faced turned scarlet and she hissed, "You weirdo! You perv! I'm tracing this call." She slammed the phone down.

Kizzy leaned across the counter. "They make you answer the phone like that?"

Brenda rolled her eyes and gave a little huff of disgust. "I told Mike it wouldn't work."

Dick left us in Mike Purdy's office, a luxurious room larger than my entire home, with rich blue carpet so plush I hesitated to step on it. An enormous desk—cherry wood Kizzy said—sat in the center of the room. Two straight-backed chairs were pulled up next to the desk. An off-white leather couch and love seat formed a conversational setting.

A huge astrological chart covered one wall, its midnight blue background splashed with stars and an iridescent moon. Beneath the chart were the words, "You must have chaos within you to give birth to a dancing star . . . Friedrich Nietzsche."

The words made the hair on my arms stand up.

Kizzy sat on the couch and picked up a magazine. I tiptoed across the intimidating carpet—checking to see if I left footprints—approached the massive desk and studied Mike Purdy's family photos, four in all. The largest was a family portrait, mother and father seated behind three kids in the foreground. My hands trembled when I picked it up.

The man had close-cropped dark hair. Was it curly when it grew out? Were his eyes green? I couldn't tell. I was waiting for a clap of thunder, the peal of bells or a sudden zap of electricity. Something that said, *Yes, Allie, this is your daddy, the man who gave you life.* Nothing tugged at my heart. He looked like a million other middle-aged guys.

I studied the rest of the family. Blond wife. Looked a little like Faye. Two pre-teen blond daughters and a little dark-haired boy. I bit my lip and set the picture down. Why had I come here? Big mistake.

Kizzy glanced up from her magazine. "We don't always get the answers to our questions, Allie. That doesn't mean they're not worth asking."

I thought about what she said as I looked at the rest of Mike Purdy's pictures. Mike, the missus and kids in ski clothes standing in front of a rustic lodge, all smiles. Mike, an arm around each daughter, standing on a beach with sand the color of sugar, the deep turquoise ocean behind.

I picked up the last photo and caught my breath. Mike and his son each held up a fish. Mike grinned at the camera. The boy gazed up at his father, his look of adoration so intense I felt a lump form in my throat. And, oh yeah, the kid looked exactly like me. Same long skinny legs, same green eyes, same dark curly hair which meant, of course, Mike was my father. I set the picture down.

"I've got two sisters and a brother." Tears welled up in my eyes. "We shouldn't have come here."

Kizzy stood up and held out her arms. She hugged me and patted my back. "The truth can be hard to handle, darling girl. What you choose to do with it is up to you."

I snuffled a little then pushed away from Kizzy. I never used to cry, not even when I smashed my finger in the trailer hitch. What was wrong with me? I swiped at my eyes, drew a shaky breath and sat down on the love seat, my heart hammering like thunder. Why had I come here?

Maybe Faye was right about leaving the subject alone.

We didn't have to wait long. The door burst open and Mike Purdy entered the room. Dressed in a sleek gray suit with a black dress shirt and gray striped tie, Purdy had filled out since he glowered into the camera in pre-Allie days. His shoulders were broader and he'd learned how to smile, even though it looked phony. He focused immediately on Kizzy, striding toward her, one hand outstretched.

"Mrs. Lovell? I'm Mike Purdy. Delighted to meet you."

At least he didn't say the "extraordinary service" thing. I was happy about that.

Kizzy stood and extended a hand, palm down, like he was supposed to kiss it. I felt laughter bubbling up. Hysterical laughter. *Not now, Allie*, I told myself.

Kizzy greeted him then pointed at me. "This is my friend, Alfrieda Emerson."

Purdy's head swiveled toward me but his eyes, green eyes, didn't really see me. "How ya doin' kid?" he said with his fake smile before turning back to Kizzy.

Follow the money, I thought bitterly. "Fine," I said.

Suddenly, he stiffened and turned to look at me again. His eyes were wary and slightly narrowed. He stared at me a long moment before his gaze darted away. "Alfrieda, huh? Bet you got named for somebody's old maid aunt." He jammed his hands into his pockets and turned back to Kizzy.

"Allie," I told his profile. I hated the way my voice sounded. Wimpy and weak. I cleared my throat. "Most people call me Allie."

At my words, he flinched slightly then spoke to Kizzy. "Tell me what you have in mind and I'll have samples brought in."

Maybe he thought if he didn't look at me, I didn't exist.

Kizzy ignored him and lifted a quizzical brow in my direction. I knew she was thinking, *This is your moment, Allie.*

I opened my mouth to speak. I thought of all the things I wanted to say. Like, didn't he ever wonder what I was like? Did he even know I was a girl? Did it bother him that Faye, who was just a kid herself, now had a kid to take care of? Was Faye just an unpleasant chapter in his life, one he wanted to forget? Obviously, the answers were no, no, no and yes.

I felt anger rise up and warm my cheeks. People are easy to find. He could have found us if he wanted to. The answer was simple. He didn't want to. All the more reason I should speak up, demand help for Faye and me. But I just sat there, tongue-tied, while this stranger in his custom-made suit chatted up a customer who would make him even richer.

Kizzy continued to stare at me. I responded with a tiny shake of my head. No matter how much outrage I was feeling, my mind was filled with the image of a little boy gazing up at his father with such love it stole my breath away.

All at once, I felt an unbearable pressure on my chest. I couldn't breath. It was as if all the air had been sucked out of the room and I'd suffocate if I didn't get out. Now.

I bolted for the door. "I need to use the restroom."

I flew out of the office. Behind me I heard Kizzy's murmur of concern followed by the deep rumble of Purdy's voice.

Brenda, scowling into the phone, looked up at my approach and pointed toward the back of the showroom with a red lacquered fingernail. I trotted by the cluster of salesmen and sought out the only uncarpeted room in Magic Mike's Carpet Heaven, the bathroom. It was a dark, crummy little room, apparently not intended for customers. A giant case of toilet tissue from a big box store sat against one wall, a waste basket and toilet brush against another.

I splashed cold water on my face and patted it dry with

a scratchy paper towel, breathing deeply to slow my racing heart. The tiny mirror hanging over the sink reflected my wide staring eyes. My face looked greenish-yellow in the dim light. Swarthy people do not pale prettily. I'd just given my cheeks a vicious pinch when I heard someone tap on the door.

"Allie? Everything okay? Mrs. Lovell wanted me to check on you."

I opened the door to find Brenda hovering just outside, her forehead wrinkled in concern.

I gave her a weak grin. "I'm fine. Just a little carpet overload."

"No kidding. The smell gets to you, huh? I'm looking for another job. I want to have a kid someday. Gotta be screwing up my eggs, workin' here. A woman only has so many egg, ya know."

We passed the leering salesmen. Brenda snickered and nudged me with an elbow. "Not that it wouldn't be a good thing if their little swimmers went belly up. Know what I mean?"

"Yeah, some people shouldn't have kids."

"Right on, girlfriend!"

We exchanged high fives.

"Tell Kizzy I'll wait for her outside."

I headed out of carpet hell thinking about my flippant remark, the one about people not having kids. Did I really believe that? If Mike Purdy hadn't reproduced, there would be no Allie.

I sat on a bench outside the store, my mind swirling in confusion. All my life, I'd waited for this moment. Father and daughter joyfully re-united. Faye and me in a cozy little apartment, funds provided by the guilt-ridden man who wanted to make up for his years of neglect. But it wasn't just about money. Maybe he'd even take me out for a hamburger and coke, get to know me better.

What *was* I feeling? Angry? Scared? Disappointed? Bingo. But not in Mike Purdy. No, I was disappointed in myself. I'd been an idiot. The fairy tale ending I'd imagined had vanished, sucked up into the noxious fumes of Carpet Heaven.

I stood and walked to the curb. Charlie jumped out and opened the door. Before I slid in, I turned for one last look at the man in the billboard. Magic Mike. Seated on a magic carpet? What was *that* about?

I hurried back into the store almost colliding with Kizzy, who Purdy was escorting to the door. Kizzy had a big carpet book under each arm.

"Mr. Purdy," I said. "That billboard outside? The one with the magic carpet? It's really cool. That's you, sitting on the carpet, right?"

Kizzy beamed like I was a gifted child.

Purdy squirmed and gazed out the window. "It's just a sales gimmick. Everybody knows the magic carpet story. That's all."

"But why do you call yourself 'Magic Mike?'" I persisted.

He shot me an annoyed look. "Like I said. Just a gimmick. Nothing magic about me."

I stuck out my hand. "Nice to meet you, Mr. Purdy."

He looked surprised but instinctively reached out. I shook his hand vigorously and gave it a quarter turn counterclockwise before I let it go. Looking puzzled, he pulled it away but not before I got a gander at his palm. And, if I'm not mistaken, he took a look at mine.

Oh yeah, he had the star.

Maybe Mike Purdy had a few secrets of his own.

Chapter Ten

Charlie loaded us into the limo and we headed for the freeway. Kizzy looked at her carpet books and waited for me to talk.

Finally I said, "Did you see it? At the base of his little finger."

Kizzy slid the carpet books onto the floor and nodded. "It's called 'the Mercury mound.' Has to be the reason he calls his business 'Magic Mike's Carpet Heaven.'"

"But why would he call himself Magic Mike then get all weird when I asked him about it?"

Kizzy shrugged. "Who knows? Maybe he's not comfortable with his powers. Sort of like you."

I winced. Yeah, it sounded exactly like me. Special powers are a double-edged sword. Part of me was proud and excited about doing things other people couldn't. But the other part screamed, "You're a freak!"

"Yeah, he's my dad alright." I sighed.

Kizzy gave me a quizzical look. "What do you plan to do about it?"

I shook my head. "He's got a new family. I bet they don't know anything about Faye and me. I keep seeing that kid, the little boy who looks like me. He loves his dad. If I make a big stink his wife might leave and take the kids. They'd lose their dad like I did."

My voice quavered and I gulped back tears.

Kizzy took my hand and squeezed it. "That's very mature of you, Allie. Putting others' needs ahead of your own."

A jet thundered overhead, startling us into silence. The body of the plane cast a huge shadow overhead, its dark presence moving across our path. In its wake came an explosion of color. Purple, bright pink and sunshine yellow. It swooped across the windshield then slithered around the side of the car. It paused for a moment and flapped like a bed sheet in the wind before peeling off and shooting skyward. I yelped and jumped about three inches off the seat.

"What is it, Allie? What's wrong?" Kizzy said, her brows drawn together in concern.

"That . . . that *thing*. It flew across the windshield," I stammered.

"You saw the shadow from the plane. That's all." She touched the back of her hand to my forehead.

"No, it wasn't the shadow." I was desperate to make her understand. "It was right there." I pointed at the side window closest to me. "It looked like a purple, pink and yellow sheet flapping away and . . . "

"You don't have a fever," Kizzy said. "But maybe the chemicals . . . "

I leaned forward in the seat. "Charlie? You saw it, right?"

Charlie glanced back at me. "All I see is a bunch of friggin' traffic."

I stared out the window. Was Kizzy right? Had sensory overload from Carpet Heaven made me hallucinate? It was then I noticed the green highway sign pointing the way to SeaTac. The Seattle-Tacoma airport. Trilby's hell on earth. Trilby with her purple, hot pink and yellow tie-dye dress.

"How far is SeaTac?"

Kizzy blinked in surprise. "It's just a few miles down the freeway. Why?"

"Just wondering."

I closed my eyes. Should I tell Kizzy about Trilby? At first, I'd believed Trilby was a dream. After the second time, I knew she was real, at least as real as a semi-ghost can be. But what would I say? *Your mother's housekeeper's daughter is my spirit guide. She's a dope-smoking, aging hippy who hangs around SeaTac waiting to go to heaven.* How could I tell that story without sounding totally nuts? Better to let Kizzy believe I was ditzy from carpet fumes.

When the limo turned into Uncle Sid's driveway, it was jammed with cars.

"Aunt Sandra's church ladies," I explained. "Every other Monday evening. They're probably peeking out the windows to see who's in the limo."

Before I climbed out, I gave Kizzy a hug. "Thanks for everything. I'll never forget this day."

I trudged down the driveway and, sure enough, I saw the curtains in the dining room window part and three faces peering out. I pointed back at the limo and mouthed the words, "Yeah, it was me in the limo. Cool, huh?"

The lights were on in the trailer. I knew Faye would be waiting for me. On the table, I'd see a paper plate with two Twinkies, each with a birthday candle. The message, "Happy Birthday, Allie," would be spelled out in chocolate chips on the table top. When I walked through the door, she'd light the candles. Our annual tradition.

I grinned in anticipation. I looked forward to telling her about my day. I'd tell her about Mike Purdy, his new family and that she was right. We'd celebrate like we always did. Blow out the candles, eat our Twinkies and have a race to see who could scarf down the most chocolate chips.

I reached for the door and stopped when I heard voices inside, the rise and fall of female voices, murmuring softly as if soothing a fussy child. Above the murmurs I heard Faye's voice, wild and shrill with panic. "No! You can't take her away from me!"

I charged through the door, my heart in my throat. Faye sat at the table, ashen-faced, a tattered University of Washington sweatshirt pulled over her pajamas. Her lower lip trembled and her eyes were wide with shock. The Twinkies had been pushed to one side, the chocolate chips scattered in a random pattern across the table.

A tall, thin woman sat on my couch bed, a briefcase open by her side. She looked up when I entered and compressed her lips into a pale, narrow line. Her steel-gray hair was styled into rigid curls and stiff with hairspray. Across from her and perched on the edge of the swivel chair sat a plump, pleasant-faced woman clad in a tan pants suit. Her eyes twinkled and the corners of her mouth curled up in an inappropriate smile. "Oh, you must be Allie."

She stood and extended her arms like she wanted to give me a hug. I ignored her. Good cop, bad cop, I thought.

I plopped down next to Faye and grabbed her hand.

"What's going on? Who are these people?"

Faye made a little sound like a cross between a hiccup and a sob. "CPS," she whispered.

"What?" I screeched. "Child Protective Services? No way! Besides, they don't come calling this time of the night. Did they show you their identification?"

I was shaking with outrage and fear. An ugly suspicion began to form in the back of my mind as I remembered the faces in the window as I passed the big house.

At my words, the two women dug out their identification. The place was so small I didn't have to get up to see that their State Of Washington ID's matched the names on their badges. Cynthia Badgley was the mean one. Pam Pettibone, our lady of the perpetual smiles, the other.

"Why are you here?" I waited for the lies to begin. CPS operates on referrals. Somebody had turned Faye in. I was pretty sure I knew who it was.

Pam regarded us with a concerned smile. Cynthia squared her shoulders and cleared her throat. "We've had a referral regarding your mother's parenting practices and feel her neglect may be putting you in harm's way."

I jumped up. "I'm fine! My mother has fibromyalgia. Maybe you've never heard of it. It's a disease that makes you hurt all over. She can't work. I'm not neglected. Do I look neglected?"

The fear was gone. Now I was just plain mad and maybe a little crazy. Never did I think I'd be defending Faye's fake illness.

Pam Pettibone fluttered her fat little fingers and clucked, "It's all right, Alfrieda When we have a referral, we have to check it out. Surely you understand. And, you look fine, dear. Just fine."

Cynthia shot her a dirty look. I continued to glare down at the women. Pam was right. Thanks to Faye, I looked pretty darn good. She'd insisted I wear her good black slacks for my big day. They looked like crop pants because they hit me mid-calf, but topped with her blue silk blouse, I looked hot. Well . . . maybe not *hot* but definitely hotter than those two.

"But . . . but . . . " I sputtered. "Faye needs . . . " I clamped my mouth shut before I could utter the rest of the sentence. *Faye needs me to take care of her.* Even though it was true, why give them more ammunition?

Cynthia, though, gave me a smug look. Maybe she could read minds. Maybe she had a moonstone like me. Too bad mine couldn't help me now.

After a long silence, Pam said, "Ms. Emerson, we understand your father lives in Vista Valley."

Faye jerked like she'd been poked with a sharp stick. "I haven't spoken to my father for . . . " She paused and glanced at me. "Fifteen years."

"We talked to him about your, er, situation," Pam began.

"He's willing to let you and Allie move in until you get on your feet."

Faye lurched forward and clutched the tabletop with shaking hands, like she was trying to hold herself back. "You have no right to go behind my back!"

"Actually, we do," Cynthia said. Her pinched lips barely moved when she talked. "We make every effort to keep families together. From all accounts, your father is financially well-set, he has a large home and . . . "

"No!" Faye shouted. "I will not take my daughter into his home. Period."

Pam cocked her head to one side and raised an eyebrow. "Are there issues we don't know about?"

She waited for an answer but Faye had shut down. I sighed. When Faye chose not to talk, she could hold out forever. If we wanted to get rid of these two before midnight, I had to do something. "Do you have Big Ed's card?"

Hope bloomed in her eyes. She hurried into the bedroom and I heard her rummaging through the papers stacked next to the bed. Pam, Cynthia and I waited in uneasy silence. The tension in the room hummed like the power poles next to Tom's Corner Market. I folded my arms across my chest and stared at Pam (the weakest link,) who squirmed in discomfort. Cynthia gazed around the trailer, a look of disapproval on her narrow features.

Finally, I broke the silence. "Talk to Susan Wright, our caseworker. She knows all about us."

Cynthia gave me a pitying look. "We have jurisdiction over all other agencies. Your mother doesn't work, drinks excessively and doesn't provide for you. That sounds like neglect to me."

I opened my mouth to protest when Faye emerged holding Big Ed's business card. I handed it to Cynthia with a triumphant flourish. "You have anything else to say to us, tell it to Big Ed."

Cynthia smirked and shook her head in mock distress. She peered around me and spoke to Faye. "Oh, yes, Ms. Emerson. I've heard you have a special working relationship with Mr. McDougall."

The fury I felt burned through my veins like molten fire, and I wanted nothing more than to punch the smug look off her face. The need to inflict pain boiled up from deep down inside me, the same feeling I'd had when Cory Philpott dissed my mother and I smacked him. I heard a moan like an animal in pain. Had I made that sound? I saw Pam's stricken face floating before me while I fought for control.

From my peripheral vision, I saw Faye sink back onto the dinette bench, two red spots burning in her cheeks. *Be smart, Allie,* I told myself. *Use your head, not your fists.*

Breathing deeply, I sat down beside Faye, brushed aside some chocolate chips and folded my hands on the table top. I focused on Pam. "Do you go to Peacock Heights Church of the Good Shepherd?"

She gulped noisily. "Yes, why do you ask?"

I turned my gaze on Cynthia "What about you?"

She blinked three times in succession and avoided my eyes. "My religious affiliation has nothing to do with the subject at hand."

I took that for a *Yes.* "I know Aunt Sandra wants us out of here. Must have been her who made the referral."

Cynthia drew herself up and huffed, "That's privileged information."

"No problem. I'll just walk over and ask her. Godly people never lie. Right?"

"Your lack of respect is just another symptom of poor parenting. Your attitude needs adjusting, Alfrieda," Cynthia said. She picked up her brief case and stood. "We'll take no action tonight but we will be making frequent drop-in visits. Let's go, Pamela."

Pam who'd been staring at me, mouth agape and goggle-eyed since I'd brought up the church issue, snapped her mouth shut and shot out of her chair.

I followed them to the door. Suddenly my mind flashed on an item from Current Events class. "Nice to know Faye and I are top priority for CPS. Too bad about the little kid in foster care who got beaten to death because his caseworkers didn't check on him. Remember that one?"

Cynthia and Pam scurried away. I waited a few beats then, in spite of Faye's protests, stepped from the trailer and into the shadows. Cynthia's tall figure was easy to track in the dark. She was heading for the cluster of cars in the driveway. Pam trailed behind like one ship following another. The *SS Cynthia*, sleek and tall-masted, sailed straight ahead, making for home port while the *SS Pam* floundered and clunked along in her wake.

They'd just reached the car when a dark figure slipped from the shadows. I was too far away to hear her words, but when she stepped into the circle of light illuminating the driveway, I could see it was Aunt Sandra. Big surprise. Though I wanted to charge up to her and scream out my anger at her lies and betrayal, I did nothing but watch helplessly as the three women, heads bent together in the dim light, discussed my future.

Happy birthday, Allie. Not!

Chapter Eleven

Morning came too soon. Before she cried herself to sleep, Faye stubbornly refused to give me any information about Grandpa Claude. Since she'd been a drama queen all her life I figured it had to be one of the following: (A) She was mad at him for naming me Alfrieda Carlotta. (B) He refused to give her money. (C) Something horrible I didn't want to think about.

Yeah, I know. I'm my mother's daughter.

Before I left for school, I checked on Faye, who'd fallen into a coma-like sleep. I ate peanut butter toast, brushed my teeth and kissed Faye's pale cheek, whispering, "It'll be okay. I promise."

Weary beyond words, I trudged down the driveway wondering if I should talk to Uncle Sid when I got home from school. After all, he was a relative, a half-assed one, but still a relative. That should count for something. I was halfway down the driveway when I heard Matt's Jeep start up. I hadn't seen Matt since the day I'd peeked into his dirty little mind.

He pulled up beside me. "What's up, Allie?"

I looked over at him. "Ask your mother."

"Huh?" he said, a look of bewilderment clouding his perfect features. It was clear he didn't know about Aunt Sandra's agenda.

"Oh, never mind. You'll find out soon enough."

"You still mad at me?"

I flashed on the ugly words he'd been thinking. Having little experience reading minds, I had no idea how to respond. "That depends. Should I be?"

He blinked in surprise. "Heck, no. I'm a lovable guy."

"Yeah, right. See ya, Matt."

He lifted a hand in farewell and peeled out of the driveway toward Peacock Heights Christian School.

While we waited for the bus, I told Manny and Mercedes about our CPS visit. Mercedes reacted in her typical manner. "No way!" she cried. "That's totally, totally screwed up!"

"Wow," I said with a weak grin. "Two 'totallys.' Must be really bad, huh?"

The ever-practical Manny said, "I've seen that woman's car in your uncle's driveway a bunch of times. I'll pass the word. Don't worry, Allie. We see that car around . . . we let you know right away. Give you time to make a plan, eh?"

"Thanks, Manny. You're the best."

I patted his chubby cheek. He flushed and ducked his head. By "passing the word," I knew Manny meant he'd inform his entire, extended family, which included dozens of people spread far and wide across the valley. A couple hundred extra eyes watching for Cynthia and Pam couldn't hurt.

Later, on the bus—thankfully Cory Philpott was absent—I dug out my algebra book to make sure my homework was inside. Folded carefully around my algebra problems was another sheet of notebook paper. I smoothed it open and read the following message, written in bright purple ink with little hearts drawn over each letter "i"

Hey Allie,

It's me, Trilby! Happy birthday, kid. Saw you in the limo—classy wheels, by the way. Did you see me? I stopped by the limo to tell you goodbye. Yeah, that's right, I'm on my way up there.

She'd drawn an arrow pointing upward

You did it, you passed the third test. So I'm outta here. Oh, yeah, I see that clueless look you get like, 'Duh, what test?' So I'll tell you. It was the daddy thing. You denied yourself something you really wanted. You put someone else's welfare and needs before your own—you know who I'm talkin' about—the scrawny little kid who looks like you. Which means, you're now fully vested in your powers. And don't ask me 'what powers?' You gotta figure that out for yourself.

Peace and love,

Trilby, your spirit guide.

P.S. If I don't like it up here, I'll be baaaaack! Bet you're wondering how I know about The Terminator. Got bored one day at SeaTac (oooh, oxymoron). Some dorky-looking kid had one of those portable movie players and I sat by him and watched. Arnie's hot!

I tucked the note away from Mercedes' curious eyes, vowing I'd think about it later when the specter of CPS wasn't hanging over my head.

"Hey, dude! Cool necklace."

I jumped, and Mercedes yelped in surprise. The voice belonged to Didier Ellsworth the Third, whose fuzzy blond head appeared over our seatback. My hand flew up to cover the moonstone. I'd forgotten to tuck it inside my shirt.

"Jeeze, Didier, you shouldn't sneak up on people like that. You almost gave Mercedes a heart attack."

Diddy didn't understand personal space. He slithered forward until his upper torso was wedged between Mercedes and me. He looked back and forth between us, smiling his goofy Diddy smile. He pointed at the moonstone. His long, thin fingers reminded me of spider legs. "So that whaddaya call that thing, dude?"

Mercedes giggled. With a little huff of irritation, I said, "Diddy. I am not a dude. Dude's are guys. Stop calling me a dude. Okay?"

His face fell. I saw the hurt in his pale blue eyes and felt like I'd kicked a puppy. Yeah, I was tired and crabby, but that was no excuse for lashing out at poor Diddy. "I got it at a yard sale."

I lowered my hand and let him take a good look before I stuffed it inside my shirt.

"Awesome, dude, I mean, Allie. Hey, if you ever need any help in algebra, I'm really good at it. I could come over to your place if you want."

"Thanks, Diddy. I'll let you know." Like when kittens and puppies grow on Uncle Sid's apple trees.

I turned away from him and stared out the window. He finally got the hint and retreated. I steeled myself for what I knew would happen next.

Sure enough, Mercedes poked me with her elbow and whispered, "Oooo, Diddy's in love! You better not break his heart. He might slit his wrists or jump in front of a logging truck."

I shook my head and smiled. The girl should write romance novels.

Later that day, we'd just finished responding to Mrs. Burke's *"Como esta?"* by saying, *"Bien, gracias,"* when Cory Philpott burst into the room. He flipped his pass on Mrs. Burke's desk and headed to the back of the room, where all the losers sit. His shoelaces, untied of course, dragged on the floor, and he shuffled his feet to keep his gigantic clodhoppers from falling off. He stopped when he got to my desk. "Hey, Allitosis. Ding dong, the witch is dead."

I wasn't in the mood for Cory. My only response was a dirty look and a dismissive flap of the hand. Not to be denied, Cory said, "Thought you'd want to know, you being so close to her and all."

A sudden chill shot through my body. I looked up at Cory. "What are you talking about?"

Mrs. Burke said, "Cory and Allie. I hope my lesson plan isn't interrupting your little chat."

Mrs. Burke could be real sarcastic at times. I felt a flush crawl up my neck. "Sorry, Mrs. Burke." I ducked my head and hissed at Cory. "Tell me!"

"It's that Kizzy woman. Somebody beat her up real bad. I was with my dad when the 911 call came in. Man, there was blood everywhere. I think she's dead."

"No!" I jumped out of my chair. "I just saw her yesterday."

"Allie!" Mrs. Burke spoke sharply. "Sit down."

My classmates watched in slack-jawed horror as I ran to the front of the room. Mrs. Burke's eyes went huge and her hands fluttered helplessly. "I have to go, Mrs. Burke. I'm really sorry. Please, it's important. I'll explain later."

Without waiting for her answer, I dashed from the room and tore out of the building at a dead run, and my only thought was, She can't be dead, she can't be dead. I felt the moonstone hard against my chest and pulled it out of my shirt. I clutched it as I ran, hoping it's magic would make everything all right.

After a block, I kicked off my flip flops and pounded barefoot down the dirty, concrete sidewalk. When the sidewalk ended I moved to the narrow shoulder of the two-lane road, wincing as I ran over bits of gravel and other debris. Blood oozed up between my toes.

I'd just slowed down to catch my breath when a car pulled up beside me. I glanced over to see Junior Martinez in his low rider. The passenger window slid down. Junior leaned toward the open window. "Hey Home Girl, hop in. I'll give you a ride."

Gasping for breath, I leaned over, put my hands on my knees. "I'm not your home girl. Why are you here? I just saw you in Mrs. Burke's class."

"Told Burke I had to go with my mom to pay bills."

"Liar," I said. "Are you stalking me?"

He shot me an amused look. "Emerson, you're a piece of work. Get in."

I approached the car cautiously, all of Faye's dire warnings flashing through my mind.

"That's it," Junior said like he was coaxing a stray dog.

He reached over and opened the door. Without taking my eyes off Junior, I slid into the passenger seat. I needed to get to Kizzy's but could I trust Junior? Granted, I liked the way he smelled, and my nose doesn't lie. A guy who smelled like fresh laundry couldn't be all that bad . . . I hoped.

He glanced down at my feet. His eyes widened in surprise. He cursed furiously in Spanish. "God Almighty, girl, your feet are all bloody. What happened to your shoes? And where are you going in such a hurry?"

I explained about the flip flops and my need to get to Kizzy's house. He made a U-turn.

Still leery of Junior, I screeched, "You're going the wrong way. Let me out!"

"Chill, Emerson. We gotta get your shoes. You gonna walk around like that with your feet all torn up?" He shook his head sadly. "Women."

The flip flops were still in the middle of the sidewalk where I'd run out of them. I started to open the door but Junior held up a hand. "Don't be stupid."

He retrieved the flip flops and handed them to me along with a towel he pulled from the back seat. "I can't believe you. Running barefoot through all that stuff. Are you crazy?"

He was right, but I didn't need a lecture from too-handsome-for-his-own-good Junior Martinez, former gang member, teenage father and seducer of ninth grade girls. As we drove toward Kizzy's house, I turned and checked out the back seat.

I clucked my tongue in disapproval. "I don't see a government-approved, child's safety seat installed in your car. I hope you don't drive around with your baby bouncing around the car like a helium balloon."

Junior slammed on the brakes, jerked the wheel sideways and screeched to a halt at the side of the road. "What the hell you talkin' about? What baby? You think I've got a kid?"

"Yeah, uh, well . . . " I stammered. "Manny Trujillo said he saw you at the mall, pushing a baby in a stroller."

"You thought it was mine?" Junior's eyes were a surprising shade of gray when filled with outrage.

Mortified, I stared at the floorboards. "It probably wasn't you."

"It was me all right, with my sister's kid."

I knew the car wouldn't move until the matter was settled.

"Really, Junior. I believe you," I said.

"All right, then. Guess we got that cleared up. Anything else?"

Oh, just the little matter of you stabbing a rival gang member, but no big deal. "No." I was bouncing up and down in my impatience. "Let's go."

Junior pulled out onto the road, driving a good ten miles under the posted speed limit. "Come on, Junior. Pick it up. This is an emergency."

"Easy for you to say. You're not on probation. I made a promise to my mom. No more breaking the law, no more gang banging. You know how hard that is around here?"

I thought about Cory getting slapped around by the Proud White Tuffs, about a Native American kid I knew who didn't have a mean bone in his body but, sick of getting pounded on, formed his own gang, the Red Posse, and I thought about the Chicanos from Southern California, whose fathers were seasoned gang bangers and expected their kids to follow in their footsteps.

"Yeah," I said softly. "I bet it's tough. Are you doing okay?"

He glanced over at me. "You really want to know?"

I nodded.

So, while Junior drove sedately down the country road like a sweet-faced old lady on her way to Senior Day at the casino, he filled me in on his life. Junior was his mother's last living son. One brother died in a car crash, the other in a violent gang fight. Seeking to avenge his brother's murder, Junior joined a gang. The bloody encounter that followed ended with his opponent badly injured and Junior serving time.

"Bottom line," Junior said. "My mother will cut my nuts out . . . oops, sorry, I mean she'll kill me in a slow, painful way if I mess up again."

I thought about Faye. "Yeah, me too. Not the nuts part, of course." I ducked my head and blushed. Time to change the subject. "What about your dad?" I almost choked on the "d" word.

Junior lowered his window and spat. "Son of a bitch left us and went to Mexico. I think he's got another wife down there."

On the "dad" issue, Junior and I weren't so different. "The gang let you out?"

His face closed up. "I had to fight my way out."

He tugged at his right sleeve and pointed to a jagged scar that started at the elbow, traversed the entire length of his upper arm and disappeared into his crisp, white tee shirt.

"Ouch." I traced the scar with the tip of my index finger. Junior inhaled sharply but kept his eyes on the road.

"Those guys still after you?"

"Let me put it this way. They're getting the message."

His eyes glittered with a fierceness that made me blink and withdraw my hand. This was a different Junior, the don't-mess-with-me-or-I'll-mess-you-up person who lurked just beneath the surface. The dimple was gone.

We pulled in behind three police cars parked in front of Kizzy's hedge. An ambulance, lights flashing, backed out of the driveway and tore down the road

I whispered, "If she's in an ambulance, she must be alive. Right, Junior?"

Junior's eyes softened. "It'll be okay, kid. Just hang tough."

I got out on trembling legs and headed for the house. When Junior didn't follow, I turned back to the car. "Are you coming?"

"Naw, I'll wait for you."

He pointed at the house. "Cops. They think I'm still runnin' with the gang."

I leaned into the open window. "Thanks for the ride. Guess I'll see you at school."

"I'll wait."

From the stubborn set of his jaw, I knew it was pointless to argue. "I don't want you to get in trouble."

"What trouble? I'm just sitting here. Go."

I dashed through the gate and ran toward the house. The broad stairs leading to the veranda were crisscrossed with yellow crime-scene tape. My stomach felt queasy, and a bitter taste rose in my throat as I stepped over it. The front door stood open. I heard men's voices and a sharp bark of laughter. Laughter? What the hell was wrong with these people?

Determined to find the source, I stepped into the living room and clapped a hand over my mouth. The room looked like a tornado had ripped through it. Tables and chairs were tipped over. Drawers hung open, their contents spilling out onto the floor. Shards of a shattered vase and a tangle of pale blue iris lay on the stone hearth in a puddle of water.

I picked my way through the mess. The men's voices were coming from the kitchen. Afraid of what I'd find, I slowly approached the kitchen. As I reached for the door, it opened and a man holding a camera stepped through. He recoiled in surprise. "Where the hell did you come from, kid? This is a crime scene. Didn't you see the tape?"

I'd come this far. No way would I back down now. And maybe he was the laugher, which would justify the lie I was about to tell. "I'm a family member. I need to see Deputy Philpott. Is he here?"

The man called over his shoulder, "Hey Dick. Some kid's here. Says she's family."

"Be right there. Tell her to wait."

The photographer pointed a finger at me. "Don't move."

He tromped through the living room and out the door. I waited a few beats then peeked through the kitchen door. Before my mind could comprehend the horror, I smelled the blood and felt the heavy weight of violence lingering in the air. Kizzy's pristine kitchen, newly updated with granite countertops and a white tile floor, was spattered with blood. Scarlet streaks stained the walls. A bloody handprint was clearly visible on the kitchen island. Three men, clad in sterile suits and booties covering their shoes, crouched over the chalk outline of a sprawled body. I cried out in horror. My knees buckled and I sank to the floor, the edges of my world turning dark and fuzzy.

"Allie!" I felt hard fingers grasp my arm. Deputy Philpott pulled me into the living room and sat me down on an overstuffed foot stool.

"Drop your head between your knees. Take some deep breathes."

I gulped air until the buzzing in my ears subsided.

"Atta girl," he said. "Now you're getting some color back."

I looked up at him, my lower lip trembling uncontrollably. "She's dead, isn't she? Kizzy. That's why the siren wasn't going. That's why you drew a line around her body."

Philpott squatted down in front of me. "I'm going to be honest with you, Allie. She was in bad shape when the paramedics got here. Barely alive. They started a transfusion. Whether she makes it or not . . . " his voice drifted off and he shook his head sadly.

"But, all that blood. How could she live and lose all that blood?" The gory scene in the kitchen played out in my mind. I had a feeling I'd be seeing it for a long time. "Do you know what happened to her?

"Somebody beat the stuffing out of her. It looks like she fought back. At some point she either fell or the assailant bashed her head against the granite counter." Philpott stood up and cleared his throat. "So now you're family, huh?"

I blushed and looked at the ceiling. "Well, I'm like family. She does have a daughter, though. Carmel. She and her boyfriend were just here last weekend. You should call her."

Philpott withdrew a small notebook from his breast pocket. "Carmel, last name Lovell?"

I nodded and pointed at the overturned table where Kizzy kept her phone and address book. "Check the drawer. Her number should be in there." I felt my strength returning and stood up slowly. "Where did the ambulance take her?"

"Vista Valley Regional. Why?"

"Just wondering." I sidled toward the door.

"You know much about her family situation? The daughter her only child?"

"Kizzy couldn't have kids. She and her husband adopted Carmel. She has a boyfriend. Teddy. Kizzy said

they only come here when they want money. You might
want to check on those two."

Philpott looked thoughtful and made another notation.

"Who made the 911 call?" I asked.

"The limo driver. She had a nine o'clock appointment
with her lawyer. He came by to pick her up. When she
didn't answer the doorbell, he went in and found Ms. Lovell
in the kitchen. The back door was standing open, and he
heard a car take off in alley behind the house."

"Gotta go." I scuttled toward the door.

"I might have more questions, later."

"You know where to find me."

I trotted to the car and jumped in.

"Back to school?" Junior asked.

"I really need to get to Vista Valley, but you don't have
to take me."

Junior made a disgusted sound. "Like I'm going to let
you run all the way to Vista Valley in flip flops!"

Chapter Twelve

Junior and I were in Regional's waiting room for family members of patients. I was now Kizzy's niece, one of her few living relatives. Who knew I had such a talent for lying? The nurse, though, had been brutally honest. "If she has a daughter, somebody better get her here. Fast."

She promised to let me see Kizzy, to say my goodbyes. "Her head wound has been sutured and she's in a deep coma. She won't know you're in the room."

Her callousness angered me. I glared at her. "How do you know that? Kizzy's strong. She's not going to die."

Unlike the other nurses, this one wore a starched hat. Her name tag said, "A. Haugen." It should have said, "Boss Nurse." She gave me a pitying look and turned to leave. "I'll come get you as soon as the other guy leaves."

"What other guy?"

"The guy in a fancy suit. Blonde hair. Good looking. Says he's her nephew. If you're her niece, you know who I'm talking about, right?"

Oops. Busted. I avoided her eyes. "Oh, him."

After a long, appraising look designed to ferret out my secrets, she left.

"You're a piss-poor liar, Emerson," Junior said from across the room, where he'd been talking in Spanish to a distraught-looking Hispanic couple.

I ignored him and tiptoed to the open doorway. I looked up and down the hall. "I'm going for a walk."

"Yeah, right," Junior said. "Want me to come?"

I shook my head and slipped into the hall. Other than a man mopping the floor, all the activity was centered at the rear of the nurses' station. It looked like a mini bridal shower was in progress. A. Haugen was nowhere in sight. Three women were gathered around a fourth, who reached inside a gift bag and withdrew a black lace teddy and a long, cylindrical item that looked like an oversized penlight. The women howled with laughter.

Grateful for the diversion, I meandered down the hall, glancing in each window for Kizzy. The last one had the curtains pulled tightly together. Silently, I eased the door open and saw a man looming over a prone figure lying in the bed. Granted, the man could have been a grieving relative saying goodbye to a loved one, but something about him made the hair on the back of my neck stand up.

My heart was racing as I pushed through the door. The man jerked upright and stared at me. I saw something flash in his eyes, something dark and predatory. A split second later, he gave me an ingratiating smile. He straightened his tie and raked his fingers through thick, blond hair. His face was lean and bronzed and filled with concern.

"Hello there. Are you here to see Kizzy?"

I ignored him and hurried over to the bed, staring with horror at Kizzy's still form. I held my breath until I saw her chest rise and fall. Thank God, she was still alive.

I glanced up at the man. "So you're Kizzy's nephew. You must be her sister's son."

Since I knew Kizzy was an only child, I looked forward to his answer.

Without a moment's hesitation, he looked deep into my eyes and said, "That's right. Christian Revelle. And you are . . . ?"

Okay, if he was claiming to be Kizzy's fake nephew, I couldn't be her fake niece. We'd have to know each other.

Right? Since, as Junior pointed out, I was a piss-poor liar, I decided to tell the truth.

"Allie." I gave his outstretched hand a tiny squeeze. His palm was sweaty. I resisted the urge to wipe my hand on my pants.

"You're family?" He ran an appraising eye over my tee shirt, jeans and bloody flip flops. "Guess we've never met."

I walked to the other side of Kizzy's bed. "Kizzy and I are close friends. Has anyone notified Carmel?"

Ha! Gotcha. I watched his face.

His eyes slid away from mine then back. He shrugged. "I assumed the hospital called her."

I could have pushed harder. I could have asked, "So, you told them how to reach her?" But I didn't. He needed to think I was a dumb, clueless kid.

Nervously, my fingers closed around the moonstone. It felt warm against my hand. Its touch filled me with a sense of peace and calmed my racing heart. It felt like Kizzy was telling me everything would be all right. Revelle's eyes followed the movement of my hand and lingered there for a long, uncomfortable moment.

"Interesting piece of jewelry." He cocked his head to one side and regarded me with a puzzled frown. "But, hold on. Isn't that Aunt Kizzy's?"

I felt my cheeks turn fiery red under his intense gaze. I had no reason to feel guilty. Revelle was the liar, not me. But something in his unspoken accusation made me feel like a sneak thief. "She gave it to me. If you don't believe me, you can ask her when she wakes up."

Gleaming white teeth flashed in a fake smile. "Oh, I believe you, kid. No problem." With a deep sigh, he sat in a chair adjacent to Kizzy's bed and bowed his head. "I pray she'll come around soon."

My fingers still clutched the moonstone. I though about Trilby's words. *You're now fully vested in your powers.* Since she didn't elaborate, it was trial-and-error time. Four days had passed since I'd tuned in to Matt's nasty little mind. With Revelle still playing the role of a grieving relative lost in prayer, I was free to experiment.

I rotated the moonstone in its setting until I felt it click. Instantly, an eerie green light filled the room, and my head was filled with a jumble of voices like two radio stations playing at once. An icy finger of fear crawled up my spine as a dark presence rose from Revelle's bowed head. Biting my lower lip to keep from crying out, I watched the specter move and change, shifting and re-forming until it hung over Kizzy's bed like a black storm cloud clinging to the rounded foothills surrounding Peacock Flats.

I moved closer to the head of the bed and grabbed the bedrails, afraid to take my eyes from the evil presence lurking over Kizzy's head. The voices faded out and I heard what sounded like static. I took two steps sideways. The jumble of voices returned. I looked down at Revelle, still slumped over in his chair. A thick lock of hair had fallen over his forehead, concealing his eyes. *What's in your mind, Christian Revelle?* Utter silence. Nothing. Nada. I felt a flash of irritation at Trilby. Fully vested? Ha!

With a sigh of disgust, I looked around for another chair. No way would I leave Kizzy alone with this guy and the evil black blob that had popped out of his head. I'd just taken two steps toward the end of the bed when I heard Revelle's voice.

I stopped, dead still, and listened as my mind picked up snippets of words.

"Damn kid! Wouldn't you know she'd come in and . . . "

His voice faded away like a radio station out of range. Frustrated, I moved a few inches to the left. Nothing but white noise. I moved toward the foot of the bed and clearly heard the word, "moonstone," and "Baxter."

Trying not to make a sound—not easy wearing flip

flops—I moved back and forth trying to pick up Revelle's thoughts. Just as I heard "kill" which, believe me, stood my hair on end, Nurse A. Haugen burst into the room. I turned the stone back to its original position and tucked it into my shirt.

"You!" She pointed a long, bony finger at Revelle, who was frozen in a half crouch. She pointed at the door. "Out!" Her ice blue eyes sliced into me like a laser. "And you! What part of 'one visitor at a time' do you not understand?"

"Sorry," I mumbled, certain she would now order me out of the room.

Revelle leaned over Kizzy and kissed her cheek. I almost gagged. After a long look at the bump on my chest—the moonstone, I mean—he said, "See ya, kid," and strolled from the room.

Hands on her hips, A. Haugen watched him leave before tending to Kizzy. I tried to make myself invisible as she checked numerous tubes and gauges. Finally, she turned to me, pointed at a chair and said, "Sit. Stay," before marching out of the room. She returned with a plastic tub of water which she plunked down on the floor next to me. She handed me soap and a towel. "Wash those filthy feet," she ordered

"Yessum, Boss Nurse," I muttered, slipping out of my flip flops.

The corner of her mouth twitched. "You're a bit of a smart ass, aren't you?" When I didn't answer, she said, "Look, I know you're not Ms. Lovell's niece. The sheriff called and gave me the information about her daughter. We're trying to reach her. But, if you want to sit with her for a while, it's okay. By the way, who are you?"

I scrubbed my feet and told her my story. That I was like a daughter to Kizzy. As I said the words, I realized they were true. Hot tears stung my eyes and spilled down my cheeks. I used the towel to wipe them away.

Her lip curled in distaste as she looked at my bloody footwear. "Shoes, too."

I dunked the flip flops, ashamed at how filthy the water had become. A. Haugen went to the door and summoned an underling to come fetch the dirty water and, when she was done, to check the bedpan in room 312.

She stared down at me. "That good-looking Hispanic boy in the waiting room wants to talk to you."

I slipped squeaky clean feet into my flip flops. "Can I come back and sit with Kizzy?"

Her eyes softened. "Someone she cares about should be with her."

I found Junior alone in the waiting room, staring out the window at the parking lot below. When I joined him, he pointed at an Escalade pulling out of the lot.

"That's the guy who came out of Kizzy's room. Slick lookin' guy. Another man was waiting for him in the car. They sat and talked a while, then they both got out of the car and Slick pointed up here. Those two are up to something, and it's not good."

Another guy? Hmmm . . . Baxter? I nodded not quite trusting Junior enough to tell him about the moonstone and the information I'd picked up from Revelle's mind. Instead, I filled him in on Revelle's fake story.

"When I walked into the room, he was standing over Kizzy." I shuddered, remembering the twisted, hateful look on Revelle's face. "Maybe he and the other guy beat her up. Maybe they want to finish the job. We should tell the cops. She needs somebody guarding her."

Junior shook his head. "We got no proof."

"Then I'll stay here. I'm not leaving her alone!" I bit my lower lip to stop it from trembling.

Junior slipped an arm around my shoulders and led me to the couch. "I got you something to eat." He thrust a shrink-wrapped bologna and cheese sandwich into my hand. "I gotta go to work. You wanna stay here, or what?"

I picked at the plastic wrap. "I told you, I'm not leaving."

Junior pulled a cell phone from his pocket. "Call your mother. She'll be wondering why you didn't get off the bus."

Though I doubted Faye had come around after her trauma-filled night, I took his cell phone and called Mercedes, who asked me about a million questions. I promised to fill her in later.

Over the blaring TV in the background, I heard Manny telling her something in rapid-fire Spanish. "Oh, yeah," Mercedes said. "Manny says not to worry about those child welfare dudes—chicks . . . whatever. They're down in the lower valley today."

Thank God for the Trujillo family. I smiled. My first one of the day. "Tell Manny thanks. Talk to you later."

Junior left for his shift at Big Bob's Burgers, promising to pick me up when he got off at nine. I finished my sandwich and headed back to Kizzy's room. She was gone!

"Noooo!" I shrieked, looking with horror at the empty bed. "She can't be dead!"

Yeah, I panicked. Big time. Guess I'd seen too many movies where someone like Sandra Bullock walks into a hospital room expecting to see her father recovering from open heart surgery only to find a freshly made bed and her father gone. I mean, really gone, like Trilby, to the other side.

But I wasn't Sandra Bullock, dammit, and I wanted answers. I stormed out the door and crashed into Nurse Haugen, who grabbed my arm and shook me. Hard.

"Stop that screeching! Right this minute."

I snapped my mouth shut.

"Your friend isn't dead. She stabilized, so we moved her. If you calm down, I'll take you to her."

I chilled and followed her through a maze of corridors, firing questions as we walked. "What do you mean, 'stabilized?' Did she wake up? Can she talk? Did she tell you what happened?"

The nurse stopped in front of room 314 and put one hand on her hip. "Stable refers to her vital signs and no, she's not conscious and no, she can't talk."

She frowned at me though I saw a slight twinkle of amusement in her frosty gaze. "Anything else?"

After cautioning me not to cause any more trouble because, after all, Kizzy wasn't the only person in the hospital who needed her attention, she turned and strode down the hall, her sensible white nurse shoes squeaking with every step.

I slipped through the open door and glanced at the first bed, where a hugely obese woman sat upright sipping water through a bendy straw. When she spotted me, her moon face lit up in a smile. "Gastric bypass," she said, pointing at her tummy. "Give me a year and I'll look like a swimsuit model. You here to visit her?"

She pointed at the white curtain separating the two beds. "She's real quiet. Great roommate!" She giggled and settled back against her pillow. I tiptoed around the curtain and pulled a chair up next to Kizzy's bed. The room faced west, and late afternoon sun poured through slatted blinds casting a striped pattern of light and dark across the bed. I reached over and took her hand and felt a thrill of surprise when her fingers tightened around mine.

Without releasing her hand, I stood and leaned over her. "Kizzy?" I whispered. "Can you hear me? Squeeze my hand."

She stirred slightly and moaned but, once again, I felt her hand grip mine. I stared down at her, trying to decide what to do. Was Kizzy coming out of her coma? Should I call A. Haugen? Was I endangering her life by standing here like a dummy? Before I could decide on a plan of action, Kizzy's eyelids fluttered and opened. Her beautiful turquoise eyes, usually sparkling and full of life, were dull and unfocused. I caught my breath. It seemed like the real Kizzy was gone and some pale stranger had invaded her body and stolen her light.

Her eyelids fell shut and she croaked, "Allie?"

"I'm here, Kizzy. Right here. Can you see me?"

I desperately wanted her to open her eyes again, to see if the real Kizzy had come back. But her eyes remained shut and her breathing became more regular. She'd gone back to wherever people go when they're in a coma. I bit back my disappointment. But as I started to sit down, her fingers clutched mine in a surprisingly strong grip.

I put my ear next to her lips.

"Don't let them have it . . . the moonstone."

"Who? Who did this to you?" My voice sounded shrill and demanding.

Kizzy jerked convulsively. Her eyes fluttered open once again. This time her gaze was focused and fierce. "Look in cedar chest . . . prophecy . . . Mama's things . . . promise . . ."

Before I could utter a word, her hand went limp. She closed her eyes and began to snore gently. Lights out!

I continued to sit with Kizzy, listening to her breathe, hoping she'd wake up and give me a few more clues. For starters—who wanted the moonstone so badly he was willing to beat her to death to get it? And—hey, I'd never seen a cedar chest in Kizzy's house, and I'd been in every room.

While I fretted over answers to these questions I must have dozed off, because the next thing I knew, Junior was shaking me awake. The delicious aroma of french fries clung to his clothes and permeated the sterile hospital air. I must have been hungry, because some primitive urge made me want to fling myself into Junior's arms and suck on his neck.

We tiptoed out of the dimly-lit room. The gastric by-pass woman stirred in her sleep and muttered, "French fries. Mmm."

I looked for Nurse Haugen but she'd gone off duty, replaced by a tiny blonde wearing pink scrubs and a ferocious scowl. When I got in Junior's car I had a sudden panic attack. "What if those guys come back? Kizzy's all alone."

I scrabbled for the door handle. Junior turned on the ignition. "Chill, Emerson. Visiting hours are over, and there are security guards at the door. She'll be okay."

Not convinced, I looked for a black Escalade as he pulled out of the parking lot. "Give me your phone."

Junior sighed and dug out his cell phone. He rolled his eyes when I called information and got a listing for A. Haugen. She answered on the first ring, "Haugen here."

"This is Allie. You know, the one with the dirty feet?"

Her sigh sounded a lot like Junior's, and she was probably rolling her eyes, too.

"I'm sorry to bother you but that guy who said he's Kizzy's nephew? He's not. I think he's trying to kill her."

"Have you called the police?"

"Well, uh, I don't really have any proof, but I thought you should know."

"Okay, Allie, listen up. Nobody's going to get killed on my watch, and the night nurse, in spite of her size, is even meaner than I am. Feel better?"

Actually, I did. I thanked her and hung up. Junior and I rode in silence. I turned my head and studied his profile, thinking about how he'd been there for me when I desperately needed help. No second thoughts. No questions asked. His sudden appearance in my life seemed right and natural, like it was meant to be. I decided to trust him.

"Junior?"

"Yeah?"

"I've got something to tell you."

The words poured out of me like water spurting out of a high pressure hose. The electric fence and Blaster the bull. Kizzy and the moonstone. Trilby. My ability to read thoughts. Kizzy's cedar chest and the mysterious letter. Everything. As I talked, I watched Junior's face. But he just looked straight ahead and kept on driving.

When the silence grew, I thought, Stupid, stupid, stupid! You and your big mouth!

I bit my lip and looked out the window, blinking back tears. Of course he thought I was weird. Who wouldn't? If only I could take the words back, swallow them and never utter them again.

What happened next totally blew me away. I thought I'd hear, "You're kidding, right?" But instead, Junior pulled over to the side of the road. He reached over and took my hand. "Hey, look at me."

I turned my head slowly. Junior squeezed my hand and gave me one of his beautiful but rare smiles. "Thanks for telling me. I always knew you were special."

His words were so unexpected, so sweet, my mouth dropped open. I slumped against the seatback, weak with relief. The heavy burden I'd been carrying alone lifted from my heart and soared away on the soft night air. I threw back my head and laughed until tears poured down my face. Junior gave me a brief, worried look before putting the car in gear.

"You okay?"

"Oh, yeah," I giggled. "Couldn't be better."

When we pulled into Uncle Sid's driveway, I pointed at the trailer. "You can pull in by the pick-up. I'd ask you in but my mom isn't feeling too well."

"Yeah, I heard." Junior glanced over at me in the dim light.

I was dying to know what he heard, but didn't ask, because if I didn't like the answer I'd have to go into attack mode, and I was feeling way too mellow for that. Instead, I leaned over and pecked him on the cheek. "Thanks so much. I guess I'll see you at school."

Instead of pulling back, I moved in closer until I felt heat radiating from his body. Junior gripped the steering wheel with both hands and stared straight ahead. Jeez, what was I doing wrong? Granted, I didn't have much experience, and I wasn't planning on being another check-mark on his, "I've screwed every freshman girl list," but a little kiss would be okay.

Finally, he sighed, put an arm around my shoulders and pulled me close. He murmured into my hair, "You'd better get out of the car before I do something I'll be sorry for."

I lifted my face to look at him. "Why would you be sorry?"

His lips were right there, just inches away. I gave him an encouraging smile.

"You're a good kid, Emerson, and we're going to keep it that way."

I must have looked disappointed, because his arm tightened and he touched his lips to mine, a warm, feathery touch that made me shiver. He leaned across me and opened the door. "Go. I'll see you tomorrow."

I smiled as I walked to the trailer. Not counting the stupid kissing game where Donny Simonson had to stand on his tiptoes to reach my lips, I'd just experienced my first almost-kiss. In spite of the awful day, things were looking up.

Chapter Thirteen

It was after school and I was sitting in the detention room catching up on the work I missed the day before. I thought Junior would be there. But Junior turned on the charm—even school officials couldn't resist him—and received clemency because he had to go to work. So, it was just me and fellow detainee, Sonja Ortega, who was painting her fingernails green, glaring at me through black-rimmed eyes and muttering threats.

"You think you're hot? You think Junior likes you? You'd better stay away from Junior, or you'll be one sorry white chick!"

Detention is what happens when you leave school without permission or, in Sonja's case, tell your chubby homeroom teacher his face looks like a pig's ass. Either way, you get to spend time with Mr. Ted Thornburg, who's a retire-rehire. That's what they call old dudes who've retired after teaching about a hundred years and want to come back part time. He told us to call him "Mr. Ted," and he wore hearing aides in both ears but took them out because the noise kept him awake. True to form, he was dozing in his chair, his chin against his chest.

I had only my wits to keep Sonja from beating the crap out of me, even though I'd briefly considered using the TKP as a diversionary tactic . . . like making Sonja's bottle of nail polish scoot across the top of her desk. I'd watch it with a horrified expression and yell, "It's an earthquake! Get under the desk. Quick!"

But I hadn't used TKP since the incident with the Poor White Trash boys. And what if Sonja (who was no dummy) figured out I'd somehow caused it? It would give her way too much ammunition. I tried using reason instead.

"Look, Sonja, Junior and I are just friends. I needed a ride and he gave me one. That's it."

Her lip curled into a sneer. "Yeah, right. I've seen the way he looks at you. Like he wants to . . . "

I leaned forward so I wouldn't miss a single word of what Sonja thought Junior wanted to do to me. Before she could finish, Mrs. Burke popped into the room. She marched over to Mr. Ted and tapped him on the shoulder. He awoke with a snort and leaped to his feet. He glared at Sonja and me. "Get to work, you two!"

Sonja and I looked at each other and snickered, a rare moment of solidarity as we faced a common enemy.

"I'd like to talk to Allie," Mrs. Burke said. "She can finish her homework in my room."

Without waiting for an answer, she headed for the door. "Come with me, Allie."

"See you around, Sonja," I whispered. "Mr. Ted will be asleep soon and you can finish your fingernails. Cool color, by the way."

Yeah, I was totally sucking up to Sonja, but who wants to get beat up in the girls' bathroom?

"See ya," she said. Her homicidal glare had softened to one of mere hostility. Hostility, I could handle.

Turned out homework was the last thing on Mrs. Burke's mind.

"How's your friend, Kizzy?" she asked after I settled into my desk.

"Still in a coma."

Junior had let me use his cell phone during lunch. Nurse

Haugen told me Kizzy's vital signs were stronger and she might not die after all. And no, Kizzy's fake nephew had not returned, but Carmel had arrived and was at her mother's bedside.

Mrs. Burke sat in the desk next to me and folded her hands. "What I'm about to tell you must be held in the strictest confidence. You can tell no one, not even your mother. Especially your mother."

I didn't know what to say. It was Mrs. Burke who told me if an adult ever said what she just said, tell a trusted adult. She, of course, was my trusted adult. I must have looked confused because she fluttered her hands nervously. "I know, I know. That sounded bad. But I don't want to get my daughter in trouble. You know Shelly's a paralegal for Big Ed and his son, right?"

I nodded, still trying to connect the dots.

Big Ed's son was known as 'Little Ed,' which was totally screwed up, because Big Ed was a dried-up little guy with fluffy white hair that looked like a dandelion gone to seed. He wore tiny, tasseled loafers and glasses that made his eyes look enormous. Little Ed, on the other hand, was well over six feet, had broad shoulders, greasy, swept-back hair and liked three piece suits.

Mrs. Burke looked around the room—checking for spies, I guess—then leaned close to me. "Shelly works mainly for Little Ed. Probate, wills, stuff like that." Her voice dropped to a whisper. "The day Kizzy Lovell was attacked, she had an appointment to sign her will." She paused and waggled her eyebrows. "Her *new* will."

"Uh huh." I wondered why Mrs. Burke thought drawing up a new will was such a big deal.

"The new will left a small amount of money to her daughter, Carmel." Her gaze darted to the door and back to mine. "*You* were named as the primary beneficiary. Had she signed the will, the rest of her fortune would go to you, Allie."

I felt the air leave my lungs in a whoosh. "Wha . . . but . . . how . . . " I stammered, trying to get my mind and mouth to work together. A sudden chill crawled up my spine, and I scrunched down in my chair.

"And that's not all." Her words seemed to bounce around the silent room.

"There's more?" I croaked.

"Kizzy's appointment was on Tuesday. On Monday, Shelly accidentally overheard Little Ed make a phone call to Carmel. He told her she was out of the will and you were in."

"Did he tell her when Kizzy was coming in to sign it?"

"Yes."

"Oh, jeez." The dots were connecting and it wasn't a pretty picture. "What Little Ed did, isn't that against the rules or something?"

"Absolutely," Mrs. Burke said. "Kizzy is his client and he supposed to maintain lawyer-client confidentiality. What he did was unethical."

I wondered if it was ethical for Shelly to "accidentally" listen in on a telephone conversation, but didn't ask. Instead, I thought about my encounter with Carmel. She seemed shallow, not evil. Sure, she'd looked at her mother with impatience and a kind of amused superiority, but I hadn't seen hatred in her eyes.

I said, "I don't want to believe Carmel would try to kill her own mother."

"People are capable of doing terrible things when there's money at stake."

"Has Shelly talked to Deputy Philpott?"

"Philpott has an appointment with Little Ed today. He'll find out about the new will, but Shelly can't reveal what she heard, or she'll get fired. But, Philpott's not stupid. He'll check out Carmel and see if she has an alibi for

Tuesday."

"Oh my God!" I jumped up. "When I called the hospital, the nurse told me Carmel was there, sitting with her mother. Do you think . . . ?"

I couldn't say it, could hardly bear to think about Carmel slowly lowering a pillow over Kizzy's face, snuffing out the tiny flicker of life she clung to so tenaciously.

Panic stricken, I started for the door. "I've got to do something."

"Use my cell phone," Mrs. Burke said.

Before I could ask for A. Haugen, the nurse's station connected me to Kizzy's room. Carmel answered, which startled me into a brief stammering fit. When I regained my wits, I said, "I just called to check on Kizzy. How is she?"

Carmel yawned into the phone. "About the same."

"Is, uh, Teddy there with you?"

"Naw, he had some business to take care of."

"Are you going to stay for a while?"

Carmel whined, "It's boring here. The doctor doesn't know when Mom will wake up. Deputy Dawg wants to talk to me then I'll probably split. The hospital will call if her condition changes. I mean, really, what can I do?"

I breathed a sigh of relief. Carmel sounded like her usual "it's all about me" self, not a daughter intent on murdering her mother. Unless, of course, Teddy planned to sneak in later and do the dirty deed. I murmured sympathetically and told her I'd be in to sit with Kizzy whenever I could get a ride into town.

"Yeah, you do that." Her tone turned snippy. "Seeing as how you're kind of like a member of the family now."

I pretended I didn't understand. "About the moonstone, Carmel. It's not like I wanted it. Kizzy made me take it and . . . "

I heard a click. She'd hung up on me. I handed the

phone back to Mrs. Burke. "Carmel's leaving after she talks to Philpott."

Christian Revelle and his sidekick, Baxter, flashed into my mind. Were they in cahoots with Carmel? Would I be able to keep Kizzy safe? Swear to God, the whole friggin' mess was making me crazy.

*

The next day was Thursday, Big Ed day. I didn't want to go home after school. With Mrs. Burke's warning fresh in my mind, I hadn't mentioned the will to Faye. Mrs. Burke was right. Faye would have been all over Big Ed for information, and Shelly's job would be history. I wondered what Shelly knew about my mother's case. Faye was too trusting, and Big Ed was pretty vague about the details.

Note to self: work up a sneaky little plan to extract Faye's info from Shelly.

Instead of getting off the bus with Manny and Mercedes, I stayed on. Oh yeah, Faye knew I was going to Kizzy's house. She didn't know I'd be alone. I'd told her a tiny, little fib. I said I'd been in touch with Kizzy's daughter (true); she considered me a member of the family (kind of true); and that she wanted me to come to Kizzy's house and pick out some personal items to take to her mother in the hospital (definite lie.) Actually, the part about going through Kizzy's personal items was not a lie. I had to find that cedar chest. But I fervently hoped Carmel would not be there. If things went according to her plan, Carmel would be gone. Not a sure thing, though. A nagging voice in the back of my mind warned, *What if her alibi did not convince Deputy Philpott and he told her to stay in the area?*

Our bus driver, Patti didn't want to let me off at Kizzy's.

"No way! After what happened to that poor woman, you're not spending the night alone in that creepy old house.

What's wrong with you, girl?"

So, I was forced to repeat the half-truth, half-lie to Patti, which made me feel twice as guilty. Not that I lie a lot. But sometimes it's better for certain people not to know the truth. Besides, I had an agenda. Since Kizzy was conscious long enough to mention the cedar chest, it had to be an important clue.

When I finished, Patti huffed her disapproval, but finally relented and opened the doors. When I scrambled down the stairs, she said, "You'd better be waiting right here tomorrow morning, G, or I'm coming in after you."

Before I could lose my nerve, I opened the gate, taking care not to look in the falcon's eye. However, I couldn't resist telling it, "I thought you were supposed to ward off evil. Well, you screwed up royally this time."

The yellow crime-scene tape was gone. No motorcycle in the driveway. No vehicle of any kind. I peeked in the window of the detached garage. Nothing but lawn furniture and a riding mower. I circled the house to make sure Teddy hadn't stashed the bike in the back yard. The image of Teddy waiting for me inside the house creeped me out so bad my legs started shaking.

Okay, Allie, suck it up. I climbed the broad stairs leading to the front door. The creaking of the stairs added to my sense of uneasiness. It felt strange, almost surreal, standing alone on the shadowy veranda, like I was violating some unwritten code. Intruding where I didn't belong. But I'd come this far. Steeling myself against rising panic, I reached up and slid my fingers across the top of the door frame until I found Kizzy's spare key.

With the bloody scene in the kitchen playing out in my mind, I stepped into the house. A heavy silence hung in the air. Without Kizzy's presence, it felt hollow and lifeless. But, someone, probably Kizzy's cleaning lady, had straightened up the living room. The furniture was back where it belonged. Fresh flowers on the mantle. I approached the kitchen on dragging feet, hoping the cleaning lady wasn't put off by blood and gore. With my eyes squeezed shut, I opened the door and sniffed. Lemon disinfectant. I opened one eye. The kitchen was spotless.

I heaved a huge sigh of relief, ready to begin my search for the cedar chest. But first, I went into every first-floor room and turned on all the lights. Then I turned on the television set in the living room.

Feeling a strong sense of purpose, I started downstairs in Kizzy's bedroom and the guest bedroom I used, even though I'd never seen a cedar chest in either place. Actually, I wasn't sure I'd recognize a cedar chest if I saw one. But, it had to be big. Right? Armed with a flashlight, I peeked under bed ruffles and pawed through closets. Nothing.

I wasn't anxious to go upstairs. I'd been up there a time or two with Kizzy, and didn't like it. The rooms resonated with sadness and broken dreams. Kizzy and her late husband bought the huge house years before, hoping to fill the rooms with a bunch of kids. But it didn't happen. They were in their forties when they adopted Carmel and wanted to adopt more. But Kizzy said raising Carmel was a "challenge." They'd changed their minds.

I raced up the stairs and dashed from room to room, turning on lights. The shades were pulled down tight in all four bedrooms. I was torn between my desire to open them and let the daylight in and my reluctance to draw attention to the fact that I was snooping around in Kizzy's house. Of course, the blaring TV and blazing lights downstairs might have been a tiny clue.

I took a deep breath and checked the bedrooms, trying to ignore the odor of mothballs and dark, shadowy recesses where the light didn't penetrate. Recesses large enough for a man the size of Teddy or Christian Revelle to hide. An involuntary shiver crawled up my spine as I opened the door to the linen closet. I pulled the string to turn on the light and found Kizzy's video library stacked neatly on the center shelf. Cool. I'd watch a movie later; get my mind off the spooky stuff.

The Sound of Music, Kizzy's favorite movie, was on top of the stack. We'd watched it together dozens of times. The last time she'd pulled it out of the box, I'd said, "If I have to watch Julie Andrews dancing across a meadow and singing, *The hills are alive* . . . one more time, I'll go friggin' nuts!"

She'd smiled and played it anyway. Maybe I was being punished, or maybe it was that karma thing I'm always hearing about, because, all at once, the *Do, re, mi*, song the Von Trapp kids sing popped into my head and refused to leave. I switched off the light, closed the closet door and headed down the hall singing, "Do, a deer, a female deer, re, a drop of golden sun," at the top of my lungs.

I had one more room to check, the largest room on the second floor. At the end of the hall, it extended across the end of the house. I'd been putting it off because it was the creepiest room of all. It didn't have a bed and dresser to fill up space. Kizzy used it to store all kinds of stuff, stuff that had sheets covering it.

But the "do, re, mi" song was working its magic. I reached for the door knob screeching, "la, a note to follow sol." Surely that would scare away the evil doers. Testing my new-found courage, I flung open the door then yipped in surprise as the sheets draped over the furniture billowed and rippled in response. For one crazy moment, I thought the things underneath the sheets had come alive and were getting ready to suck me into an alternate universe, where I'd be stuck forever and never see Faye or Junior again.

After a few heart-stopping seconds I finally realized, *C'est moi.* (Mrs. Burke would be proud!)

It was me. *I* had caused the air to rush into the room

when I threw the door open. Feeling like an idiot, I flipped on the light.

Humming loudly, I scanned the room and decided to tackle the scariest object first. I marched over to the shrouded, man-shaped object lurking in the corner and peeked under the sheet to discover an ancient floor lamp with odd little pointy bulbs and no cord. I continued my search and found the following: a rusty exercise bike, a treadle sewing machine, a set of dusty encyclopedias and a baby crib. The crib made me feel sad. Was Kizzy hoping Carmel would give her grandchildren? Carmel and Teddy reproducing? *Eewww!*

I'd just lifted the lid on an old steamer trunk when I heard a sound that made the blood freeze in my veins. The creak of a floorboard. Like somebody was creeping up the stairs, trying not to be heard. Panic raced through my body like wildfire. I stopped humming and turned slowly toward the door, resisting the urge to jump in the closet and hide. It was then I heard the thump. Omigod, was it coming from the closet? The very closet I intended to hide in?

The hell with it! I screamed and dashed down the stairs, intent only on putting as much space as possible between Kizzy's house and yours truly. I threw open the front door and crashed into Junior, who was standing on the porch, one hand raised to knock.

Chapter Fourteen

I grabbed Junior and held on like he was the lone life raft in a storm-tossed sea. His arms tightened around me. "Whoa, Emerson, you're shakin' like a leaf. You see a ghost?"

I managed to gasp, "Heard a noise. Somebody on the stairs and . . . and . . . thumps in the closet . . . and . . . and"

To Junior's credit, he didn't laugh at my panic-induced hallucination. He stroked my hair and patted my back. "Your heart's bangin' away like crazy. It feels like it's gonna jump right out of your chest. Don't be scared. I won't let anybody hurt you."

Junior gently pulled away from me and stepped back. He cupped my face in his palms and looked into my eyes. "You okay now?"

Not trusting myself to speak, I nodded.

The corner of his mouth twitched and he winked. "How about we go inside and check out that closet? See if we can find the boogey man and throw his ass out. Whaddaya think?"

Embarrassed, I nodded again and avoided his eyes.

"Don't worry about it, girl. This spooky old house would scare anybody. *Muy horripilante!*"

I trailed behind Junior as he climbed the stairs and checked every room. The fear and panic that sent me screaming from the house vanished, lost in the onset of hysterical laughter. A fit of giggles bubbled up in my chest.

I could hardly hold it back. But, we'd been down that road before, the night Junior took me home from the hospital. He'd think I was a real nut case if it happened again. I pinched myself hard to nip it in the bud. "Ouch. Damn, that hurts."

Junior spun around. "What?"

"Paper cut." I pointed at my thumb. "English class."

Junior frowned and started back down the stairs. "Miz Kizzy's bedroom on the first floor?"

I nodded.

"You're looking for a cedar chest, right?"

"I already checked her room. No cedar chest."

"I want to see it anyway," Junior said.

I stepped in front of him to lead the way. A strange phenomenon had occurred with Junior's presence in Kizzy's house. The relief I felt swelled into a helium balloon of euphoria. The dark corners now looked like cozy nooks; the creaking floors were simply the sounds of a tired old house settling in for a good night's sleep. As I opened the door to Kizzy's room, I burst into spontaneous song.

"Do, a deer, a female deer, re, a drop of golden sun. Mi . . . "

"Whaddaya singin', Emerson?"

I turned to face Junior. "Have you ever seen *The Sound of Music*?"

Junior frowned. "How the hell can you see a sound?"

"No, no, it's a movie. We can watch it later if you want."

Junior remained silent as he gazed around Kizzy's bedroom, taking in the antique, four-poster bed, the massive bureau, the white-lace curtains, the elegant dressing table, the overstuffed thing Kizzy called a "divan" in the corner, her lacy blue shawl draped across one end. He gave an appreciative whistle. "Nice."

I crossed to the divan and picked up Kizzy's shawl. It smelled like lavender, Virginia Slims and the spicy potpourri she loved. Suddenly, nothing seemed funny, and I desperately wanted Kizzy back home, to feel her gentle touch and hear the words, "You're a special girl, Alfrieda." Kizzy, who'd moved heaven and earth to help me find my father. Kizzy, whose garbled memories held the secret to the moonstone tucked inside my shirt.

"Hey, Emerson. Do you even know what a cedar chest looks like?"

Junior's voice, loud in the silent room, pulled me back into real time. He was peering into an old steamer trunk Kizzy used to store extra bedding.

"Well, I know that's not it," I said. "It has to be made of wood 'cause cedar's a tree. And since it's called a chest, I guess it would be big."

Junior looked at me and grinned. "So I'm guessing you don't have a clue."

I smiled back at him. "Pretty much."

He wandered over to the closet and opened the door.

"No room in there for a cedar chest," I pointed out.

Junior ignored me and pointed at the shelf above the hanging rod, a shelf stacked high with cardboard boxes. "Might be some important papers in the boxes."

I gave a little huff of disapproval. "I don't think we should be pawing through Kizzy's private stuff."

I might as well have been talking to the wall. He hooked his fingers under the uppermost box and slid it forward. As he pulled it free, the box tipped and an avalanche of papers cascaded over his head. Swearing in Spanish, Junior staggered under the weight of the box and let it drop to the floor. I burst out laughing. "Serves you right for being nosy."

He glared at me and began pawing through the papers. "Sometimes it pays to be nosy."

I picked up a bundle of envelopes held together with a rubber band. Bank statements. Old bank statements dated in the 1980's. Why would Kizzy save bank statements that old? I felt a flash of annoyance as I glanced over at Junior still sifting through the box. Weren't we supposed to be looking for a cedar chest? "We're wasting our time. It's just Kizzy's old bank statements."

Junior gave a grunt of surprise then looked up at me, a look of triumph on his face.

"What?" I made no effort to hide my irritation.

"Cedar chests are big, huh, Emerson?"

"Well, duh! What else could they be?"

"Not big." Junior held up a small wooden chest. The lid was fitted with a metal hasp and fastened with a tiny padlock.

"Oh," I said in a small voice. Part of me didn't want to admit Junior was right. "Well, I got the impression it was *much* bigger. Besides, it's locked, and you don't have the key."

Junior smirked. "Can't handle it when you're wrong, huh?"

"Who says I'm wrong?"

Junior walked to Kizzy's dressing table, picked up a nail file and began working on the padlock. I watched, fascinated, as he probed the slotted opening at the bottom of the padlock. "Looks like you've done that before."

"Graduate of a life of crime." Junior gave the padlock a yank. It popped open. He set the chest on the table and lifted the lid. I peeked over his shoulder, expecting to see a lock of Carmel's baby hair tied up in a pink ribbon or pictures of Kizzy's old boyfriends. But all I saw was a rolled parchment, yellow and crumbling with age. Was this what Kizzy wanted me to find?

I unrolled it carefully while Junior looked over my shoulder, his breath warm on my cheek. "What the hell?" he muttered.

The handwriting was spidery, the ink faded and

smudged and written in a language that might as well have been Greek.

"Not Spanish," Junior said.

The only words I could make out were *Nicolae Romano* and *1755*. My mouth dropped open. Was I looking at a document written in 1755? By Nicolae Romano? Directly below the signature, was a smudged hand print. Apparently this Nicolae dude had dipped his hand in ink and pressed it against the paper so that every crease and whorl from his palm appeared on the paper. But why? He'd signed it. Why the palm print?

I set the paper on Kizzy's dressing table. "Great. Just great! We find the cedar chest, and all that's in it is a piece of paper written in some language that probably doesn't even exist now, and a hand print."

I went over to the divan and plopped down with a heavy sigh. Yeah, I was disappointed, but more than that, I was scared. How could I keep her from dying if I couldn't find the directions or whatever it was Kizzy wanted me to find?

When Junior didn't answer, I looked up and saw him bent over the wooden chest poking at something with the nail file. I heard a metallic *ping* and Junior's triumphant cry, "Yes!"

"What?" I vaulted off the divan.

Junior was studying the blue-velvet lining inside of the lid, turning it this way and that. He pointed at a tiny hole in the center of the liner. "Somebody put a screw right there. No reason to have one there."

"But why would . . . ?" I stopped mid-sentence and watched as Junior stuck the point of the file into the narrow crack between the lid's wooden edge and the lining. One quick twist and the liner popped off.

"That's why." Junior pointed at the compartment hidden under the lining. A narrow metal band bisected the center of the lid. Tucked beneath the band was an envelope.

I beamed a smile at Junior. He handed me the envelope without saying a word.

I opened the envelope and found a single piece of paper folded in half. No ink blotches, no spidery writing. Nothing but a solid block of neatly-typed text. I scanned it quickly. Nicolae Romano's name was typed at the bottom. My hand shook as I read words and phrases that had a familiar ring. I'd heard them before. From Kizzy. From Trilby. I'd found the prophecy.

Though my heart had leaped into my throat, I calmly handed the paper to Junior. "It's a translation." My voice sounded strange, like it was coming from a different person.

Junior gave me a sharp look before his gaze dropped to the paper. He began to read aloud:

I am Nicolae, the cutter of stone. Tonight, I awake from a deep slumber to see the moon slip beneath a thick veil of darkness and disappear. By the light of a candle, I write the words that follow, words I seem compelled to write for I have heard the murmuring of the moonstone in my dreams. Just yesterday, I freed it from its homely prison. It was cut and shaped by these rough hands to reflect the glorious light of the moon. I am but a simple man and, as such, cannot fathom the true meaning of the words I write. I am only the vessel.

As Junior's words washed over me, seasoned by his native Spanish, I pulled the moonstone from my shirt and watched the reflected light play across its surface. In my mind, I was transported back to the simple hut of the stone carver. I could see him hunched over a circle of flickering candlelight, dipping his quill pen into an inkwell, scratching out words that would inextricably tie us together across the years. When silence filled the room, I heard my own exhalations and came back to the present. Junior was studying my face.

"Read the prophecy." My voice was voice husky with

emotion.

"You okay?"

I nodded. He cleared his throat and began, reading . . .

I am the moonstone and this is my destiny. I will pass through many hands before I reach the one whose heart holds the key. Brought to life by the stone cutter, my shimmer of light attracts the Gypsy, who takes me for his own. Though he casts me in silver, my position is not fixed. I wax and wane like my namesake moon. The Empath's will is strong but her heart is selfish. In her hand, my magic sparks to life, but heartache and sadness follow. Tossed aside like an orphaned child, my wayward path leads to the Slacker, a careless woman who defiles my purpose and tarnishes my name. When finally, I am passed to the Guardian, she holds me fast while seeking the one whose palm bears the mark of the star. At journey's end, I lie close to her heart, the maid who is strong of mind. Tested by the power of three, she is the Keeper of the light. Our destinies become one.

It all made sense. Magda, the Empath. Trilby, the Slacker. Kizzy, the Guardian. Me, the maid who was strong of mind. The three tests.

"There's more," Junior said. His face looked grim. He traced the words with his finger and read, *I look to the sky and see a miracle. The moon has emerged from its dark thrall. What lies beyond is hidden in the mists of time, but this I know . . . the maid who is strong of mind will determine the course that follows. Two paths appear. One brings great glory, the other, death. I pray she chooses wisely. By my signature and the mark of my hand, I swear what I have written is a true account.*

In the year of our Lord, 1755.

Nicolae Romano

I felt the hair on my arms prickle. "But why the palm print?" I whispered.

Junior shrugged.

I set the palm print directly beneath the small lamp on Kizzy's dressing table. With my index finger, I traced the

clear, deep lines etched in the hand of the man who'd
shaped the gemstone tucked inside my shirt. I knew about
the heart line, head line, fate line and life line. Kizzy had
taught me. They all appeared as they should . . . strong,
unbroken lines A series of smudged chains, crosses, islands
and tassels dotted Nicolae's broad palm. These were the
small but important details, according to Kizzy, that filled
in the rest of a person's history, revealing their secrets,
traumas, good and bad fortune. And I didn't have a clue
what they meant. Why hadn't I paid closer attention?

I shook my head and sighed.

"Try this." Junior picked up the magnifying glass next
to Kizzy's chair, where she read the morning paper. I held
the magnifying glass over the paper. After a brief stomach-
lurching moment of blurriness, I moved it closer and was
rewarded with a much larger and clearer view of Nicolae's
palm print. That's when I saw it. The star. At the base of
his little finger. I inhaled sharply. The magnifying glass
slipped from my hand and clattered onto the table top.

"What?" Junior said, a frown furrowing his brow.

"He has it too." I pointed at the star on my palm.

Junior took the paper from me and scanned it again.
"The Keeper. She guards me well while seeking the girl
whose palm bears the mark of the star." He set the paper
down. "So that's you. You got the star."

He paused and scratched his head. "And this guy's got
the star. So, does that mean this old dude's like your great-
great grandfather?"

I shook my head. "Not from my mother's side. Her
people came from Norway."

"Maybe your dad's?"

I thought about Mike Purdy's hand and shrugged. I
reached for his hand. "Hey, maybe you've got a star on
your palm. Maybe that's why we're here, together, trying
to figure this out."

Junior stepped back and jammed both hands into his pockets. "Naw, I don't have nothin' like that."

Why wouldn't Junior let me look at his palm? Jeez, he acted like I was trying to steal his soul. What was he trying to hide? Definitely weird.

I set the palm print aside and picked up Nicolae's prophecy. The words, "The maid who is strong of mind will determine the course. Two paths appear. One brings great glory, the other death. I pray she will choose wisely," jumped from the page.

I moaned. "I chose the wrong path. Kizzy's going to die!"

"You don't know that," Junior said. "It might be part of a test, you know, to see if you can figure out who did this to her."

"But . . . but . . . "

Junior gripped my shoulders, gave me a little shake. "Listen to me! We're making progress. We found the cedar chest, didn't we?"

"I didn't. *You* found it."

"Doesn't matter. Remember, you're the maid who's strong of mind."

"Who can't even find a cedar chest? How pathetic!"

The irony of the situation hit both of us at the same time. We looked at each other, grinning like fools. As if this situation was totally normal. As if we were just two teenagers out on a Friday night date, not an ex-gang banger and a trailer-dwelling, moonstone-wearing, fatherless girl forced to make life and death decisions.

"You're a piece of work, Emerson." Junior wrapped me up in his arms and I nuzzled his neck, savoring his smell. Naturally my stomach chose that moment to growl so loudly Junior must have felt it clear down to his toes.

I felt his smile against my cheek. "I've got food in the car."

I pushed away from him. "What are we waiting for?"

Before we left Kizzy's room, we put everything back exactly as we'd found it. Since Kizzy had gone to such great lengths to hide the prophecy, the least we could do was keep it from falling into the wrong hands, even though it was unclear whose hands they were.

Junior had just reached the door when the phone rang. He froze, one hand reaching for the knob. "Answering machine?"

I nodded and stared at the phone like it was a ticking bomb. After three rings, Kizzy voice instructed the caller to leave a message.

"Carmel? Chris Revelle. I need to talk to you. I'm parked in front of your house. Can I come in?"

Chapter Fifteen

At the sound of Revelle's oily voice, my stomach clenched into a burning knot, driving away all thoughts of food. Revelle paused, the brief silence filled with the sound of a car engine idling in the background. Junior crossed to the phone and stood over it. Scary Junior was back. His muscular body was all hard edges, coiled for action like a big jungle cat ready to pounce. The glitter of menace in his eyes made me shiver.

"I was driving by and saw the lights," Revelle continued. "I have something important to discuss with you. Something that would benefit both of us . . . money-wise."

Junior snapped, "Pick the phone up. Say you're Carmel. Tell him you can't come to the door right now."

I saw my hand obeying him, reaching for the phone. When my mind caught up, it screamed, *Are you nuts? He'll know it's you! Maybe Baxter's with him and they'll come after us.*

The image of Patti, the bus driver, discovering our bloody, bullet-riddled bodies danced through my mind in living color. I snatched my hand back and shoved it into my pocket.

Junior took a big breath, let it out. The warmth returned to his face. "Come on, kid. You can do it."

Before I could change my mind, I grabbed the phone and in Carmel's little girl voice said, "Oh hi there. Who are you again?"

Junior reached over and hit the speaker phone button.

I jumped about six inches when Revelle's voiced boomed, "Is this Carmel Lovell?"

"Yes," I squeaked.

"My name's Chris Revelle. Revelle Investments. We need to talk. Can I come in?"

I gave a little shriek of horror. "God, no! I'm a mess. You got me out of the shower. Can't you just tell me over the phone?"

"I've been asking around. I hear you could use some dough."

I breathed into the phone, trying to gather my thoughts. "Well, yeah, who doesn't?"

"I'm talking a big score. Not just your mother's estate which, by the way, I heard she's not leaving to you. Millions, even billions."

"How do you know about my mother's estate?"

"Look, we need to talk in person. Cell phones conversations are tricky."

I pretended to think it over. "Well, Mr. Revelle," I cooed. "Maybe you should give me a teensy little clue as to what you're talking about."

Dead silence. I looked at Junior and shrugged.

Revelle said, "It involves the kid with the moonstone. You know who I mean?"

I gave a Carmel-like snort of disgust. "Oh, yeah. Her! She's always over here sucking up to my mom like she's family or something." I paused for a minute. "Did you say millions?"

"Yeah, maybe more. Where do you want to meet?"

Oops! What was I thinking? I was seriously not cut out for espionage. Panicky, I looked at Junior.

"Tell him to pick a place."

I covered the receiver with my hand and whispered, "No way!"

"Just do it."

I jotted down Revelle's information. My hand trembled as I set the phone down. We went to the window, cracked the drapes and watched the Escalade pull away.

"Now what, smart guy?"

I was kinda pissed at Junior. Obviously, I couldn't show up at a coffee shop named Jumping Bean Espresso, in Vista Valley pretending to be Carmel.

"Now, I talk to some people who owe me," Junior said with a wolf's grin. "Has Revelle ever seen Carmel?"

"No, but I'm pretty sure he knows she's not Hispanic."

"Newsflash, Emerson. I know people who aren't beaners."

He smiled to take the edge off the words. I looked at the floor, embarrassed.

He put his hands on my shoulders and gave me a little shake. "I'll take care of it. You go to school like a good little girl."

Damn! The last thing I wanted was for Junior to think of me as a good little girl. I jerked out of his grasp. "Hey, I'm the one with the moonstone. Don't give me that 'I'll take care of it' stuff."

"Better you don't know."

I glared at him. "I'm not a little kid, Junior . . . remember, I'm the maid who's strong of mind."

His face hardened again. "Then you better polish up that moonstone 'cause that's the only way you'll get the information out of me."

We stared at each other for a long minute, neither of us blinking. Then, Junior took a deep breath, and the tension left his body. Right on cue, my stomach growled again.

Junior grinned. "I'll go get the food."

While I ate, he took his cell phone, stepped into the kitchen and shut the door like he was on some big, friggin' secret mission. Junior. Secret agent man. It's not like I couldn't keep my mouth shut. And who's problem was it, anyway!

When he emerged from the kitchen, I was sitting on the sofa, still ticked off.

"So what's the plan?" I asked.

He sat down next to me and mulled it over for a while. Finally he said, "Okay, listen. There's this girl that owes me a favor . . . "

"Why?" I interrupted. "Why does she owe you a favor?"

Junior sighed. "See, I knew this would happen. Exactly why I didn't want to tell you."

"Okay, okay. I'm sorry. Go ahead."

"You said Carmel was a good-looking blonde. This girl is too. And she's smart. She'll meet Revelle tomorrow and pose as Carmel. Then, we'll know what he's planning to do."

I tried to get past the image of Junior and the good-looking blonde who owed him a favor and think objectively, but it wasn't easy. It required a heavy-duty mental slap upside the head. *Get real, Allie. Junior has a past. He knows lots of girls and he's trying his best to help you.*

"Okay," I said. "That might work."

"So tell me everything you know about Carmel and her family."

After I filled him in on Carmel, Kizzy, Magda and the moonstone, we watched *The Sound of Music.* About the time Maria was outfitting all the little Von Trapps in outfits made from window curtains, Junior fell asleep and slumped sideways with his head on the arm of the sofa. I threw caution to the wind and curled up next to him, my head on his chest. He shifted in his sleep and draped an arm across my body. Startled, I made a little sound and pulled away. Junior reached up with his free hand and patted my cheek. His voice was hoarse with sleep. "Relax. You're safe now. Go to sleep."

I snuggled closer. Swear to God, my plan was this: cuddle with Junior for five minutes, then brush my teeth and bed down in Kizzy's guest room. But, the next thing I knew, it was morning. I awoke with sleep-jumbled thoughts and a left leg with no feeling in it. I thought I was back in the trailer in my couch bed. It felt funny, warmer than usual, and I heard static. I remember thinking Faye must have left the TV on. I opened one eye to check the time and was amazed to see sunlight streaming in through the tall, narrow windows flanking the fireplace in Kizzy's living room.

Ohmigod, I'd slept with Junior! I rolled off the sofa and crashed to the floor with a little screech of surprise. Junior shot to his feet, instantly awake and poised for action. His gaze darted around the room, looking for danger.

"What happened? Somebody try to get in?"

I rubbed my numb leg and tried to figure out what to say without sounding like a complete dork.

"No, no, nothing like that," I stammered. "I just woke up and there you were, I mean, there *we* were, you know, together on the sofa, uh, sleeping . . . "

Junior looked down at me and grinned. He rubbed his eyes then held out a hand and hauled me to my feet. The grin grew into an outright chuckle.

"Well, damn, Emerson. We spent our first night together."

I snatched my hand away and sneaked a peek at my jeans. Zipper was up and locked. I felt my cheeks burn with embarrassment and confusion.

"Okay, fine," I snapped. "You can stop laughing now." I glanced at the clock. "The bus will be here in twenty minutes. I need to take a shower and get ready."

Junior sobered quickly and took a step back. An awkward silence hung between us, as thick and palpable as a storm cloud.

"Yeah, well, I should get going too." He rubbed a bristly cheek. "I'll be at school later. See you then."

I made a point of looking away while he gathered up empty fast food cartons, stuffed them into a paper bag and headed for the door. The same door I'd blown through last night, panicky and scared out of my wits. Straight into his arms.

"Junior, wait!" I called softly.

He turned toward me. His expression looked exactly like Uncle Sid's when Aunt Sandra was in one of her snits. Kinda like, "Damn, what got into her?" I felt like an ass.

I cleared my throat. "Thanks, Junior. I was really scared last night. If it hadn't been for you, I would never have found the cedar chest. I really appreciate it."

I was treated to a full-out, no holds barred, genuinely glorious Junior Martinez smile.

"Don't mention it, kid. See ya later."

He put his hand on the door knob then whirled suddenly and strode toward me.

"Give me the moonstone."

Startled, I took a step back. My hand flew up to cover the gemstone tucked inside my shirt.

"No way. I'm supposed to wear it all the time. Kizzy said."

Junior's eyes narrowed. "Don't argue. Just give it to me."

I tilted my head back and glared at him. "What's your problem, Junior? You think you can run my life? The moonstone's mine. Now, back off!"

Junior blinked in surprise but he stepped back. He lifted his hands and grinned, "Sorry, I didn't mean to scare you."

"I'm not scared. I'm mad!"

He brushed my cheek with the back of his knuckles. "I wanna keep you safe, Allie. As long as you have the moonstone, you're in danger. You heard what that Revelle guy said. He wants it. He and that other guy could hurt you bad."

His voice was husky with emotion, his eyes soft and pleading.

"What if they come in the middle of the night? Break into your trailer? They might even hurt your mom. I know you don't want that. Nobody will find it, if that's what you're worried about. I'll hide it good," he said.

He took another step back and waited for my decision.

I tried to sort it out in my mind. After reading the prophecy, I knew I was the Keeper, that I was meant to have the moonstone. But when Kizzy gave it to me, she didn't know about Revelle and his buddy. Junior was right. As long as Revelle and Baxter were around, Faye and I were in danger. The moonstone was my responsibility. I needed to keep it safe. My hands were shaking when I slipped the moonstone off and handed it to Junior, but, somehow, the decision felt right. However, I was still ticked off about Junior's macho behavior. I narrowed my eyes and glared. "One more thing, Junior. Stop bossing me around and acting like I don't have a brain in my head. Yeah, I was a little scared last night, and I'm glad you were here but I can take care of myself."

Junior looked like he was trying not to laugh. "Got it."

"Okay, then. I guess we're clear on that."

Junior stuffed the moonstone in his pocket and headed for the front door.

I watched him go, my hand automatically reaching up to hold the moonstone. Instead of its sleek, warm presence, I felt the thudding of my heart. I thought about the stone cutter and the prophecy, how every word of it had come to pass. Panic rose in my chest like startled birds. I hoped my choice had been the right one.

I shivered as I recalled the words, Two paths appear. One brings great glory, the other death. I hope she chooses wisely.

I breathed a little prayer. *I hope so too, Nicolae.*

Chapter Sixteen

I climbed on the school bus and smiled at Patti's greeting, "Good morning, gorgeous!" and did my best to ignore Cory Philpott sprawled in the first seat across the aisle from Patti, where she could keep an eye on him. The trouble-maker's seat. Cory had kept his promise not to bug Manny and Mercedes, but I was still fair game. No problem. I could handle Cory Philpott any old day of the week.

Apparently he'd had a new dining experience, because he snickered and said, "Hey, Alfredo Sauce! How's your fettuccini?"

I pretended to lose my balance and staggered sideways. My back pack swung around and whacked Cory in the head. He rubbed his head and glared at me.

"That hurt, Allie."

"Oh, did my back pack hit you? Sorry."

I made my way down the aisle and slipped in next to Mercedes.

Manny leaned across the aisle and said in a conspiratorial whisper, "Ya know those two ladies?"

"Two ladies?" I repeated, my mind still on Junior, the moonstone and the prophecy.

"The ones who came to your house that night and want to put you in a foster home."

I inhaled sharply and stared at Manny. "What about them?"

"I heard they're gonna be in Peacock Flats today."

The air whooshed out of my lungs, and I shot to my feet. Faye! I had to warn her! I grabbed my back pack and lurched out into the aisle, almost falling when Patti rounded a sharp curve.

Manny grabbed my arm to steady me. "It's okay, Allie. I told your mom. She knows."

He blinked and looked away but not before I saw the pity in his eyes. I thanked him and settled back into my seat, a flush of embarrassment warming my cheeks. Last night had been "Big Ed night."

How long did Manny have to pound on the door before Faye answered? Was she hung over and reeking of vodka? Were her eyes red from crying? Did she thank him? I wanted to know but couldn't ask. Mercedes picked up on my mood and stopped her interrogation.

Once we got to school, a sense of relief swept through me. I'd had enough of the unexpected, the anxiety of being powerless, of not knowing which way to turn. I needed the familiar routine of fifty-five-minute class periods with five-minute passing time and a forty-minute lunch break.

So, I put the moonstone, Junior, the CPS ladies, the whole darn thing out of my mind. Instead, I filled it with algebra formulas, Ms. Burke's cultural lesson of the day— *Ogenki desu ka* which means, *How are you?* in Japanese— and ran an extra lap in physical education.

By lunchtime, I was shaky with hunger. Thankfully, Manny and Mercedes had two big thermoses of their mother's chicken and rice and well as a stack of homemade tortillas wrapped in foil. We sat outside at a picnic table next to the alley, the late spring sun warm on our faces.

Diddy, our other lunch mate, gulped down his alfalfa sprout sandwich and headed for the cafeteria to practice his herky-jerky dance moves. Though he still clung to his ghetto-speak, my classmates had come to accept him, sorta like you get used to an uncomfortable pair of shoes. They rub you the wrong way but you like them anyway.

Manny and Mercedes each ate two tortillas heaped high with chicken and rice and left the rest for me. I was already on my third when I realized I was the only one eating. Embarrassed, I pushed the foil wrapped stack of tortillas over to Manny.

"Naw, that's okay," Manny said. "We had a big breakfast."

Mercedes giggled, "Girl, do I look like I'm going hungry?"

She stood and waggled her chubby little butt in my face. Manny turned away, gazing out into the street, where two cars had pulled up, one a plain, tan sedan, the other a red Toyota Camry. Two men got out of the sedan. Both wore jeans, polo shirts and dark-blue baseball caps with white lettering.

"Gang intervention," Manny said. "County guys. Wonder why they're here."

I watched the two men walk toward the building. One Latino, one Caucasian. Husky guys with big, muscular arms and the flat, appraising gaze of law enforcement officers. Both had guns on their hips. When they got to our table, they stopped and focused on Manny.

The Latino guy said, "How ya doin,' kid? I'm Gabe."

He paused and jerked his thumb at the other guy. "He's Ray. We're with the county gang intervention."

Manny nodded solemnly. "Uh huh."

"You know a kid named Junior Martinez?" Gabe said.

I froze, my hand halfway to my mouth. Butterflies fluttered through my recently ingested lunch.

Manny nodded, "Yeah, I know him."

"He at school today?"

"Nope," Manny said.

The tortilla fell from my nerveless hand, chicken and

rice spilling out across the table top. Two curious gazes swung over to me, one set of brown eyes, the other blue. My stomach rolled with a sickening lurch.

Ray braced one foot against the bench. He leaned toward me with a friendly smile and cold eyes. "What about you, honey? You know Junior?"

"I, uh, well, I . . . " I stammered. My lips felt numb. Involuntarily, I sucked in air with a loud, shuddering gasp.

Ray grinned and exchanged a look with Gabe. "I think that's a *yes*."

Manny stood up. "'Course she does. We all know him. Why you want him?"

But the men weren't looking at Manny. Their attention was focused on the low rider cruising slowly up the alley and into the parking lot. Junior's car. My fingers closed convulsively around the edge of the table. Should I call out? Warn him? But what if it was nothing bad? Maybe the men were here for another reason. Like to say, "Good job, Junior, for leaving the gang life behind." Somehow I didn't think that was the case. So I did nothing.

Sonja Ortega had no such conflict. When Junior stepped out of his car, she called out, "Hey Junior, the cops are here."

I shot to my feet. Junior's head swiveled back and forth between his car and the drug intervention team.

"Noooo," The cry ripped from my throat and hung in the air between us. Junior's gaze locked onto mine. I saw the anguish in his eyes as the men sprinted toward him. I trailed behind them, followed by Manny and Mercedes. The kids who'd gone across the street to smoke, drifted closer.

The men approached Junior cautiously. I heard Gabe say, "Somebody reported you hanging at an old lady's empty house last night. You carrying, Junior?"

Junior shook his head and lifted his hand, palms up.

He stood stoically as the men patted him down, staring off into space, his chin jutted in defiance.

Our principal, Mr. Hostetler, burst out of the building and trotted toward the men. "Hold it, guys. Are you arresting this boy?"

Before they could answer, Sonja Ortega peeled away from the crowd and yelled, "Yo, fuzz. He was with me."

Emily Murphy, a pale-skinned, freckled redhead who'd apparently made Junior's list spoke up, "Like hell, Sonja. He was with me, and you know it."

The two girls exchanged dirty looks. Emily pushed Sonja, who grabbed a handful of stringy red hair and screamed, "Keep your hands off me, bitch!"

The boys began to chant, "Chick fight! Chick fight!"

Mr. Hostetler used his cell phone to call for reinforcements as the girls tumbled to the ground, throwing punches and screaming obscenities. Two teachers ran out and pulled them apart. Sonja, still spoiling for a fight, shouted at Emily, "This isn't over! After school. The park."

Mr. Hostetler clapped his hands and yelled, "Okay, everybody. Let's get to class."

Somebody whined, "But the bell ain't rung yet."

Hostetler ignored the comment and turned his attention to the gang-intervention guys. "What's this about? Is Junior in trouble?"

Gabe said, "We want to ask him some questions. We have a witness who saw a kid coming out of the Lovell house this morning. Description sounds like Junior. The neighbor thinks he broke in and was robbing the place."

Sonja Ortega just wouldn't give up. "I told you, he was with . . ."

"Shut up, Sonja!" Junior snarled.

I watched in horror and guilt as the men began to lead Junior away. This was all my fault. With my heart hammering in my chest, I stepped forward and yelled, "He didn't do anything wrong! He was with me!"

After a brief shocked silence, an excited murmur rippled through the crowd.

"Knew she was a skank," Sonja told Emily. Both the girls glared at me with murder in their eyes.

Ray raked me with a curious glance before turning back to Junior. "You got yourself a whole lotta groupies, kid. Part of your gang? Makes it a little hard to believe anything you say, though."

Junior's eyes glittered and a knotted muscle twitched in his jaw. Through clenched teeth, he spoke to Gabe. "I did my time. I'm out of the gang. Talk to my PO if you don't believe me."

This wasn't going well. I had to do something else. I walked over to Mr. Hostetler and tugged on his sleeve. "Mr. Hostetler, I was there, in Kizzy's house, and so was Junior. I can clear this up." I looked around at the crowd of students pressing in. Some looked at me with pity, some with avid curiosity and others with downright hostility. "But not out here."

Mr. Hostetler stared at me for a long moment, then gave a brief nod. "Go to my office and wait."

It took most of the afternoon to sort it out. Junior was put in a separate room where Kizzy's neighbor, Mrs. Hawkins, identified him as the person she'd seen leaving Kizzy's house. She was then brought into Mr. Hostetler's office, where I leaned against the wall looking like a prisoner waiting for the firing squad. When asked if she knew me, she said, "Of course I know her. She's Kizzy's friend, Allie. Allie stays with Kizzy every Thursday night."

She narrowed her eyes and shook her finger at me. "Allie Emerson, shame on you! Kizzy's in the hospital and you bring that boy into her home and did God knows what with him all night long!"

I pushed away from the wall. "We didn't do anything!

Nothing happened. I was scared to stay by myself, that's all."

I squirmed in embarrassment, mad at myself for caring what this woman thought.

Mrs. Hawkins glared at me for what seemed like an hour. "I have Kizzy's front door key. I will accompany the law enforcement gentlemen into her house where we will check to see if anything's missing."

"I would never steal from Kizzy," I said hotly. "And neither would Junior."

Her lips curled with scorn. "You're not a very good judge of character, Allie."

She whirled and reached for the door.

"You're wrong," I said to her back. "Just because I'm a kid doesn't mean I can't tell whose character is good. And, guess what? It's not yours!"

Mr. Hostetler made a little strangled sound, sort of a snort laugh disguised as a cough. Mrs. Hawkins didn't turn around. But as she marched through the door, I saw the back of her neck turn red.

After she left, Mr. Hostetler droned on and on about "personal responsibility" and "potential" and "making good choices." I nodded my head vigorously, but his words washed over me like crashing waves. All sound, no meaning.

Then he said, "Since you don't have a telephone, I'll be sending the school social worker to speak with your mother about this incident."

I snapped to attention. Faye! I'd told her I was at Kizzy's with Carmel. She knew nothing about Junior. She was going to kill me! And what about the women from Child Protective Services? Wouldn't they just love to hear about this little episode?

I bit my lip and swallowed my pride. "Mr. Hostetler, please let me talk to my mother first. It's . . . well, it's complicated. Could you give me a couple of days?"

He took off his glasses, rubbed the bridge of his nose and sighed heavily. "Today's Friday. You've got the weekend, Allie. That's it. Now, get out of here."

I thanked him and scooted out of his office. "Talk to your mother," he called after me.

My knees were shaking when I walked down the hall to my Washington State history class. I knew people were saying stuff about me. Like "Junior finally nailed her," or "He'll dump her now, like he did the others." I'd heard it all before, but now they'd be talking about *me*. My hand shook as I opened the door. The room was dark. A video played on the wall-mounted television set. Something about Grand Coulee Dam. Other than a few curious glances, I was pretty much ignored as I slipped into my seat. Thank God for Movie Friday!

I didn't see Junior until later. His car was parked in front of Uncle Sid's house when the school bus pulled up to let me off. Cory Philpott saw it too. He smacked his lips loudly and said, "Oooo, Allie's got a boyfriend."

As I climbed down the steps, I heard someone mutter, "Don't be a dumb ass, Cory. You're messin' with Junior's girlfriend."

Suddenly, I had what Mrs. Burke calls "a light bulb moment." I knew why people weren't giving me grief. They were afraid of Junior. The thought made me uneasy. That and the fact I had to face the music with Faye. I'd been thinking of possible excuses during the bus ride home. Could I make myself look like an innocent victim instead of a sneaky little liar? Probably not. And, if I compounded the original lie with more lies, I'd trip myself up. Plus the fact that Faye would know I was lying. So, I was back to square one.

These thoughts weighed heavily on my mind as I trudged along the side of the road toward Junior, who leaned against his car and watched me approach through hooded eyes. I stopped, leaving some space between us.

"Hey." I watched his face carefully. Junior was good at hiding his feelings. I couldn't tell if he was mad, sad, glad or something in between.

"Hey," he said, pushing away from the car. When we stood toe to toe, he reached over and brushed back a strand of hair that had escaped from my pony tail. When he spoke, his voice was hoarse with emotion. "I gotta go to work."

He blinked hard and looked at the ground. When he lifted his gaze back to mine, his gray eyes were fierce. "No way I'll ever be locked up again. I want to thank you for what you did."

I drew a shaky breath. "Well, it was kinda my fault you were in that house."

"Hostetler told me I'm in the clear. That old biddy checked and said nothing was missing." He grimaced like he was in pain. "I knew I should have stayed away from you. You're a good kid, Emerson. Soon as I start hanging around, you get in trouble."

Say what? Was Junior dumping me? Oh sure, he was looking all heart-broken and pretending like it was his fault. Probably one of his well-practiced dumping techniques put to use after he added the potential dumpee's name to his list. And, dammit, I wasn't even *on* his list!

Furious, I shrugged out of my back pack and stamped my foot. "That's bull, Junior! If it hadn't been for you, I'd have run out of that house and never looked back."

Junior reacted to my anger like he always did. He smiled.

I glared at him. "So if you're trying to dump me, you better think of another way."

A brow shot up. "You think I'm trying to dump you?"

He was either a very good liar or . . . could it be I was wrong? It was my turn to look at the ground. Junior cupped my face in his hands and forced me to look into his eyes.

"You're crazy, girl. You know that?"

Embarrassed, I pulled away. "Okay, okay. I'm crazy. Now tell me what happened this morning. Did your fake Carmel meet with Revelle?" Without saying a word, he dug a mini cassette recorder out of his pocket and handed it to me. "No way!" I exclaimed. "She taped Revelle?"

Junior nodded. "Yeah, she had it in her purse." He rested both hands on my shoulders. His expression was scary serious. "When you hear what Revelle said, you'll know I was right to hide the moonstone." He released me and stepped back. "Gotta go to work. Talk to you tomorrow."

Before he left, he let me use his cell phone to check on Kizzy. Nurse Haugen informed me, "Her vital signs are stable."

"So, is that a good thing?"

Deep sigh. "Allie. I believe we've covered this ground before. Stable means exactly that. Nothing has changed."

"Has her daughter been in to see her?"

With a derisive snort, she said, "She's gone back to Seattle. Said to call her if the old lady got worse. That's what she called her . . . the old lady."

After Junior left, I headed for the trailer, dread and anxiety churning in my belly, not knowing what to expect. The CPS woman's car was not in the driveway but maybe they'd dropped in on Faye earlier. I tried to imagine the possible scenarios following these words, "Yeah, Faye, I was at Kizzy's last night, but her daughter wasn't there. I was with Junior Martinez, who's kinda like my boyfriend, but nothing happened. Really. Oh yeah, and the school social worker visitor will be coming to see you because Kizzy's neighbor thought Junior stole stuff from Kizzy's house, so I had to step up in front of the entire student body and say he spent the night with me."

Her reaction would probably be one of two things.

She'd collapse on her bed and cry for three days or . . . she would take my side and charge into school like an avenging angel.

If there was a third option, I knew it wouldn't be good.

Chapter Seventeen

Faye was gone.

My first clue . . . the truck was missing. The second clue was the note taped to the front door. The third was the newspaper on the spool table, opened to the "Help Wanted" ads, several of them heavily underlined. I smiled as I read the note. Though it was addressed to me, the words were obviously written for the prune-faced Cynthia and her cheery assistant, Pam. Thank God for Manny Trujillo and his early warning system.

Dear Allie, Even though I'm not feeling well (FIBROMYALGIA!) I've risen from my sick bed to search for a job. I have several hot prospects, so keep your fingers crossed. If you're hungry, there's a nutritious snack in the fridge. I'll be home later to prepare dinner. Your loving Mother.

Part of me was relieved. I'd temporarily dodged a bullet. The other part—the guilt-ridden part—wanted to get it over with. I opened the door, and a business card fluttered to the ground. Cynthia and Pam had indeed paid us a visit. Somebody, probably Cynthia, had written on the back of the card, "Ms. Emerson. Sorry you're not home to discuss Allie's future."

The words seemed vaguely threatening, but I had more pressing problems to deal with at the moment. Cynthia would have to take a number. I tossed the card on the dinette table and checked to see if Faye had lied about the nutritious snack. Carrots. A plastic bag full of carrots, not the baby ones, big giant ones, like the kind you feed to horses.

The air inside the trailer was hot and stuffy. I cranked the windows open, grabbed the carrots and went outside. After checking for Blaster, I sat under the apple tree and turned on the tape recorder. I'd told Junior everything I could remember about Kizzy's family. Hopefully, he'd relayed the information to the wannabe Carmel.

I gnawed on a carrot and listened. After a few seconds of static, I heard the whoosh and gurgle of an espresso machine, shuffling footsteps and a woman's voice ordering a double skinny latte. Revelle was easy to recognize.

He said, "Grande Americano, two shots of chocolate . . . no, no, put your money away. My treat."

I suffered through ten more minutes of small talk before they got to the good stuff.

Carmel: (in a breathy, little girl voice) "So, Mr. Revelle, what's this big mystery all about?"

Revelle: "How much do you know about your grandmother?"

Brief moment of panic! Had I told Junior about Magda?

Carmel: (heavy sigh) "Why are you asking about *her*? You said this meeting was about us getting rich."

Revelle: "It starts with her."

Carmel: (incredulous squeak) "This is about Magda?"

The breath I'd been holding escaped in a gusty sigh of relief.

Revelle: "Magda stole a bunch of money from my grandfather."

Carmel: "No way! You trying to shake me down?"

(Sound of chair scraping across the floor)

Revelle: "No, no, I'm not after money . . . at least not from you. This is about Magda's pendant . . . the moonstone she wore around her neck."

Carmel: (snort of disgust) "That gaudy old thing?"

Revelle: "What I'm about to tell you, I've heard from my grandfather hundreds of times. You can believe it or not. Your choice."

He paused. When the silence grew unbearable, Carmel said, "What? Tell me!"

"My grandfather was a full partner in a successful investment firm in New York. A native of Hungary, he was pleasantly surprised when a young woman, your grandmother, appeared in his building selling the pastries he remembered from his childhood. Pastries with strange-sounding names. *Kiffles, linzes, beigs, mezeskalacs.* Before long, the woman had access to my grandfather's corner office, where he met with his most important clients. Grandfather said Magda would slip silently through the door with her basket of goodies, so unassuming he'd forget she was in the room."

Revelle slurped some coffee. "One day, Magda stopped coming. She'd vanished. Completely and utterly."

Thirty seconds went by before Carmel said, "So she disappeared. So what!"

Revelle's voice was cutting. "So guess what else disappeared, Carmel." When she didn't answer, he said, "After she left, the shit hit the fan. Unauthorized withdrawals from wealthy clients' accounts began to surface. Remember, nothing was computerized in those days, so it took a while to figure it out. The word got around. People began to pull money out of the firm. It all but ruined Revelle Investments. It took years to re-build it."

Carmel said, "And you guys blame my grandmother? It was probably some clerk who had access to the account numbers."

"Every employee was thoroughly investigated. Magda was the common denominator. All of the victims remembered Magda's presence in Grandfather's office."

"So, you think she was memorizing account numbers or what?"

"There was no possible way she could have accessed personal information. The men were not introduced to Magda. When she passed around her pastries, my grandfather made sure all the documents were out of view."

"Then she didn't do it," the fake Carmel said.

Revelle heaved a heavy sigh. "Here's the weird part. Every person who lost money remembered the moonstone. They thought it strange that a plainly dressed immigrant woman would wear such a thing."

"Probably the only thing she had of value," Fake Carmel said, still defending her fake grandma. She was actually a pretty good actress.

"Each of the men who had money stolen was interviewed separately. Each one of them said exactly the same thing. After Magda passed out the goodies, she stepped back away from the desk where she stood with one hand covering the moonstone."

With a huff of disgust, Fake Carmel said, "Oh, please! Next you'll be telling me Magda used the moonstone to beam information from the files into . . . what? Her goody basket? This is too ridiculous!"

When Revelle spoke, his voice had changed. It had an eerie quality that caused the hair on the back of my neck to prickle in alarm.

"Oh, Magda used the moonstone all right. My grandfather was first and foremost a Hungarian. As a child, I heard stories about gypsies, their uncanny ability to read palms, tea leaves and other such nonsense. But, when it came to money, he used his head, not his heart. Nonetheless, he was convinced that Magda used the moonstone to read minds; that she somehow accessed the information she needed to make withdrawals."

Fake Carmel snorted. "Okaaaay," she said, drawing the word in disbelief. "Let's assume this really happened—not that I ever heard a word about it from my mother—but, oh, well, if it's true and you don't want the money paid back, what *do* you want?"

"My grandfather spent a life time looking for Magda, but she changed her name and moved across the country. And she was smart. She made small withdrawals from a lot very rich people on the chance they wouldn't notice. Revelle Investments wasn't her only target."

"Let's cut to the chase. Why am I here?" Fake Carmel said.

Revelle chuckled. It wasn't a pleasant sound. "The moonstone, of course. Magda was small potatoes. Think about the potential, Carmel. Think big."

I could hear him breathing.

"Imagine being able to look into the minds of the rich and powerful, learning their secrets, their weaknesses."

"So you could . . . blackmail them?" Carmel said.

"No, that's too dangerous. What I have in mind is a consulting firm. Picture yourself as an advisor to the power brokers of the world. For an exorbitant fee, of course." Revelle chuckled again. "Which they would be willing to pay because we'd be privy to information they couldn't get anywhere else."

"But, wouldn't they want to know *how* we got it?"

Revelle said, "Trust me. The wheelers and dealers of the world only want to win. That's all they care about."

"But maybe my grandmother was all, you know, some supernatural chick who knew the secret of how to use the thing. It might not be as easy as you think," Carmel said.

"There's one way to find out."

Carmel sighed. "I suppose you want me to get it from the kid . . . Allie."

Even though I was expecting it, I jumped at the sound

of my name.

"She knows you. Right?"

"Yeah. She's my mother's little friend."

"Who has the moonstone," Revelle finished. "Why did your mother give it to her?"

"Hell if I know," Fake Carmel said. "Probably because she didn't want *me* to have it."

I listened intently as Revelle instructed Fake Carmel how to get the moonstone from me. It felt weird, like I was eavesdropping on my future. Totally removed, yet an integral part of a whole.

I turned the recorder off and leaned back against the apple tree. I thought about the moonstone and how strange my life had become since it entered my life. There was so much I didn't know. Would the moonstone's magic work only for me? If that was true, I would gladly hand it over to Revelle, knowing his greedy plan would fail.

But then I thought about Kizzy; how she'd fought through layers of pain and unconsciousness to whisper her urgent message. The prophecy said *I* was meant to have the moonstone. Not Revelle. I would do everything in my power to keep it out of his hands.

*

I must have dozed off, because I awoke to the sound of wind chimes and found Trilby hovering above the ground directly in front of me. She was dressed in a flowing pink thingy that kept floating upward, revealing bright, red, bikini panties. She glowered at me and slapped angrily at the billowing garment.

"About time you woke up," Trilby snapped. "I haven't got all day, ya know."

I sat up and stretched. "Nice outfit. They give you that in heaven?"

Trilby plummeted to earth with a grunt of surprise, her pink gown fluttering and settling around her like it had a life of its own. "Everything's color-coded up there. White's the biggie but you have to *earn* it." She said that with finger quotes and a sneer.

"Why are you here? I passed the three tests."

Trilby scrunched up her face in concentration and thought for a long moment. "Why? I was sitting in class listening to a lecture from this short dude named Saint Arthur. When he gets upset—which is most of the time—his big old wings ruffle up and flap like crazy. Anyhow, I got bored and started flirting with the class assistant, Micah. I mean this guy is seriously hot! Long, golden hair. Big, furled wings. Talk about your heavenly host!"

I giggled. "So it's okay to hook up with guys in heaven?"

"Don't know yet. I'm still on the first floor. First floor's like pre-heaven, and let me tell you, there's no hanky-panky going on there. And you know what pisses me off?"

Without waiting for my answer, she said, "I have to get at least a C average, or the elevator doors won't open and I can't get rid of this damn dress until I get to the second floor."

She used her thumb and fore finger to pluck at the distasteful garment, one side of her mouth turned down in disgust. I'd forgotten how easily Trilby's mind wandered. "So you're here to tell me . . . " I prompted.

"Oh, yeah, you're in danger. They sent me to warn you."

"Can you be more specific?"

Her mouth turned down in disgust. "What's with all the questions! It's not like I have a photographic memory. Just be careful. Okay?"

I nodded. I knew Revelle was dangerous. So far, Trilby hadn't told me anything I didn't already know.

"Oh, I almost forgot." Trilby floated to her feet, her voluminous gown billowing and swirling around her.

"You're supposed to practice. Your life may depend on it."

Swear to God, Trilby was making me crazy. I shot to me feet and yelled, "Practice what? Concentrate, Trilby. Practice the piano? My multicultural lesson of the day? Bull riding?"

"Jeez, chill out, girl," Trilby said in an offended tone. "I was going to tell you. Practice moving stuff with your mind. You know, the TKP."

"Oh," I said in a small voice. "That's why they sent you here?"

With a solemn nod, Trilby said, "So I'm guessing it's important. Just do it. Okay?"

Before I could answer, she was sucked into a vortex of flapping pink fabric and borne away, apparently back to pre-heaven and a sexy angel-in-training named Micah.

Practice, she'd told me. My life depended on it. And so I began.

Chapter Eighteen

I was scared. Yeah, tough little Allie who stood up to bullies, ran barefoot down a country road, provided an alibi for a former gang banger in front of the entire student body and bravely spent the night in a spooky old house (well, maybe not so bravely) was scared of her own power. What if I couldn't control it?

Picture this: It's harvest time. Allie is picking apples to earn money for clothes. She decides it would be faster to make the apples fly off the tree into the bin. She has an unfortunate power surge and apples begin flying through the air like hailstones. The other pickers panic and run screaming from the orchard. Uncle Sid loses his apple crop and has to go on welfare.

Telekinetic power in the hands of a novice . . . scary.

Despite my misgivings, I couldn't afford to be scared. Granted, Trilby was a ditz, but past events had unfolded exactly as she'd predicted. The words, "Practice, your life depends on it," resonated in my mind as I glanced around to make sure I was alone. I'd seen Uncle Sid earlier, sidling into the house. The only living creatures around were the dogs, Lewis and Clark, who always returned from their explorations at precisely 5:30 p.m. for dinner. They'd been fed, and were both lying in the grass chewing on big, meaty bones.

I set a carrot on the spool table and tried to make it roll. Nothing happened. I could hear the thudding of my heart, the rumble of a passing truck, a distant siren. I felt a soft breeze ruffle my hair, saw the sun's downward descent in the west and the yellow flash of a goldfinch in the apple tree. *Too much distraction. Concentrate, Allie.*

I closed my mind to everything except the sound of my beating heart. Taking deep breaths, I began to count the beats. *Bump. Bump. Bump.* The steady rhythm soothed me. The world fell away, and my vision grew dark around the edges. My eyes saw nothing but the carrot. My ears heard nothing but the sound of my heart. My mind contained nothing except my desire to make the carrot move. And then it did. The carrot rolled across the table and fell to the ground. I took another deep breath and re-focused my energy, thinking only, *lift, lift.* Yes! I pumped a fist in the air as the carrot rose and plopped down on the table top.

Before darkness fell, I'd made a garden hose slither through the grass like an enormous snake, which scared the crap out of Lewis and Clark who dropped their bones and ran for the back porch. I'd just moved a lawn chair from one side of the table to the other, when Blaster announced his presence in his usual fashion.

I turned my head slowly and found him staring intently at me through mean, little eyes. It was like he remembered when I fell off the ladder, and he wanted another crack at me. I wondered if I could make him levitate and float to the other end of the pasture. Worth a try. I took a step toward the pasture.

I was concentrating so hard, I didn't realize Faye was home until I heard the truck door slam. Her appearance jolted me back to reality and my date with doom. Confession time. I walked to the trailer on dragging feet, a dull ache blooming in the back of my skull.

It was then I had a stroke of brilliance. As Faye walked toward me, I put my hands on my hips and glared. "Where have you been? And don't tell me you've been interviewing for a job. Not at this time of night."

Faye folded her arms across her chest and studied my face. "What's with the attitude, Allie? You got something to tell me?"

I'd forgotten Faye knew every trick in the book. She'd probably used them on Claude, my off-limits grandpa. I knew when I was whipped. I gulped in some air. "Yeah, actually, I do. Let's go inside."

I turned toward the door, but stopped when I heard the unmistakable sound of a low rider slowly bumping down Uncle Sid's driveway. Junior? Here? Now?

Faye's head whirled toward the sound. Junior pulled up next to our pick-up, killed the engine and stepped out of the car.

"Hey, Allie." He flashed me a smile.

Faye's eyes narrowed in suspicion. "Who the hell are you?"

Junior stepped forward and extended a hand, "I'm Allie's friend. Junior Martinez."

I held my breath. Faye ignored his outstretched hand. Her head swiveled back and forth between Junior and me. "Allie's friend?" Her voice held a warning. She turned to me, her eyes blazing. "Please don't tell me you have a boyfriend."

I opened my mouth to answer, but Junior stepped around Faye and stood next to me. "It's not like that. We're just friends."

Oh, crap, I thought. I'm just Junior's friend.

Hastily, I added, "Yeah, it's like he said. I needed a ride to go see Kizzy. He helped me out. He's helped me out in other ways too."

Oops, wrong thing to say.

"Helped you out, huh?" Faye studied Junior like he was a dead frog under a microscope. "Exactly how did you help her out?"

Junior lifted his palms and turned on his megawatt

smile. "Nothing bad. I'll swear on a Bible if you want."

I saw Faye's shoulders relax and the corner of her mouth twitch. Junior was getting to her. She opened the trailer door, stepped back and waved Junior inside. "I'll see if I can find one."

Her voice wasn't exactly dripping with sarcasm, but it had a tone I recognized. What she really wanted to say was, "This better be good or Allie will be stuck in this trailer for a month."

I was usually embarrassed when people saw the way Faye and I lived. I never invited friends over. But with Junior, it was different. He seemed perfectly comfortable sitting on my couch bed, flashing his dimples at my mother, whose expression had softened considerably. I sat down next to him. Faye sat across from us.

"And you're here because . . . ?" Faye prompted.

Junior and I both started to speak then stopped.

Junior leaned forward and spoke earnestly, "Did Allie tell you what happened today?"

Faye's eyes narrowed. "No. Why?"

Junior launched into the story, starting with me running, screaming, out of Kizzy's house. At that point, I had to confess I was there alone, not with Carmel, as I'd told her.

"But I had to," I said. "Kizzy only came to for a few minutes, and she wanted me to find that cedar chest. I knew you wouldn't let me stay there alone. I'm sorry I lied."

Faye shook her head slightly and sniffed, a sure sign of hurt feelings. At this point, it was more about me not trusting her. I felt my lower lip quiver in response. Junior took my hand and squeezed it.

"Nothing happened, Ms. Emerson. Honest." His clear gray eyes willed her to believe. "I haven't known Allie very long, but I know she's a good kid. If she lied to you, it's because she was trying to help."

"Maybe you better tell me the rest," Faye said.

Taking turns, we filled her in. Not wanting to worry her, I down-played Christian Revelle's role in the moonstone drama. I squeezed Junior's hand to clue him in. He picked up on it immediately.

"Revelle thinks he's a player but we've got it covered."

He told her about the fake Carmel's meeting with Revelle but skipped most of the back story, saying only, "Next week, Revelle will be getting what he *thinks* is the moonstone. But it will be as fake as Carmel."

I looked at him curiously. "You won't be able to match it. He'll know it's not the real deal."

Junior said, "You told me he didn't get a good look at it. You covered it with your hand. Right?"

I tried to remember exactly what had happened that day in Kizzy's hospital room. I nodded. "After I covered it with my hand, he sat down by Kizzy's bed like he was praying. That's when I moved the stone one click."

"And you read his mind."

Faye's eyes got big. "Is that true, Allie?"

I nodded. "Just bits and pieces. When the words faded out, I put the moonstone inside my shirt."

"You're sure he didn't see you move the stone?" Junior said.

"I made sure he wasn't looking when I moved it."

"The meeting's set for Monday," Junior said. "The woman playing Carmel will give him the fake stone. She'll tell Revelle she's been trying to read minds, but there's nothing magic about it. Remember, she mentioned it might not work for him when they met yesterday."

I grinned. "Oh yeah, the 'supernatural chick' comment."

Junior smiled back at me. "Revelle will take it and leave town. When it doesn't work, he'll toss it in the nearest garbage can. End of story."

"Not quite." Faye rose from her chair and looked down

at the two of us. "I need more information. You two spent the night together. Where did *you* sleep, Allie?"

I blushed and stuttered, "Uh, uh, on the couch."

"And what about you, Mr. Martinez?"

Junior flashed his gleaming smile again. I felt myself responding to it until I remembered; it was his charm-freshman-girls-out-of-their-panties smile. I glared at him while he attempted to steer Faye in a new direction. "Allie wanted me to watch a movie, something about music, but I got bored and fell asleep."

Faye was not easily fooled. "On the couch?"

Unfazed by Faye's unblinking stare, Junior replied calmly. "It's a big couch, Miz Emerson. Nothing happened."

Faye stayed silent for a long moment then flapped a hand at Junior. "You! Go home." She turned her gaze on me. "You! Go get the mail."

I jumped up and followed Junior outside. I tugged at his sleeve. "Think it will work? The fake moonstone?"

He guided me to the car. "Hop in. I'll drive you to the mailbox."

Risking the wrath of Faye, I scrambled into the low rider. Junior started the engine and backed slowly down the driveway before he answered my question. "It should work. Got a better idea?"

I shook my head. Junior stopped at the end of the driveway and took my hand. I felt the warmth of his touch clear down to my toes. "You and your mom okay now?"

"I think so. Thanks for coming over. It helped a lot."

He raised the back of my hand to his lips. Filled with a yearning I didn't fully understand, I caught my breath, a little frightened by the sensations sweeping through my body. Maybe I wasn't the only person in the car blessed with magic. I pulled my hand away and opened the door. "See ya, Junior."

"See ya, kid."

He stayed until I picked up the mail and walked back down the driveway. Caught in the bright beam of his headlights, I turned and waved, watching as he pulled slowly onto the road and drove away. At that moment, flushed with warmth and happiness, I knew I'd fallen in love with Junior Martinez, and that I trusted him not only with the moonstone, but with my life.

Chapter Nineteen

I stood under the yard light and went through the mail. A flyer from Tom's Corner Market. A *No Bull!* catalog featuring mail-order bull sperm, put in our mailbox instead of Uncle Sid's. Another tan envelope from Social Security addressed to Faye, and a small, padded envelope addressed to Allie Emerson. I tucked it into the pocket of my jeans to read later.

I climbed into the trailer. Faye sat at the table slashing a file across her fingernails, ominously quiet. When I entered, she looked up at me, her expression unreadable. Had we put the "boyfriend genie" back in the bottle, or was I about to be royally chewed out? With Faye, one never knew.

"Anything interesting?"

Without a word, I handed her the tan envelope. She slipped the pointy end of the nail file under the flap and ripped it open. She withdrew a single sheet of paper and unfolded it carefully. Her eyes moved back and forth across the page. I watched her face, praying it was good news. Bad news would trigger a week-long crying jag. I didn't need that right now. I didn't need that ever.

She blew out air and tossed the letter onto the table. "Thanks for nothing, Big Ed."

I snatched up the letter and scanned it. The words "benefits denied" practically jumped off the page. I braced myself, but Faye surprised me. Not a single tear. She stood

up, slammed her fist down on the table and started cursing
Big Ed. She started at the beginning of the alphabet—A is
for A-Hole, B is for Bastard—and so on. A couple of the
letters stumped her, so she skipped over them. She finally
ran out of steam after Turd and Son-of- a- Bitch. But she
had only just begun.

I watched, goggle-eyed, as she picked up Uncle Sid's
No Bull! catalog, tore out each page and stacked them
together, carefully aligning the edges to form a neat pile.
Then she folded her hands and smiled. It wasn't a pleasant
smile. Was my mother losing her mind?

"Do you have a magic marker and a big envelope,
sweetie?"

Without saying a word, I found the requested items.
Slowly and methodically, she began scrawling, I HATE
BIG ED! across the studly bull featured on each page, then
folded the pages in half and stuffed them one at a time
into the envelope. I guess we all deal with disappointment
in different ways. Who was I to judge?

"Need some help with that?" I said. At the rate she
was going, we'd be up all night.

She nodded. "Just make sure you put the message *on*
the bull."

"Why?"

She gave me a dark look. "I have my reasons."

I found another pen and slid into the bench across from
her. We sat in companionable silence, scrawling our
invective across various-and-sundry bull parts, a real
mother-daughter Kodak moment. I noticed Faye's hands
had stopped shaking. In fact she looked eerily calm.

I cleared my throat. "You're not planning to mail this,
are you?"

"Thought I would."

"Maybe you should wait a few days, you know, until
you cool off a little."

Faye dropped her pen and reached for my hand. She pressed it against her hot cheek. "How did you get so wise, Allie? With a mother like me?"

I searched her face. Still no tears.

"You do okay." My voice suddenly thick with emotion.

She dropped my hand and winked. "But I'm still going to mail it to Big Ed."

Faye got up and poured herself a glass of wine. She set the glass down on top of the torn SSI envelope. "It's not the end of the world."

"True," I agreed and crossed my fingers under the table. Maybe this was Faye's . . .

"Wake-up call," she said. "That's what it is."

I kept my face carefully neutral but in my head, I was dancing a jig and screaming, "Yes!"

She picked up the business card from Child Protective Services and set it on top of the brown envelope. "Two wake-up calls."

She tapped her index finger on the card and mused, "I need a job."

I held my breath and waited for her to continue.

"I really did have an interview today, Allie."

"That's good, Mom," I said.

She beamed. "You called me 'Mom.'"

"Oops," I kidded. "That's good, Faye."

We finished up our hate mail, and Faye went to bed. I was feeling pretty good, having dodged two bullets. Faye hadn't lapsed into a blue funk, and her anger was now directed at Big Ed instead of me. And furthermore, the moonstone was out of my control at the moment. I felt lighter than air for the first time since my tumble off the ladder.

When I pulled off my jeans, I remembered the envelope I'd stuffed into my pocket. I slipped into PJ's and curled up on the couch before opening it. No return address, but the postmark said, Portland, Oregon. Curious. I knew no one in Portland, Oregon. My name and address were typed and centered perfectly.

Using Faye's nail file, I opened the envelope and removed a tiny, bubble-wrapped cellular phone, a charger and a type-written note, unsigned. When I read the note, my euphoric mood evaporated faster than a drop of water on a sizzling hot sidewalk.

Allie,
This phone has a pre-programmed number. Hit Send and listen carefully. It's important. Good luck.

I stepped outside and leaned against the side of the trailer, the heavy mantle of responsibility settling, once again, on my shoulders. I punched Send. After a bit of static, the message started. The tone was eerily distorted. Had to be somebody I knew who didn't want to be identified. Man or woman? I couldn't tell.

"Listen carefully. This message will not be repeated. Because Kizzy Lovell is your mentor, you know about the prophecy passed along by her mother, Magda. You are the girl whose palm bears the sign of the star. You, Allie, are The Keeper. Your legacy cannot be denied. But first, you need to know why you must guard the moonstone with your life."

I felt a frission of fear scamper down my spine. Who was this person and how did he/she know the intimate details of my palm? And, the words "guard the moonstone with your life" sent me on a huge guilt trip. I didn't even have the darn thing!

The voice stopped, and I heard breathing, as if the speaker was gathering the courage to give me bad news. I bit my lower lip and waited, listening to the sounds of the night . . . a passing car, the distant lowing of cattle, the incessant barking of a neighbor dog, the sound of a plane passing overhead. I imagined myself on that plane, flying far, far away from Peacock Flats and the screwed-up mess my life had become.

The message continued.

"Long before the moonstone came into existence, two societies were formed. One group, the Star Seekers, have a star located somewhere on their palms. A star on the palm indicates psychic abilities of varying degrees. Yours, because of its placement in the exact center of the lunar mound, is extremely rare and the most powerful of signs. In the early days, psychic powers were thought to be signs of witchcraft. The Star Seekers met secretly and had a common goal: to use their powers to fight the evil in the world. Their history has been passed down through the generations by word of mouth, and their secret is still closely guarded. Their oral history includes the story of a powerful gemstone and the maid who is meant to have it. The Star Seekers are determined to see this prophecy fulfilled."

Okay, I thought, with a sigh of relief. *This isn't so bad.* I'd have to start checking palms, see if any of the Star Seekers were hanging around Peacock Flats and watching out for me. What I heard next blew away my happy thoughts.

"The second group is called the Trimarks. They are identified by an inverted triangle on their palms, the sign of an evil, twisted personality. The point of the triangle faces downward toward the wrist and may appear anywhere on the palm partially or fully formed. The most dangerous of the Trimarks have a perfect inverted triangle located where the head line and fate line intersect. Trimarks have varying degrees of supernatural ability, but they share a single philosophy: 'What's mine is mine. What's yours is mine. And I will take it by whatever means possible.'

"The Trimarks may be white-collar criminals or

common thugs. They're dangerous and unpredictable but *all* of them have the uncanny ability to relate to their victims using charm, vulnerability . . . whatever works to gain that person's trust.

"Allie, here's the part that affects you; they know about the moonstone. They want it. It's possible they know you have it."

The speaker paused again. I realized the airplane fantasy wouldn't cut it. I needed a rocket ship to carry me to another planet. The sudden chill I felt had nothing to do with the soft May night and everything to do with the impenetrable shadows next to the barn. I continued to listen as I stepped inside the trailer, shut and locked the door. I dived onto the couch and pulled the comforter over my head, the phone still pressed to my ear.

"The Trimarks have devoted their lives to chaos and evil, hoping to profit as a result. They were at the crucifixion of Christ, the Nazi death camps, the Kennedy assassination, Hurricane Katrina. One can only imagine what might happen if they get their hands on the moonstone. Trust no one. Remember . . . you are the maid who's strong of mind."

On that note, the eerie voice ceased, and I heard nothing but static. I dashed out from under the covers and buried the phone at the bottom of my backpack.

Sleep did not come easily that night. The night sounds I usually found to be soothing morphed into something far more sinister. In my troubled state, the wind in the trees blew to disguise the sound of approaching footsteps. A car door slammed. Had a carload of Trimarks pulled into the driveway? A tumble weed, tossed by the wind, brushed against the side of the trailer like clawed fingers scrabbling for an opening.

Not only was I scared out of my wits, I didn't have the moonstone. What if I'd broken some cardinal prophecy rule, and the result would be chaos and destruction? It was too horrible to think about. Though I tried desperately to ignore it, a seed of dark suspicion began to sprout, its tangled roots spreading like poison. Junior. His reluctance to let me see his palm. Junior. Who now had the moonstone.

When my exhausted mind finally gave up, I drifted off to a landscape of nightmares in which every single person I knew appeared before my eyes like some weird, psychedelic slide show. Faye, Mercedes, Manny, Patti the bus driver, Cory Philpott, Junior, Mrs. Burke, Diddy, Mike Purdy, Mr. Hostetler and more. One by one they paraded through my dreams. The pounding of my heart provided the percussive background for the message I could not forget. "Trust no one."

*

Saturday. Dump day once again, which suited my frame of mind. Crappy. I was sleep-deprived and worried sick. Since Faye no longer had her fake illness she was free to drive, even though I was now the proud possessor of a Washington State Learners' Permit, thanks to Deputy Philpott.

We hitched up the trailer and headed for Friendly Fred's. I considered using the mother-daughter time to fill Faye in on the whole thing. The cell phone. The Trimarks and Star Seekers. My doubts about Junior. I needed to unburden myself. I decided to play it by ear.

We took a side trip to the post office so Faye could mail her special package to Big Ed, even though I tried to talk her out of it. That's when all hell broke loose again. I don't know why, but when Faye and I were together in the pick-up, disaster followed. Bad karma, I guess.

The post office parking lot was jammed with cars. It was a small lot with an entrance at one end, the exit at the other, designed to get people in and out quickly. It wasn't designed for Faye and I pulling our house behind us.

Even though it was Saturday, the lobby was open so people could access their post office boxes. Faye handed me the package. It was plastered with enough stamps to send it around the world and marked "CONFIDENTIAL," in big, black letters.

"Just scoot on in there and drop it in the outgoing mail. There's no place to park, so hurry."

"Yeah, yeah." I was tempted to dump the package in the nearest trash can.

"Lose the attitude!"

I slammed the door and moseyed into the post office. Mrs. Burke, carrying an armload of mail, was coming out.

"Allie!" She was delighted to see me, as usual.

Part of me hated what I did next, but I had to know. I waved Faye's package.

"Could you hold this for a sec? My shoe's untied."

Mrs. Burke, always accommodating, stuck out her hand, palm up. I bent over to re-tie my still tied shoe and got a gander at her palm on the way down. Sigh of relief. No inverted triangle. No star. Nothing unusual at all.

"Thanks, Mrs. Burke," I chirped.

"How's your friend, dear? Has she improved at all?"

I was about to answer, when I heard honking horns and yelling coming from the parking lot.

"Gotta go. Catch you later." I shoved Faye's package through the mail slot and hustled outside. "Oh, no," I groaned.

A huge semi, loaded with hay, blocked the exit lane. Our pick-up and trailer stretched from one end of the tiny lot to the other, effectively keeping all the cars from backing out. Faye was yelling at the truck driver, who was tightening the tie-downs holding a giant tarp in place. He pretended to be deaf. The people who were blocked in their parking spaces began to mutter and curse. I spotted a couple of kids from my class, pointing and laughing. My face burned with embarrassment.

Mrs. Burke ran up to me. "Oh my goodness, what a mess! Can your mother back the trailer out into the street? Once she's out of the way, the rest of us can get out."

Faye had a number of talents, but backing a truck and trailer wasn't one of them. I pointed at the truck driver.

"He's the one messing things up. Why can't he move?"

"His motor conked out," somebody yelled. "Back the trailer out!"

I trotted over to the driver's side. Faye sat, staring straight ahead, clutching the steering wheel so hard her knuckles were white.

"You have to back up, Faye. People are getting mad."

"You know I can't back."

"Yes, you can," I insisted. "I'll tell you which way to turn the wheels."

I tried to sound confident, even though my backing ability was more pathetic than Faye's. We usually planned our route so we could pull forward at all times.

After Faye managed to get the trailer jack-knifed, and all I wanted to do was bury myself under the load of hay, Deputy Philpott arrived. Of course.

"You two, again?" I could tell he was trying to act all tough and disapproving. But I saw a brief smile beneath his billy-goat whiskers.

Faye clutched her throat and fluttered her eyelashes. "Oh, thank God you're here. Can you help me?"

A blush bloomed on Philpott's lean face. "That's why I'm here, ma'am. Just slide on over."

Yeah, it was sickening. By the time we were on our way, I couldn't resist saying, "You just *had* to mail that stupid package, even though I told you not to. You *knew* that parking lot was too small for the trailer."

"Oh, give it a rest, Allie. It's over now. No harm, no foul."

"Oh, really?" I shrieked.

"What the hell's the matter with you?"

And so it continued, all the way to Friendly Fred's and back home. By then, I was so angry there was no way I would confide in Faye.

We parked the trailer and hooked up the water and electricity without speaking a word. I made a peanut butter sandwich and sat outside with a book. Sometime later, Faye came out of the trailer.

"I'm driving to Vista Valley to see about a job. If you want, I'll drop you off at the hospital."

Her voice was subdued, apologetic. I cleared my throat and closed the book, but didn't look at her. "That would be great. Thanks."

She dropped me in front of the hospital. "I'll pick you up here in an hour."

I nodded and shut the door, carefully this time. I watched her drive away and decided, when she came back, I'd tell her about last night. The Trimarks. The Star Seekers. I needed to talk to somebody, and Faye was all I had.

Chapter Twenty

The third floor was teeming with visitors, some somber-faced, others laughing and joking. A toddler ran down the corridor, an older brother giving chase. As I walked past the nurses' station, I looked for Nurse Haugen. But the ferocious little blond was on duty today, the one A. Haugen called the night nurse. Her gaze swept over me, lingering on my feet. The bloody-foot-dirty-flip-flop story must have spread through the hospital like wild fire. Thankfully, my feet were squeaky clean and clad in sneakers. I guess I passed inspection, because she returned to her paperwork.

One door down from Kizzy's room, a woman began to wail, the volume increasing exponentially as the pitch grew higher. I clapped my hands over my ears, wondering how people could get well in a place like this. They probably died just to get some peace and quiet.

When I got to Kizzy's room, the door was closed. My over-active mind began to dream up possible reasons for this anomaly. Like I'd walk in and see an empty bed as I did before, or find Kizzy lying dead with a sheet pulled over her face, or see a team of doctors and nurses wielding scary medical implements, standing around her bed yelling, "Stat! Stat!"

Such was my state of mind when I opened the door a small crack and peeked in. Two people stood by the window, deep in conversation. My first thought was, *Wow, what a good-looking couple. Both tall and blond. Both well-dressed. Could be movie stars.* A millisecond later, my reluctant brain caught up, and my heart leaped from my chest into my throat. Christian Revelle and the real Carmel Tigani were in Kizzy's room with their heads together, no doubt having a nice little chat about Revelle's rendezvous with the fake Carmel and puzzling out who was behind that little scheme. From their expressions—Carmel's sneer, and Revelle's flushed face and jutting jaw—I gathered they knew . . . *C'est moi!*

Revelle's eyes flicked over to the door and narrowed suspiciously. Panicky, I stepped back into the hall, pulled the door shut and took off at a dead run, knees high, arms pumping like some crazy cartoon character churning up clouds of dust. I peeked over my shoulder to see if Revelle was a step behind me. He wasn't. A crowd of people stood by the elevator. I briefly considered joining them, the whole safety-in-numbers thing. But what if Revelle strolled out of the room and darted into the elevator at the last moment? If he was a Trimark—and I was pretty sure he was—he would grab me and convince our fellow passengers I was his out-of-control, junky, teenage daughter. Heck, they'd probably help Revelle load me into his Escalade.

Skirting the crowd, I headed for the stairs. I slammed through the door and crashed into a tall, thin guy wearing scrubs and carrying a large drink in one hand, a sandwich in the other. With a grunt of surprise, his hands flew up as we collided. Our arms and legs flailed frantically in an effort to keep from falling down the stairs. We ended up in a tangle of limbs pressed up against the wall, his sandwich mashed against my chest. The soft drink cup landed upside-down on the concrete stairs in a violent explosion of ice and cola.

"What the . . . !" the guy yelled as I tried to extricate

myself.

"So sorry," I gasped. "Emergency."

I jerked free and started down the stairs, one hand holding the railing, the other picking the bologna sandwich off my chest. I really did feel bad about the guy's lunch but then again, maybe the spilled cola and ice would slow Revelle down.

I'd just reached the second floor landing when I heard a door open above me and men's voices. Could it be Revelle asking the scrubs guy if he'd seen the teenage girl who'd lifted his wallet and run away? In a matter of time, security would be looking for me.

I picked up speed, taking the stairs two at a time, almost dizzy from rounding the corners so fast. Later I kicked myself for being so stupid. I should have popped out on the second floor and ducked into an empty room. But no, Allie was scared spitless and the only thought in her head was, "Run! Run!"

I kept going until the stairs ran out. I burst through the door and looked for the main entrance, but nothing was as I remembered. No gift shop. No espresso bar. No cheery volunteers pointing the way to the elevator. Disoriented, I took in the confusing maze of dim, unfamiliar corridors with growing panic. Where in the hell was I? Or . . . was I in hell?

Deep breaths, Allie. Calm down and get your head on straight.

I nearly jumped out of my skin when I heard a "ding," and the elevator door began to slide open. I froze in my tracks and prayed it wasn't Revelle. Sometimes God listens. The door opened to reveal a middle-aged couple. The man started to step out. The woman grabbed his sleeve and pulled him back.

"For crying out loud, Frank, we're in the basement. You pushed the wrong button."

Okay, I was in the basement. In my haste, I'd missed the first floor. My relief was short-lived when I realized I'd compounded my problem. If I galloped back *up* the stairs to the first floor, I might encounter Revelle running *down* the stairs. I'd have to hang around the basement for a while until the coast was clear.

I looked up and down the hall. No patient rooms to duck into. Just solid doors leading to God knew what! Probably dead bodies and harvested organs. The very thought made me queasy. Maybe I could find a restroom to hide in. I was on that very quest when an official looking woman with glasses on a chain around her neck and a pencil behind her ear came around the corner, stopped dead and fixed me with a stern look.

"Are you looking for the main entrance?"

Before I could answer, she covered the space between us in two long strides, grabbed my arm and marched me toward the elevator. I tried to pull away, but she clung to me like a crab on steroids.

"Oh, don't bother," I babbled as she dragged me along, her steely fingers digging into my upper arm. "Just go about your business. I'll find my way out."

The elevator door slid open and we stepped in. I really didn't have a choice unless I clocked her a good one, but that would just make things worse.

"No problem," she said. "It happens all the time. People hit the wrong button and think they're on the first floor . . ."

I found out why she had a death grip on my arm when the elevator doors opened. A chubby, baby-faced security guard and the guy whose lunch I'd ruined stood side by side in front of the elevator. "That's her!" The scrubs guy said. "She's got mustard on her chest."

Apparently, destroying an employee's bologna sandwich was a hanging offense at Regional.

The woman released me and strode away.

Desperate to get out of the limelight, I lifted my hands helplessly and smiled at the security guard, whose name tag read "R. Johnson."

"Listen, R, I'm really sorry. If I had any money, I'd buy him another sandwich."

R. Johnson blushed. "My name's Reggie. They only put the first initial on the name tag. Saves money, I guess."

I fluttered my eyelashes a la Faye. "Oh really? I didn't know that."

Scrubs Guy shifted his weight from one foot to the other and cleared his throat.

Reggie drew himself up and tilted his head back so he could look down at me. "Young lady." His voice was a full octave lower. "You cannot run in the hospital, especially on the stairs. Someone could have been severely injured."

I nodded briskly, hoping he'd get the hint and hurry it up. When he continued to stare at me without speaking, I prompted, "And . . . "

The pump was primed, and the words poured out. I glanced up and down the hall while he droned on about "reckless abandon" and "insurance claims."

This wasn't good. We were drawing a crowd. The back of my neck got that crawly feeling. What if Revelle was on his way down? He'd step out of the elevator and find me there, gift-wrapped and tied up with a bow.

But Revelle didn't take the elevator. He took the stairs. The door to the staircase was down the hall to my left. Out of the corner of my eye, I saw a door open. Revelle stepped out and looked around like he was trying to figure out which way to go. I gasped and slid behind Reggie's bulky body, looking around frantically for a hiding place. When my gaze landed on the sign pointing to the chapel, I knew I'd found my salvation. No God-fearing American— which I was pretty sure included Reggie—would deny me this inalienable right.

"Reggie!" I cried. "I need to pray. You know, ask for God's forgiveness."

I whirled and headed for the chapel. Reggie trailed behind. With a snort of disgust, Scrubs Guy wandered off.

I slid into a wooden pew next to a middle-aged woman, folded my hands and bowed my head. R. Johnson sat next to me. I prayed Revelle wouldn't find me there. I really did. Pray, I mean. After what seemed like an hour, but was probably only five minutes, Reggie's pager went off. He leaned toward me and whispered, "Gotta go. Remember our little talk, okay?"

After he left, I counted to one hundred and stood. The woman next to me took hold of my hand and murmured, "God bless you, child."

Her face was so sweet, her words so sincere, I felt a pang of guilt for using this sacred place for my own selfish needs. I thanked her and tiptoed out.

After making sure the lobby was Revelle-free, I dug around in my pockets for change and went in search of a pay phone. I had to warn Junior. Last night, I'd added him to my list of possible bad guys. And, he did have the moonstone. But, in the clear light of day, I'd seen it differently.

If Junior was a Trimark, would he go to all the trouble of finding a fake Carmel to meet with Revelle? I didn't think he would, and I had to trust somebody. I had to let him know Revelle was on to us.

I called Bob's Burgers. Junior had the day off to take care of important business, his boss informed me. I opened the phone book to the M's and counted ninety-seven listings for Martinez. Since I was pretty sure Junior lived on Willow Lane, I tried M. Martinez on Willow Lane and got lucky.

Junior's mother was not thrilled to receive my phone call.

"Junior not here," she screeched. "Gone! Gone!"

Before I could say another word, she slammed the phone down. Out of time and money, I headed for the main entrance and saw our truck parked close by. I kept a sharp look-out for Revelle as I trotted out the hospital entrance. In fact, I was looking back over my shoulder when I yanked the door open.

"Hey there, you must be Allie!"

My head whipped around at the sound of the deep, masculine voice. I turned slowly and, with a sinking heart, checked out the guy sitting in the passenger seat. Broad shoulders. Longish blond hair tucked behind his ears. White tank top and jeans. The name "Mona" tattooed on his right forearm. His left hand resting on Faye's thigh.

I stifled a groan. Faye had a new boyfriend. Sometimes, it sucks to be me.

Chapter Twenty One

"Hi, I'm Roy."

The jerk jumped out of the truck and offered me his hand. I ignored it.

"Are you getting out here?" I asked hopefully.

"Nope, thought you'd want to sit next to your mother."

"I don't." He gave me a sickly grin and lowered his hand. I glared at Faye. "Tell me you're not taking him to our house," I said.

Faye glared right back. "He needs a lift to the lower valley. Is that all right with you, Miss Smarty Pants?" She patted the seat beside her. "Jump in, Roy. Allie likes the window."

Yeah, right, I thought bitterly. I'll sit by the window and hang my head out like a dog sniffing the breeze.

Roy sat next to Faye. I climbed in and pressed my body against the door, as far away from Roy as possible. Faye shifted into first and hit the gas. We shot forward, all three heads snapping back simultaneously, and almost sideswiped an ambulance pulling slowly out in front of us. Faye peered around Roy and shot daggers at me with her eyes.

"Not that it's any of your concern, *Allie...*" She paused to make sure I knew she meant business. "Roy's car is in Peacock Flats. A friend of his is working on the motor."

I ignored Faye's danger signs. "Will it be done soon?"

Faye hands tightened on the steering wheel, probably

to keep from slapping my face. I knew I was pushing it but couldn't seem to stop.

Roy lifted his hands and grinned. "Hey, girls! No fighting over Roy."

As if. I turned and stared out the window the rest of the way home. As soon as Faye pulled in by the trailer, I jumped out of the truck and headed for the Trujillos'.

I heard Roy say, "Man, she's one angry little chick."

Faye murmured, "She'll get over it."

Juanita gave me a bowl of her chicken molé, and I watched *General Hospital* with Mercedes for a while When I calmed down, I tried calling Junior again. Twice. The last time, his mother's voice reached new levels. "I tell you, Junior not here! You bad girls! Always after my Junior!"

I paced the Trujillos tiny living room and tried to figure out what to do next. Thankfully, Mercedes was in her fantasy world and didn't fire a million questions at me. After pacing, fretting and mumbling a few well-chosen words, I could draw only one conclusion. I had to keep Junior away from Revelle.

I thanked Juanita, waved bye-bye to Mercedes and started down the driveway. Faye and Roy were nowhere to be seen. Matt was hosing mud off his Jeep. Good old dirty-minded Matt. Probably harmless enough in broad daylight. Aunt Sandra sat in a lawn chair under a tree sipping lemonade. She watched me approach, a phony smile stuck on her face like clown make-up.

"Where are you off to, Allie?"

"Just checking to see if Matt can give me a ride somewhere."

The words surprised me as much as it did her.

Her smile disappeared.

Matt grinned. "Sure."

Aunt Sandra spoke sharply. "Aren't you supposed to pick up Summer?"

The very mention of Summer's name made me grind my teeth.

Matt dug a cell phone out of his pocket and punched in a number. He turned away but I heard, "Gotta run an errand . . . I'll be late . . . aw, come on, baby, don't be like that." He turned to face his mother. "I took care of it. Hop in, Allie."

Like the gentleman he wasn't, he opened the door for me. I could feel Aunt Sandra's disapproving gaze on my back as we pulled away.

"Your mother doesn't like me." I said.

"Yeah, well, that's her problem, not mine."

We reached the end of the drive way.

"Where to?" Matt said.

"Willow Lane. I think it's that way."

I waved my hand in a vague southerly direction.

Matt glanced at me and turned right on Peacock Flats Road. "Willow Lane, huh? I saw Junior Martinez here the other night. Are you going to his house?"

With residual anger at Faye still boiling through my veins, I almost said, "What's it to ya?" Instead, I bit my tongue and nodded. But Matt couldn't leave it alone. His gaze flicked over my body.

"Is he your boyfriend?"

I recalled the ugly things he'd thought about me, about wanting to be the "first," and decided to yank his chain.

"What if he is?"

"Junior runs with a gang. You could get hurt."

"Guess you never hurt anybody, huh?"

Matt's blue eyes widened in feigned surprise. "Me? Heck, no. I'm a good guy."

He reached over, took my hand and made slow circles with his thumb. "You gonna be home later? Maybe we could get together, you know, do something."

I decided to act like a dumb kid. I gazed at him with

wide-eyed innocence. "Do what?"

He squeezed my hand. "I'm sure we'll think of something."

I pulled my hand away. "Gee, do you think that might hurt Summer?"

Caught in his own trap, Matt said in an offended tone, "Jeez, Allie, why are you so mean to me?"

I pointed at an intersection ahead. "There's Willow Lane."

"I know where Junior lives," Matt snapped.

He pulled up in front of a small, blue house surrounded by a cyclone fence. The front yard was freshly mowed, the flower beds planted with colorful petunias. I thanked Matt for the ride. He drove off without saying a word.

Risking the wrath of Mama Martinez, I marched up to the front door and knocked. No answer. Was she inside, peeking through the curtains, muttering Spanish oaths? I knocked again.

"My mother's not home. Are you looking for Junior?"

The voice belonged to a pretty, young Hispanic woman with a baby in her arms, standing on the other side of the fence. She smiled.

"I'm Silvia. Junior's sister. We live next door. I saw you drive up."

I stepped off the porch and grinned back at her. "I guess a lot of girls come here looking for Junior. I'm Allie."

"Oh yeah, I've heard Junior talk about you."

"I bet you say that to all the girls."

Silvia laughed. The baby clapped his chubby little hands and gurgled. I walked to the fence.

"Do you know where I can find Junior? It's important."

She raised an eyebrow and glanced at my belly. I blushed when I realized what she was thinking.

"I'm not pregnant or anything. Junior and I are just friends. He could be in danger. I really need to talk to him."

She thought it over for a long moment then sighed.
"He went to Vista Valley early this morning. Said he had
to take care of some business. You wanna leave him a
note?"

"Is it okay if I sit on the porch and wait for him?"

Silvia shrugged. "Suit yourself. I gotta go run some
errands."

"What about your mom? Will she be back soon?"

I wasn't anxious to go toe-to-toe with Mama Martinez.

"Not until tomorrow. She just left to go visit her sister."

Silvia put the baby in his car seat then brought me a
pen and some paper in case I got tired of waiting and wanted
to leave a note for Junior. She folded her arms and stared
down at me like she was trying to make up her mind about
something.

Finally she said, "Oh, for God's sake, you look like a
lost puppy. Junior will be pissed if he comes home and
sees you sitting on the front steps."

She brushed by me and unlocked the front door.

"Go on in," she ordered.

"Are you sure it's okay?"

With a snort of impatience, Silvia waved me into the
house and left before I could thank her.

Standing in Junior's living room, I felt like an intruder.
It reminded me of a dream I have at least once a month,
where I'm standing in a stranger's house, a house I shouldn't
be in. A car drives up. I hear heavy footsteps on the porch,
a key in the lock. When I try to run, my feet are stuck to
the floor. Terror-stricken and unable to move, I wait,
knowing something awful is about to happen. That's when
I wake up screaming. Maybe if I knew what happened next,
I wouldn't have the dream again.

I tried to shake my feeling of unease as I stood in
Junior's living room. Even though the house was old and
the furniture shabby, it was spotlessly clean. An olive green

area rug hid most of the yellowing linoleum floor. The windows facing the front and north side of the room were covered with voluminous, dark gold drapes, closed tightly against the sun. A brown davenport, matching loveseat and two gold recliners were angled to face a large TV setting on a shelf against the south wall.

Hanging from the wall over the TV, was the largest crucifix I'd ever seen outside a church. The cross was rough-hewn and carved from a solid chunk of wood and featured a realistically rendered Jesus who was obviously close to death. Droplets of blood dotted his forehead from the crown of thorns. His body sagged lifelessly, and his eyes were closed against the pain. I tried to picture Junior's family, gathered together around the TV, watching their favorite show. Maybe even laughing at a sitcom. Call me crazy, but that crucifix would definitely suck the joy out of my TV watching.

I checked out the rest of the house. Three bedrooms, one bathroom and a tidy kitchen. Looked like a mansion compared to my place. I wondered where Junior might have hidden the moonstone. I briefly considered launching an all-out search, but it felt too much like snooping. I wandered back into the living room and almost turned on the TV but decided against it. Somehow, it didn't seem right to enjoy myself with Jesus hanging there.

Finally, I curled up on the brown davenport and settled in to wait for Junior, wondering what his reaction would be when he opened the door and found me in his living room. Joy? Anger? None of the above? A fleeting thought raced through my mind. What if Junior really was a Trimark? I remembered the words, "All of them have the ability to relate to their victims using charm . . . etc." Without question, Junior was a bonafide charmer. *Don't go down that road, Allie.*

I'd just picked up a Spanish language newspaper when

I heard a car pull into the driveway. Had to be Junior. I ran to the door, preparing to fling it open and yell, "Surprise!"

My hand was resting on the doorknob when I heard muffled voices. Men's voices. I snatched my hand away, unsure where to go, what to do. I stood frozen in place and listened to the approaching footsteps. I pinched myself to make sure I wasn't caught up in my awful dream.

A heavy fist banged against the door. Since I wasn't dreaming, and my feet weren't stuck to the floor, I went to the front window and parted the drapes a fraction of an inch. Revelle and another guy—probably Baxter—stood on the front porch. My mouth went dry. I tried to fight the panic I knew would keep me from thinking straight. Had I locked the door when I came in? I couldn't remember! No time to waste. I crossed to north wall and ducked behind the drapes, my heart thudding painfully in my chest.

Filled with dread, I waited to see what Revelle and his buddy would do next. I heard the door knob turn, the squeak of a floorboard. Oh my God, I hadn't locked it!

"Hello," Revelle said. "Anybody home?"

He waited a beat and muttered, "We're in luck, Baxter. Nobody here."

I peeked through the tiny opening where the drapes didn't meet and saw Revelle step into the living room, his gaze sweeping the room. Baxter had a shaved head, a thick body and darting black eyes. His big-knuckled hands were curled into fists.

When Baxter spotted the crucifix, he gasped and jumped back. Revelle whirled around at the sound. His body tensed and his right arm shot out, palm forward, toward the crucifix. He turned his head to the side. His lips curled away from his teeth, his mouth opened, and he hissed, a reptilian sound that made my skin crawl. Baxter, his eyes rolling in fear, did the same. They held the pose for maybe thirty seconds then lowered their arms and turned their backs on the crucifix, which meant they were facing *my* wall. I didn't dare twitch, much less breathe.

Baxter's face was ashen, his forehead beaded in sweat. He swiped the back of his arm across his forehead and drew a shaky breath.

"I'm not up for this, man," he told Revelle. "That thing's huge, and this house is tiny. We need to get out of here."

"Suck it up, Baxter," Revelle snarled. "In and out fast. The kid said Allie hasn't been wearing the moonstone. She's real tight with Junior, so he could have it stashed here."

The kid? What kid? I must have missed something.

"Check the bedrooms," Revelle said. "I'll take the kitchen."

Baxter grumbled but walked toward the back of the house. When Revelle left the room, I took a couple of deep breaths and tried to make sense of what I'd seen. I was dealing with Trimarks. No doubt about it. The crucifix was a huge threat. Baxter was obviously scared out of his mind. Could it be his power wasn't as strong as Revelle's?

And what was the deal with the palm? Had the mark of the inverted triangle somehow deflected the danger? An involuntary shiver swept through my body as I recalled bared teeth and the hideous hissing sound. I tried to remember my monster lore. Did vampires hiss? Werewolves? My frazzled brain had no answers.

Then another thought occurred to me. What would happen if I stuck *my* hand out and flashed my star? I felt a little silly, but poked my hand through the drapes anyway, palm facing the crucifix. Of course, I didn't hiss or turn my head away. That would be stupid. Nothing happened. In a way, I was relieved.

I heard the sound of breaking glass in the kitchen. My head turned toward the sound. Revelle muttered a curse. When my gaze swung back to the crucifix, the hair on my arms stood up and I gasped in shock. The crucifix had changed. The roughened edges of the cross were burnished with gold. It glowed with a soft light that seemed to emanate from deep within.

And, oh yeah, Jesus' eyes were opened, *and he was looking right at me.*

I must have made a sound, because Revelle stopped banging around. I could feel him listening. I dropped my arm and ducked back behind the drapes. Through the crack, I saw Revelle and Baxter come into the room.

Baxter said, "What's up?"

Revelle held up a hand for silence and gazed around the room, his eyes darting around the room. He took a step toward my hiding place. Then another. Paralyzed with fear, I watched him approach, my heart stuttering in my chest. Could kids my age have a heart attack? I considered making a run for it, but he was too close. Too close!

Without thinking, I raised my hand behind the draperies, palm forward. My only rational thought was *oh, please, no, oh, please, no.* The words played over and over in my mind, like a mantra. I held my breath as Revelle hesitated then stopped. Suddenly the crucifix flew from the wall, crashed off the TV and landed, Jesus side up, on the floor.

With a shout of fear, Baxter ran from the house. Revelle whirled, extended a palm toward the crucifix and began edging toward the door, his gaze averted, his teeth bared in a grimace. When he slipped out and closed the door behind him, I collapsed in a boneless heap.

Chapter Twenty Two

I heard Revelle's car back out of the driveway and spray gravel as it tore away from Junior's house.

My mind screamed, "Move, dummy. What if they come back?"

I tried to obey, but my legs were like two limp noodles. Maybe fettuccine noodles. I remembered Cory's Fettuccine Alfredo remark and fought off a fit of hysterical laughter. Compared to Revelle and Baxter, Cory seemed as harmless as a teddy bear. With the sound of Revelle's car receding in the distance, the strength returned to my legs, and I struggled to my feet.

Warily, I approached the crucifix. What if Jesus was still staring at me? Should I thank him? I hadn't spent much time in church, so I didn't know the protocol. I needn't have worried. Jesus' eyes were closed. With a sigh of relief, I lifted the heavy wooden cross and, teetering under its weight, slid its looped hanger over the thick nail protruding from the wall.

I checked the rest of the house for damage. Chunks of broken glass littered the kitchen floor. I cleaned it up and checked the bedrooms. After tucking Mama Martinez's undies back in the drawer, I scribbled a quick note to Junior and stepped out onto the porch. The sun was slipping behind the foothills, its slanting rays bouncing off the roof of a passing car. Dark, scudding clouds gathered to the north. A storm was blowing in, and it would soon be dark.

With adrenalin still pumping through my system, I jogged down Willow Lane to the intersection and turned north toward home. I'd lay low tonight and try to catch Junior tomorrow.

Peacock Flats Road was not designed for pedestrians. With each oncoming car, I had to leap over a drainage ditch to avoid being road kill. Adding to my anxiety was my worry over Revelle. Back in the house, he seemed to sense my presence. Maybe Trimarks could smell fear. The crucifix would keep him away from Junior's house, but he might come looking for me.

I trotted down the road past orchards, hay fields and lush pastures. A wizened old guy in bib overalls stood on a flat bed wagon hitched to a green John Deere tractor, tossing hay to his cows. He leaned on his pitchfork and watched me jog by. I waved, and he touched a finger to his straw hat.

As the distance grew between Junior's house and yours truly, my body responded by falling into an easy, rhythmic lope. My mind, no longer faced with eminent danger, relaxed, and I tried to make sense of what I'd seen and heard. I didn't dwell on the crucifix scene. It had no logical explanation, so why spend time agonizing over it? One thing I *had* learned from the experience: a crucifix strikes terror into the heart of a Trimark.

I was still puzzled over Revelle's comment about "the kid," as in, "The kid said Allie hasn't been wearing the moonstone." Clearly, he wasn't referring to Junior, since Revelle called him by name in the very next breath. Other than Kizzy and Faye, I'd told nobody else about the moonstone. Of course, that meant nothing in light of what I'd been told last night.

"The Trimarks know about the moonstone. They want it. It's possible they know you have it."

I stopped suddenly and thought about the ramifications. Surely Trimarks did not pop into the world fully grown, any more than Star Seekers did. If I was a Star Seeker, there could be teenage Trimarks hanging around John J. Peacock High School. But who? Cory Philpott? No way. The message said Trimarks could be charming or vulnerable, anything to win a person's trust. Cory was just plain obnoxious. I'd known Manny and Mercedes all my life and they were no more Trimarks than Blaster the bull. Matt? Possibly, although his charm was wearing thin.

The gathering darkness nipped at my heels. The wind rising from the north tried to blow me back to Willow Lane. I broke into an all-out run, hoping to get home before pitch dark and/or the storm moved in. When I heard the sound of a tractor coming up behind me, I glanced over my shoulder and spotted the old guy who'd been feeding his cows. He pulled up beside me, and we chugged along together at the same pace for a while.

Finally, he said, "Hold on there, girlie," and hit the brakes. I stopped and put my hands on my knees to catch my breath.

He spat a stream of tobacco juice and scowled at me. "The name's Willard. You're gonna get yourself killed out here in the dark. Where ya headed?"

I assessed the situation. The flat bed wagon behind the tractor was now empty. And since Willard looked about two hundred years old, I figured he wouldn't try any funny stuff. Most of all, I was too just too tired to take another step. "Sir, do you know where Sid and Sandra McNeil live?"

He cackled, then adjusted his upper plate, displaced by his burst of hilarity. "Course I do. Climb on the wagon, girlie. I'm slow but steady. Nothin' runs like a Deere!"

He cackled again

Truthfully, I could have jogged home faster, but "slow and steady" was a whole lot safer than running down a country road in the dark on a Saturday night. I was grateful for the ride. Willard stopped in front of Uncle Sid's house and gave me another lecture, something about "young girls out after dark." If he only knew that was the least of my worries.

I thanked him and trudged down the driveway toward the darkened trailer. The truck was in its usual spot. I opened the door and switched on a light. No sign of Faye . . . or Roy.

I looked around for a note. Faye always left a note. Not this time. I figured she was still mad about the way I acted in front of Roy. Maybe they'd gone out for dinner and a movie. I tried to be happy for her. She'd been out of the dating loop for a long time. I fixed another peanut butter sandwich and curled up on the couch, too exhausted to think about the strangeness of the day.

At two in the morning, a hard rain pelted the metal roof of the trailer, the sound weaving seamlessly into my dream. I was marching down Peacock Flats Road, beating a drum and leading a parade of John Deere tractors when a Hispanic woman burst from the crowd of onlookers, shot me in the face with a squirt gun and screeched, "Bad girl! Always chasing my Junior!"

The blast of cold water running down my face turned out to be rain blowing in through an open window, not a squirt gun attack by Senora Martinez. I closed the window and dried my face with a dishtowel. Still groggy with sleep I wondered if Faye had come in and decided not to wake me. She hadn't. I pulled the shade to one side part and looked outside. Nothing had changed.

Okay, I was now officially worried. Never, in the entire fifteen years of our bizarre mother-daughter relationship, had Faye left me alone at night. Never. Ever. She has strong feelings on the subject and never fails to express them, especially when I'm bummed about something.

"Allie," she'd say. "I may not be the best mother in the world, but you're stuck with me, and I'm sticking to you like Elmer's Glue. That's how it is. That's how it will always be. So, get over yourself."

Wide awake now, I listened to the sounds of the night, imagining danger in every variation. Why had the frogs stopped croaking? I'd always felt safe in our snug, little home. Cramped and inconvenient, but safe. I glanced at the door and its flimsy lock, the windows I'd climbed through more than once when Faye misplaced her key. Might just as well put out a sign saying, "Come and get me. Don't bother to knock."

I went to Faye's bedroom, sat on her bed and tried to fight the panic rising within me like an oncoming wave.

Deep breaths, Allie. Relax and breath deeply, so you can think, make a plan.

As my heart rate slowed, my brain began to function again. If Faye wasn't home by morning, I'd talk to Uncle Sid. Check and see if he saw Faye leave and with whom. If he had no answers, I'd use Trujillos' phone and call Cory's dad. Though I didn't want to think about it, maybe she'd been in an accident.

I crawled under the covers and buried my face in Faye's pillow. It smelled like the baby shampoo she used on her blond, flyaway hair. My throat ached with the effort of holding back tears, so I quit fighting and let them flow. Never had I felt so helpless and alone. My life had spun out of control since the day Kizzy placed the moonstone around my neck. I was traveling down a twisted trail without a map, a journey with no destination.

I rolled onto my back and held my hand up to the light. I caught a tear on the tip of my index finger and touched it to the star on my palm. Why, of all the people in the world, had the fates chosen me? Why was I the one with the Gift, a gift I didn't want?

I was just a kid and, right now, all I wanted was my
mother.

*

At exactly seven a.m., I woke up, face down, on Faye's
soggy pillow, still dressed in yesterday's clothes. I splashed
cold water on my face and changed into jeans and a tee
shirt. The wind had picked up where the rain left off. I
opened the blinds and watched a tumbleweed bounce down
the driveway and come to rest against the pickup.

Uncle Sid was an early riser. I'd probably find him in
the barn or leaning against the fence, talking to Blaster. I
grabbed a sweatshirt and opened the door. A gust of wind
caught the door and pulled me forward. I held tight,
teetering on one foot, reaching for the step with the other.
I looked down and stopped mid-stride. A plastic sandwich
bag weighted down by a rock had been placed on the
cement block step.

Puzzled, I hopped over the step and closed the door.
When I moved the rock and saw what was in the bag, the
air whooshed out of my lungs. Faye's locket . . . the locket
she removed only to take a shower . . . the locket holding
my baby picture. With shaking hands, I opened the baggie
and pulled out a piece of paper, folded in half. My name
wasn't on it, but I knew it was for me.

I read, "Go to the phone booth at Tom's Corner Market.
Wait for a call. Tell no one. We'll know if you do."

An inverted triangle was scrawled at the bottom of
the note.

Still clutching the locket, I ran into the trailer to get
the pick-up keys. They were gone. Frantic to get to the
phone booth, I flew out the trailer and started down the
driveway. That's when I spotted Tiffany's Barbie bike
leaning against Uncle Sid's house. Although it was made

for a ten-year-old, it would surely be faster than running. With any luck, I'd have it back before it was missed.

I hit the road, pedaling furiously against a stiff wind. The seat was too low and my legs were too long. I must have looked like a dork, hunched over the tiny bike, pink streamers flying from the handlebars, knees bobbing up and down like pistons. I didn't care. I needed to get to Tom's Market before something awful happened to my mother.

Twenty minutes later, out of breath and scared out of my wits, I hopped off the bike and pushed it across Tom's asphalt parking lot. I was heading for the phone booth tucked up next to the store when my right calf muscle seized up in a fiery ball of pain. I groaned and leaned over to massage it.

"Hey, Allie, how's it hangin'?"

I knew that voice and stifled a groan. "Call me Diddy" was standing in the door of Tom's Market, clutching his groceries in a cloth, re-usable bag.

"Cool bike," he said, walking toward me.

What kind of idiot would think I owned a pink Barbie bike? Diddy, that's who.

"It's not mine," I snarled.

But Diddy was not deterred. "You got a cramp?" he asked, stepping out of the store.

I muttered a very bad word under my breath and kept rubbing. Diddy blinked rapidly several times and added, "Probably because the bike's too small for you."

Immobilized by the throbbing pain in my leg, I was forced to make conversation. "Your mom lets you shop here? I thought you vegans only bought organic stuff."

Diddy blushed and held up the bag. "We needed rice."

I straightened up and gingerly tested my right leg. Yes! I was cramp-free and soon to be Diddy-free.

"Gotta go, Diddy. See you around."

I limped over to the phone booth. I stepped inside and watched Diddy meander across the parking lot. He turned, gave me a goofy smile and dug a cell phone out of his pocket. Probably calling his mother because he was too lazy to walk home. .

The inside of the phone booth was filthy, littered with empty beer bottles, fast food cartons and unopened packets of condiments. It stunk of old grease and rancid sweat. I stared at the phone, willing it to ring. Fifteen minutes crawled by. Two people drove up and wanted to use the phone. In anticipation of this happening, I'd opened a packet of catsup and smeared it on the phone.

"Bloody nose," I said, pointing at a red stain next to the dial. "I've got hepatitis B. My mother went to get disinfectant."

Consequently, I was the only one around when the call came through. I lifted the receiver and held it to my ear. "This is Allie."

"Okay, Allie, listen up." Revelle's voice was low and menacing. "You give me the moonstone, and mama gets to go home."

My hand clenched convulsively around the receiver. "Let me talk to Faye."

"Why would I do that?"

"Maybe you killed her and dumped her body somewhere." I almost choked on the words.

"Hold on a minute."

Revelle's voice was muffled like he had a hand over the mouthpiece.

"Hey, Baxter. Allie wants to know if her mother's still alive. Take the tape off her mouth for a sec."

I heard footsteps followed by a brief pause. Then, the scrape of a chair, the sound of a blow and my mother's piercing scream. The receiver slipped from my nerveless fingers and banged against the wall. I was shaking so hard,

I had to use both hands to grasp it.

I heard Revelle laugh." Sounds to me like she's still alive."

The cruel indifference of Revelle's laughter while Faye screamed in pain tapped into the part of myself I'd tried desperately to deny. Last night, I'd been a scared little girl who cried for her mother. That girl was gone. Like a flower bursting into bloom, my heart opened and accepted the gifts I'd been given. At that moment, I became Allie, the strong-minded . . . Allie, who'd proven her mettle three times . . . Allie, the star seeker who would fight Revelle with every ounce of power she possessed.

"Put Faye on the phone or I'm hanging up." A half-baked plan was already forming in my mind.

Revelle sighed. "Oh, please. Do you really think you're calling the shots?'

"Do it and I'll help you find the moonstone."

"Find it? What the hell are you talking about?"

"Put Faye on."

He uttered a muffled curse. The phone banged into something. I heard Faye whimper and the words, "Talk to your daughter."

"Allie?" Faye voice was choked with fear. "Are you there?"

"I'm here," I said. "Stay strong. I'm coming for you."

Chapter Twenty Three

Back on the itty-bitty bike, pedaling fast. This time heading south in bright sunshine with the wind at my back. Having embraced my super-power status, I decided the sun's appearance and the wind blowing me toward Faye were good omens.

Between Tom's Corner Market and our place, a narrow dirt lane veered left off the road and wound through an abandoned orchard. The roadside mailbox was battered, the post leaning at a forty-five degree angle, having been bashed once too often by local guys playing "mailbox baseball." The name "Bradford" was barely visible.

The Bradford place had once been a thriving apple operation, complete with warehouse, pickers' shacks and its own packing plant. But that was years ago, before I was born. As the story goes, Mr. Bradford hung himself in the warehouse and everything fell apart. The rest of the family split the fortune and took off. Cory Philpott insisted the place was haunted, that he and his dad had seen the ghost of old man Bradford wandering through the weed-choked, dying orchard. Not that I believed him.

"No Trespassing" signs were posted along the perimeter of the property. I waited until the road was free of cars—Revelle had insisted—and pushed the bike down the lane, muddy from last night's cloudburst. I was heading for the Bradford warehouse as I'd been instructed to do.

The lane curved to the right behind the orchard then

ran parallel to Peacock Flats Road. The old wooden warehouse was still standing, but barely. Pieces of the roof were missing and the right side of the building was caved in. A loading platform stretched across the front with stairs at both ends. The wide double doors at the front of the building were warped with age and didn't quite meet in the middle. Sitting by the door on a wooden nail keg, was Didier Ellsworth Thompson the Third.

At first, I couldn't wrap my brain around it. Why was Diddy here? Had he heard about the Bradford ghost and wandered down the lane to check it out? If so, I had to get rid of him before he got hurt.

"Diddy!"

I dropped the bike and ran up the stairs. I started to ask, "Why are you here?" but the words died in my throat when I looked into Diddy's eyes. The soft, vulnerable look was gone, replaced by the cold gaze of a predator. The dark pupils seemed to grow larger in his pale eyes as he stood and watched me approach. The gangly limps and endearing clumsiness were gone. His wiry physique, clenched fists and squared shoulders told me all I needed to know.

Diddy was a Trimark.

Maybe I should have been afraid, but all I felt was anger at his betrayal. Diddy was "the kid" Revelle mentioned. Diddy had called Revelle to let him know I was at the phone booth. And, Diddy probably noticed when I stopped wearing the moonstone.

I marched up to him until we were toe to toe. "So you're a tough guy now, huh? Well, big, friggin' deal! I'm not scared of you Didier . . . or Diddy . . . or whatever the hell your name is."

I jabbed a finger into his chest, narrowed my eyes and leaned closer. "Word of advice. Get out while you can. I hear Bradford's ghost hates Trimarks. He loves to burn them alive. Trimarks have no power over ghosts. Did you know that?"

My bogus story had the desired effect. His lip curled in a snarl, but Diddy backed away from me and looked over my head toward the lane leading out to the road. I moved closer. He took another step back. The hunter was now the hunted.

The door creaked open, and Revelle appeared. He rubbed his hands together and smiled. "Ah, the guest of honor has arrived."

Diddy shuffled his feet and glanced at Revelle. "Guess I'll take off, if you don't need me anymore."

Revelle's right eyebrow shot up. "You don't want to stay around for the party?"

Diddy edged around me and headed for the stairs. "That's okay. Catch you later."

Much better odds with Diddy gone. Still two to one, but if things went according to plan, the odds would soon be even. But first, I needed to convince Revelle I was a scared, helpless kid. Lucky for me, he hadn't witnessed my scene with Diddy.

Revelle stood by the door and waved me inside. "After you."

Like an obedient child, I walked by him into the warehouse. It smelled of mouse droppings, dust and decay. Dim light leaked through the cracks in the roof. I stepped around a rickety table filled with bottles of insect spray and rusty paint cans. Apple bins lined the wall to my left, stacked from floor to ceiling. Reinforced with metal at the corners, each heavy, wooden bin was large enough to hold twenty-five boxes of apples.

Next to the bins, toward the back, Baxter perched on an up-turned apple box, his hairy, muscular forearms resting on his knees. I spotted Faye a few feet from Baxter, her pale face and light hair like a beacon in the diminished light.

Revelle grabbed my arm. "Let's go say hello to mommy."

Meek as a lamb, I let him pull me along. I looked down, so he couldn't see my eyes. They would tell a very different story. Then I lifted my head and saw what they'd done to Faye. She was tied to a chair. A purple bruise bloomed high on her cheekbone; her right eye was swollen shut. A strip of duct tape covered her mouth, and tears streamed from her left eye. At Revelle's approach, a shudder ran through her body.

I gritted my teeth to control the rage coursing through my body. Shaking with fury and my need to kick and punch Revelle, I disguised my anger as fear.

"No!" I screamed. My knees buckled and I sobbed.

Revelle jerked me back up.

"Get the chair," he told Baxter.

Baxter disappeared into the shadows.

I gazed up at Revelle through my tears. "Please, Mr. Revelle. Faye doesn't know anything about the moonstone. I'm sure you don't enjoy hurting innocent people."

I heard Baxter chuckle.

Revelle looked down at me, his handsome face twisted in a sneer. "Guess you don't know me very well."

Baxter appeared with a folding chair. "Want me to tie her up?"

Revelle nodded. I glanced at Faye. Her head was down, her shoulders sagged. I needed Faye, if this plan was going to work. But not like this. I needed Faye, the fighter. I knew she was in there somewhere.

With my free hand, I groped around in my pocket and pulled out Faye's locket.

Cowering, I lifted my tear-stained face to Revelle's. "Before you tie me up, can I please give my mother her locket?"

Revelle gave me a cold stare and thought it over.

Finally, he shrugged. "Go for it."

He released my arm. I walked over to Faye, leaned down and put the locket around her neck, prolonging the process by fumbling around with the clasp. It wasn't an act. My hands were still shaking.

As I bent over Faye, I whispered, "Keep acting scared but get ready. We'll be out of here soon. Okay?"

I straightened up, my body between Faye and the two men. She lifted her head and winked her good eye. I gave her a quick thumbs up.

"Tie up the girl. I'll get Mama ready," Revelle told Baxter.

Okay, that comment made my blood run cold. I looked over at Faye. Her face was ashen, but I saw a slight tilt to her chin. She was trying to be strong.

Baxter said, "Did you check the kid's hand? See if she has the star?"

Revelle gave me a dismissive look. "Doesn't matter. She's nothing without the moonstone."

Hah, that's what you think, Mister. After my internal gloat, I flashed my palm at Baxter.

He didn't touch me but his nostrils flared. Whoa! Was that a sign of fear in a Trimark? Apparently not, because he gave me a nasty grin and held up his palm.

"You showed me yours, so I'll show you mine."

His palm was huge. The lines were dark and deeply etched, encircling puffy, deep red mounds. I looked for the inverted triangle and found it at the base of his little finger. Poorly formed with jagged, broken lines, the two sides failed to meet at the apex of the point. Clearly, Baxter was not high up in the Trimark chain of command.

He closed his hand and pointed at the chair. "Sit."

"Hands front or back?" he asked Revelle, who was bent over Faye. I heard her whimper and barely resisted the urge to kick Baxter in the family jewels.

"Front's fine," Revelle said. "She's not going anywhere."

"She's got the star," Baxter said.

"But not the moonstone," Revelle said.

He turned, his body still blocking Faye. "You ever see a mama horse with a colt?"

"Huh?' Baxter said, tying my hands together in front of my body.

"The colt won't leave its mama, not for anything. When it's weaned, it has to be put in a separate pasture, but it still runs up to the fence and cries for her."

"So?"

Revelle smirked at me. "So, Allie here, is like that baby horse. As long as we've got Mama, she'll stick like glue."

I'm sticking to you like Elmer's Glue. Faye's words echoed through my mind. I'd heard them all my life. Revelle was right. I wouldn't leave my mother.

Baxter finished my hands then started on my feet. I studied his sun-speckled shaved head and thick neck. Strong as an ox but dumber than dirt. Revelle, on the other hand, was no fool. If my plan worked, one of them would be my adversary. Brains or brawn?

Baxter finished tying my feet then lumbered over and stood behind Faye's chair.

Revelle stepped away from Faye. I looked at what he had done and nearly screamed in horror. Her right hand was duct taped to a small table, fingers splayed apart and immobilized. Her other arm was bound to her body.

Revelle grinned at me and held up a small tube. "Super glue. Great stuff."

But what held my attention was the razor-sharp hatchet lying on the table next to her hand. My mouth went dry. I tried to speak but no words came out. Faye turned her face away.

Revelle said, "Here's the rules. I ask the questions. If I don't like your answer, Faye loses a finger. Got it?"

Unable to speak, I nodded. Revelle stroked his chin thoughtfully then crossed the six feet that separated my chair from Faye's. He leaned over me, close enough to feel his breath which, strangely, felt ice cold. I shuddered, thinking of rattle snakes.

"You said you'd help me find the moonstone. Does that mean you don't have it?"

I nodded.

Revelle glanced over at Baxter. He grinned and picked up the hatchet. My heart stopped beating.

"Be careful, Allie," Revelle said. "Does that mean 'yes,' you don't have it or 'yes,' you know where it is, or 'yes,' you don't know where it is, but you'll help me find it?"

I struggled against the ropes and wailed, "You're confusing me. Make him put the hatchet down, and I'll tell you everything you want to know."

Revelle gestured to Baxter, who reluctantly set the hatchet down.

The whole story poured out. Kizzy giving me the moonstone, Junior's involvement, the fake Carmel, the taped conversation. I spoke the truth until we got to the last part. I had no idea where Junior had stashed the moonstone. But I knew how badly Revelle wanted it. I had to make him believe me.

"It's at Kizzy's house," I blurted.

Revelle stared at me. I hoped Trimarks couldn't read minds. When I couldn't stand the silence any longer, I said, "You're the ones who beat her up. Right?"

Revelle nodded. "But she'd already given the moonstone to you. I was going to finish her off that day in the hospital but then you walked in, with the moonstone around your neck."

"She might still wake up," I said.

"We'll be long gone by then, because you're going to tell me exactly where to find it in Kizzy's house."

"Yeah, well, it's not exactly in her house."

Revelle's face turned ugly. "Stop jerking me around, Allie."

Baxter picked up the hatchet.

"Okay, okay," I cringed back in my chair. "I'm not jerking you around. You're making me nervous."

"Last chance," Revelle said. "Tell me exactly where to look."

Revelle was right. I'd been jerking him around, trying to think of a worthy, fictional hiding place. A time-consuming, fictional hiding place.

"It's in Kizzy's back yard. In a little glass jar buried under the birdbath."

Revelle's lip curled in disgust. "How deep?"

"About a foot down, and, oh yeah, there're four birdbaths."

Revelle grabbed my pony tail and yanked. "Which one?"

"Ow! Ow! Let go, and I'll tell you."

"Which one?" he said through clenched teeth.

"I . . . I think it's the second one. I didn't bury it. Junior did."

"Want me to pick him up?" Baxter asked.

I knew Junior could take care of himself. His criminal past had given him a built-in early warning system when it came to danger. A man as dumb as Baxter didn't stand a chance.

Revelle shook his head. "I'll check it out first."

He stared down at me. His eyes were cold and pitiless. "If I don't find it, Baxter gets a call on his cell phone, and Mama loses a finger. Maybe even two. Got it?"

My stomach clenched in fear, but I nodded.

Before he left, I asked, "The story about Magda stealing from your grandfather . . . was any of it true?"

He chuckled. "There's no question Magda used the moonstone to siphon money. The bit about Revelle

Investments and my dear old grandfather was a fabrication."

"Was your real grandfather a Trimark?"

He sneered. "Such a nosy little girl! I suppose you want a look at my hand."

When I didn't answer, he held out his palm. I saw it. A fully formed inverted triangle at the intersection of the fate line and head line.

"You know what that mark means, little girl?"

I bit my tongue.

"It means you can't win, little girl."

He spun around and headed for the door. I held my breath until I heard the sound of a car driving away. Revelle, of course, would not find the moonstone. But he'd also made a serious miscalculation. He assumed I had no power without the moonstone. I was about to prove him wrong.

I tried to figure out a time line. Revelle had to drive to Kizzy's house. Five minutes on a good day. On a Sunday, factoring in church traffic, maybe ten. I hoped he would dig under all four bird baths before he made the call to Baxter. But maybe not. The clock was ticking.

Chapter Twenty Four

I slumped in my chair and watched Baxter from beneath half-closed eyes. He licked his finger and ran it down the length of the hatchet blade, like he was dying to cut something . . . probably one of us. His black eyes darted over to me, then back to Faye. I could almost see the wheels turning in his head. *No chopping in the immediate future. Might as well squat and drop it.*

He set the hatchet on the table next to Faye's glued-down fingers and retreated to his apple box. It squeaked under his weight as he plopped down and flipped open his cell phone, no doubt waiting for a call that would lead to fun stuff with the hatchet.

Faye lifted her head and looked at me with her good eye. I gave a slight nod, the unspoken signal for "Get ready!"

I marshaled my strength and looked over at the apple bins stacked behind Baxter. Could I do it? A myriad of doubts nibbled away at my mind like ravenous mice attacking a piece of cheese. What if nothing happened? What if I lost control and unleashed a swirling vortex of death and destruction. What if . . .

No! I had no choice. The only other option was to watch my mother lose her fingers, one by one, and possibly bleed to death. Then they would start on me.

To clear my mind, I imagined a broom sweeping my dark thoughts into a dustpan which, in turn, poured them into a metal box. I visualized a rocket strapped to the metal box and . . . Lift off! The box flew deep into outer space and disintegrated into a million pieces.

Almost immediately, I felt a strong current of power flow into me like liquid mercury. I could see and feel the silvery liquid pour into the core of my being and spread to all parts of my body. My arms. My legs. The quiver I felt clear down to my bones had nothing to do with fear and everything to do with the knowledge that I was Allie, the maid who was strong of mind. Allie, who could summon and control the power needed to set us free.

I focused my newly harnessed energy on the stack of apple bins directly behind Baxter, thinking, *Now! Now!* In response, the bins jiggled briefly then exploded outward as if flung by a giant hand. With a shout of alarm, Baxter jumped up. His cell phone skittered across the floor. Before he could scramble to safety, an avalanche of apple bins buried him alive. One part of my mind heard his cries for help, the other part watched in horror as one last bin careened off the others and sailed through the air toward Faye.

"No!" I screamed. "No, stop!"

The heavy wooden bin hovered in the air a scant few inches from Faye's head then crashed to the floor, coming to rest against her chair. I gulped air and offered a brief prayer of thanks. I tried to cover all the deities so I included God, Jesus, the Virgin Mary, Allah and Buddha. I even threw in Zeus, Minerva and Odin.

Baxter had fallen silent. The only visible body part was an arm. It extended out from under the pile of bins in a puddle of blood, palm up, as if pleading for help.

I looked over at Faye, pleased to see a bit of color return to her face.

"Okay, that was step one. How did you like it?"

She nodded once then tilted her head toward the errant bin.

"Oh yeah," I said. "Little slip-up there. Sorry about that."

Faye was trying to tell me something. It sounded like, "Ope, ope."

"Rope?"

She nodded.

"I'm working it out."

The hatchet was the obvious choice. But trying to move it with telekinetic power was too risky. No room for error. I could end up slicing more than rope. And that wasn't the only problem. My head was pounding like a jungle drum. Was I running out of juice like a flashlight left on too long?

Faye's arms and legs were tied to the chair. Mine were not, although a single strand of rope secured my body to the chair. If I could just get to the hatchet . . .

I stretched my bound legs out as far as they would go, dug my heels in and pulled. The chair scraped forward a few inches.

"Yes!" I shouted.

I looked up at Faye. She nodded her head, urging me on.

"Hang on! I'll be there soon."

The six feet separating us looked as vast as an ocean. Unlucky for me, this particular ocean was made of wooden planks with cracks between them. As I scooted forward, the front legs of my chair got stuck in a crack. My heart sank. I couldn't slide forward. I'd have to rock back and forth and hope I wouldn't tip over. If I did, I'd be as helpless as a turtle on its back.

Beads of sweat popped out on my forehead and dripped off the end of my nose as I shifted my weight back and forth, trying to free the chair legs. At one point, I pushed back too hard and teetered precariously on the back legs, almost tumbling over backward. Faye made a frightened sound deep in her throat. As the chair started forward, I lunged with all my strength, almost crying with relief when the front legs landed ahead of the crack.

I began inching forward again, picking up speed after I figured out how to hop the front legs of the chair over the cracks. The back legs weren't a problem since I could shift my weight forward and pull them free.

I had no idea how much time had elapsed. Five minutes? Twenty? Desperate to get to Faye, I scrunched, scraped, rocked and hopped my chair to the table where the hatchet was lying on the table.

Shaking with fatigue and sick to my stomach from the relentless pain hammering the back of my skull, I reached out with my bound arms, grasped the handle of the hatchet and wedged it between my knees, blade up. I rubbed the rope binding my wrists against the razor sharp blade. In a few seconds, I was free.

Using the hatchet, I cut the rope binding my feet then reached over to Faye.

"Sorry, this is going to hurt."

I ripped the duct tape from her mouth. After a yelp of pain, she said, "Hurry! Cut me loose so we can get out of this place."

I cut through the ropes and removed the duct tape binding her hand to the table top. Faye tried to jerk her fingers free. They were stuck tight. Her eyes rolled in panic.

"Look for a solvent. A gas can. Anything. Hurry!"

I dropped the hatchet into the bin next to Faye and ran to the table by the door. Frantically, I pawed through the mess on the table. Paint cans and insect spray tumbled to the floor. Nothing! I'd have to try insecticide and hope it wouldn't poison us both. I leaned over to pick up a spray bottle and spotted a square metal can lying on its side under the table. I pounced on it.

"Paint stripper!" I cried.

I ran to Faye, averting my eyes from the bloody arm

sticking out from under the pile of bins. I tried to twist off the cap. Corroded and rusty, it wouldn't budge.

"The hatchet," Faye gasped. "Chop it open. Hurry!"

I retrieved the hatchet, punctured the can and poured the spurting liquid on Faye's hand. A split second later, three things happened simultaneously. An anguished howl rose from beneath the bins, a hand like a steel trap closed around my ankle and Baxter's cell phone rang.

No! This couldn't be happening! Faye, glued to a table. Me, held prisoner by a man who was supposed to be dead. Revelle, calling Baxter's cell phone, furious because he couldn't find the moonstone.

"Oh my God," Faye screamed, desperately trying to loosen her fingers. "Do that thing with your mind, like you did with the apple bins. Make him let go."

It should have been a piece of cake. Right? Concentrate on Baxter's hand. Make it relax and loosen its grip. I'd pull free and off we'd go, away from this hellhole with cracks in the floor, pools of blood and sharp implements.

Lack of motivation was not the problem. I tried with everything I had, grunting with effort. *Turn me loose! Now!* Over and over. It didn't work. My strength was gone, my power sapped. I kicked and stomped the brutal hand holding me fast, to no avail. I was growing weaker by the moment. My head pounded and starbursts fired in my field of vision as blackness closed in.

Baxter's phone had stopped ringing, which meant Revelle was on his way back to kill us. Faye was our only chance of survival.

"Faye," I called weakly. "I can't do it. It's up to you."

Faye lifted her gaze to mine, her eyes fierce with determination. I willed what little strength I had left to my mother.

"You have to get your hand loose. You can do it. Keep looking in my eyes."

"No pain, no gain," she said with a shaky grin.

She braced her left hand against the table top and jerked free with a yelp of pain.

"Get Baxter's phone!" I said. "Call 911. Then call Junior. Tell him to bring the moonstone."

I rattled off Junior's number. Faye spoke into the phone and tucked it into her pocket.

"Bring me the hatchet."

The thought of what I had to do next made me nauseous.

Faye ran to me, the hatchet clutched in her hand. Her face was pale but she took a deep, shuddering breath and said, "I'll do it."

"No!" I grabbed the hatchet and screamed, "You need to go! Now! Not down the driveway, through the orchard. Go left when you hit the road. Revelle will be coming from the other direction. Flag down a car."

I paused, breathing hard.

Faye's eyes brimmed with tears. "I'm not leaving you."

"It's okay, I'll be right behind you. Now, go!"

"Not without you!"

I tried to think of the worst thing I could say to her.

"If you don't leave right now, I'll call Cynthia and what's-her-name at Child Services and tell them I want to live with Grandpa Claude."

Even though my statement made no sense in our present situation, it had the emotional impact I hoped for.

Faye's eyes widened in shock then narrowed into slits. "You wouldn't dare!"

"Oh, yeah? Wanna wait around and find out?"

After one last furious glare, she turned and took off like she had afterburners hooked to her fanny.

I sank down to the floor, a feeling of peace stealing over me. Faye was safe. She might even bring help. Somehow, it didn't matter. Whatever happened next was meant to be.

I was tired. So tired.

Just grab the hatchet, Allie. Raise it high and bring it down on Baxter's wrist and you'll be free.

I wrapped my fingers around the handle and tried to lift it. My arm shook under its weight and the hatchet slipped from my hand. I knew Revelle was on his way. How much time did I have? Five minutes? Ten? A wave of dizziness swept over me, and time stood still.

My senses returned when I heard a shuddering gasp coming from beneath the bins. Baxter's grip loosened. I pulled free, staggered toward the open door and collided with a violently angry Chris Revelle. Stark terror swept away my lethargy, and I backpedaled quickly. He was on me in a flash.

Revelle grabbed my left arm and screamed, "Lying bitch!" followed by a bunch of names I hoped I'd never hear again. His right arm whipped across my face in a vicious backhand. My head snapped back and I tasted blood. He doubled up his fist and drew it back. Sobbing, I lifted my right arm in an effort to deflect the blow.

"Revelle!"

He tightened his grip on my arm and he turned toward the voice. I peered around Revelle. Junior stood in the open doorway, backlit by the sun. His body was outlined in a halo of light, his dark hair sparked with gold. In my entire life, I'd never seen anything more beautiful than Junior at that moment.

"I've got the moonstone, Revelle." Junior's voice was clear and strong. "Let her go and it's yours."

Revelle let me go alright. With strength far greater than a mortal man, he picked me up and threw me toward the jumble of apple bins. A piercing scream ripped from my throat as I sailed through the air.

I landed on my left side on an upturned bin. My head

whipped back and bounced off a sharp corner, and I slid down to the floor. Agonizing pain slashed through my body, and my world turned dark around the edges.

I gritted my teeth against the pain, even though I wanted to give in to the darkness and the blessed oblivion it offered. Instead, I focused on Junior standing in the doorway, one hand outstretched, holding the moonstone. Sirens wailed in the distance. Faye peeked around the corner of the door. Revelle grabbed the moonstone and ran.

Chapter Twenty Five

I must have blacked out for a moment. When I came to, I was cradled in Junior's arms, his tears wet on my face. I tried to breathe, but with each inhalation, a knife-like pain ripped through my body. Soft lips brushed across my cheek.

"You're gonna be fine, Emerson," he murmured. "Just fine. You know why? 'Cause Junior said so."

Faye's worried face swam into view. Her voice sounded like it was coming from the bottom of a well. "I love you, baby."

She brushed a strand of hair from my cheek. One of her fingers was bleeding.

"Did it hurt . . . when you pull your hand loose?" I croaked.

"I'm fine. The paint stripper did the trick."

I had something important to say. "I didn't mean it," I gasped. "The part about living with Grandpa Claude."

Faye bent over me. Her tears, soft as a warm summer rain, fell on my face, mingling with Junior's. "I know, baby. I know."

I tried to lift my head, but it hurt too much.

The rest of that awful day is a jumble of memories. The sound of sirens. Footsteps scraping across the wooden floor. Gentle hands probing my body. A flashlight shining in my eyes. A deep male voice saying, "Hey there, cutie. How about a ride in your very own limo?"

I felt the prick of a needle and was borne away, blissfully pain-free, my face bathed in the tears of love.

*

It took three days before my head worked properly. Strangely, faces are the only thing I remember from those lost days. Faye . . . pale and haggard, black eye turning purple. Junior . . . angry eyes and set jaw. Deputy Philpott . . . lips moving, no sound. An assortment of doctors and nurses.

The third day—actually it was the middle of the night— I opened my eyes and looked up into the face of A. Haugen, boss nurse, mistress of the bedpans, the giver of orders.

"Hi, A. Haugen. Why are you here? Are my feet dirty?"

She looked down at me and sighed. "Alice, not A. In case you've forgotten, I work here."

She raised the head of the bed and stood over me while I drank two full glasses of water.

I handed her the empty glass and took stock of my body. My left arm was in a cast. An IV was attached to my right arm. My ribs were taped, and I had a severe pain in my butt.

Nurse Haugen recited my injuries. "Moderate to severe concussion . . . that's why you're still in the hospital. Broken left wrist. Three broken ribs and a cracked coccyx . . . that's your tailbone. Other than that, you're good as new."

She winked to let me know she'd made a little joke.

I smiled my appreciation, shifted slightly and felt my cracked whats-it scream in protest. In days to come, this injury would give new meaning to the term "butt crack."

Nurse Haugen helped me to the bathroom, fed me broth and tucked me back in bed.

"Sleep," she ordered. "Your mother will be here in the morning."

As she marched to the door, I remembered.

"Hey, boss nurse. I thought you worked days."

"I do." She didn't bother to turn around. "Had a hunch you might wake up tonight."

Faye arrived with a big smile and a balloon bouquet. Nurse Haugen had called Uncle Sid, asked for Faye and told her, "Allie's awake and, judging from her smart mouth, on the road to recovery."

My mind slowly connected the dots. Uncle Sid . . . Aunt Sandra . . . Matt . . . Tiffany.

"Tiffany's bike! I couldn't find the keys to the truck."

"It's fine, Allie," Faye said. "Sid drove over to . . . " She paused and shuddered. "He got the bike." Faye pulled a chair up next to my bed and held my hand. "You need to know what Junior and I told the police."

She pulled a newspaper clipping from her purse. The headlines read, "Heroic Teen Saves Mother."

"Oh, please," I muttered.

I read through the article twice and looked at Faye in disbelief. The details were sketchy and totally wrong. "Mistaken identity? That's what you came up with?"

"People wouldn't understand about the moonstone."

Faye's abductors, according to the article, believed she was the wife of a wealthy fruit grower who would pay big bucks to get her back. The article went on to say, "Emerson's fifteen-year-old daughter, Alfrieda, at great risk to herself, went to the abandoned warehouse where her mother was being held. The quick-witted teen sent one of the men on a bogus search for the ransom money. In his absence, a wall of apple bins collapsed, killing the second man. The fortuitous accident enabled the teen and her mother to escape. The other alleged kidnapper evaded apprehension."

No mention of Junior. The article closed with a list of the injuries I'd suffered in a tussle with one of the men.

"Wow," I said. "Talk about creative writing. Fortuitous accident, huh?"

I had some issues about causing a man's death. True, he was bent on maiming and/or killing us, and the purpose of the Star Seekers is to fight evil in the world. But does that mean it's okay to squash a person with flying apple bins? For the umpteenth time, I wished my paranormal powers came with an owner's manual.

Later, I had a parade of visitors. Manny and Mercedes, shy at first, warmed up enough to share the latest gossip. Apparently Diddy and his mother had vanished. Big surprise. Mrs. Burke stopped by with homework, a new vocabulary list and this week's multicultural lesson. Like I really needed to know how to say, "Delighted to meet you," in Ukrainian.

Before she left, she whispered, "I'm so glad Carmel wasn't involved in her mother's attack. You'll keep our little secret about the new will . . . right?"

After she left, I tried to wrap my mind around the big picture. One piece of the puzzle was missing. Junior and the moonstone. Overcome by exhaustion and questions without answers, I closed my eyes, just for a minute.

Three hours later, I woke to find Junior sitting by my bed. He cupped my face in his hands and brushed his lips across mine. He smelled of french fries. My stomach growled. Some things never change.

I raised the bed and fired questions at him.

"Where were you Saturday?"

"Did you know Revelle and Baxter were in your house?"

"How did you know where to find me?"

"Whoa, Emerson. Slow down. Saturday, I was with the guy making the fake moonstone. I got your note late that night and yeah, I knew somebody had tossed the place. I figured it was those two."

I told him I was there, in his house, hiding behind the

drapes, and how Revelle and Baxter got scared off by the crucifix falling off the wall.

"Say what?" Fascinated, I watched an array of emotions play across Junior's face. Surprise. Disbelief. Wonder. "Tell me again about the crucifix," he said.

"It terrified Revelle and Baxter. They held up their palms and turned their faces away, like they were trying to put up a protective shield. That's what gave me the idea."

Junior's gaze was intense. "What idea?"

"While Revelle and Baxter were looking for the moonstone, I stuck my hand through the crack in the drapes and raised my palm toward the crucifix."

Junior leaned forward. "And . . . ?"

"Jesus opened his eyes."

Junior crossed himself and muttered, "*Madre de Dios.*"

"The second time I did it . . . "

"What do you mean, the second time?"

"Revelle was coming for me."

I shivered, remembering the terror I'd felt as Revelle approached my hiding place. "I knew I couldn't get away. I raised my hand again, and the crucifix fell off the wall. Revelle and Baxter couldn't get out of there fast enough."

Junior looked at me and smiled, like he wanted to tell me something but was waiting for the right moment. I waited, but he simply took my hand, turned it over and traced the star with one finger. I felt a little tingle. Guess I was going to live after all.

I hated to spoil the sweet moment we were sharing, but I had to know.

"Remember the morning in Kizzy's house when you wouldn't let me see your palm?"

Junior ducked his head in embarrassment. "Yeah."

"For a while, I thought maybe you were one of them . . . you know, a Trimark."

Junior released my hand and turned his palm up. His

wrist was covered with a bandage.

"Didn't want you to see my tattoo from when I was runnin' with the *Sureños*. Just had it sanded off."

He held his palm out for me to see. "Check it out, Emerson. No triangle."

I smiled. "You're right. No triangle."

"Any more questions?"

"Yes," I said. "How did you get to the Bradford place so fast?"

"I went to your trailer and found the note. I was on the way to the phone booth when your mother called."

I was quiet for a moment. "So you gave Revelle the moonstone."

"Correction," Junior said. "I gave Revelle the fake moonstone."

He pulled the real moonstone out of his pocket and held it by the silver chain. It swung back and forth, a shimmer of light on its opalescent surface.

I gasped in surprise then laughed out loud, my first laugh in a long time. It hurt my ribs, but it was worth it.

Junior fastened the chain around my neck, took my hand and wrapped my fingers around the moonstone.

"Back where it belongs." His voice was husky with emotion.

I smiled and ran my thumb over its satiny surface. "Do you think Revelle will be back?"

"I doubt it. Too many people looking for him. Besides, he thinks he has the real thing."

"And he's trying to figure out how it works," I finished.

He nodded. "I better go before that mean nurse throws me out."

"One more question. Where was the moonstone hidden all this time?"

Junior looked at me and smiled, his eyes dancing with delight, as if he had a wonderful secret to share. He crossed himself again, leaned close and whispered, "In the crucifix."

My mouth fell open. He kissed my cheek and left. Later, as daylight crept away and the first stars appeared, I was left with one more question. Saturday, in Junior's house, the crucifix had kept me from harm. Was it Jesus or the moonstone? Or both?

*

The next day, I had a visit from the FBI. That's right! Alfrieda Carlotta Emerson working with the Federal Bureau of Investigation. Actually, I didn't help them at all. The man, Special Agent Tom Jenkins, was fish-belly white, had a bad comb-over and looked like he should be driving a hearse.

He asked questions like, "Young lady, is it possible your mother had social discourse with one or more of the alleged kidnappers?"

I didn't like the way he said "social discourse." Not that I knew what it meant.

"No, never!" I replied hotly. "No discourse at all. She doesn't have discourse with strangers."

He kept asking stupid questions until Nurse Haugen came in, took a look at my face and ordered him out of the room.

The other agent, a woman, didn't say a word until Jenkins left. Haugen glared at her and said, "Two minutes. That's it!"

Her name was Ruth Wheeler. She had soft blue eyes and shoulder-length brown hair. Her voice was soothing. "You've had a rough time, Allie. When you feel better, maybe we can talk."

She set her business card on my bedside table. What she did next left me speechless.

Special Agent Wheeler lifted her hand and held it so I could see her palm. I inhaled sharply and nodded. The star was fully formed and visible in the exact center of her palm. Ruth Wheeler was a Star Seeker.

She took my hand and touched her palm to mine. "You're not alone."

When she walked to the door, she turned and smiled. "We've been waiting for you, Allie."

I touched a finger to the star on my palm, wondering what the future would bring. Unbidden, the words written beneath the astrological chart in Mike Purdy's office appeared in my mind, a beacon of light in a murky sea of confusion.

You must have chaos within you to give birth to a dancing star.

Later, Nurse Haugen pulled some strings and moved me into Kizzy's room. Kizzy had come out of her coma. The light was back in her eyes, but she had no recollection of her attack or attackers.

"Perfect roommates," Haugen said, snapping the curtain open between our beds. "She's trying to remember, and you're trying to forget."

Kizzy and I talked for a while. When she drifted off to sleep, I reached up to turn off the light. The phone rang. Tired and cranky, I hoped it wasn't some idiot asking me how it felt to be a hero. I didn't feel much like a hero. I just wanted to sleep.

"Hello," I snapped.

"Allie?"

The man's voice was familiar.

"Yes, this is Allie. Who's this?"

When the man spoke again, his voice sounded strained. "I read about what happened to you."

I waited, trying to put a face with the voice.

After a long silence, he said, "It's just the beginning."

"What's just beginning?"

I heard him breathe into the phone.

"I'm hanging up now," I said.

"Don't hang up. We need to talk. It's Mike Purdy . . . your father."

I caught my breath. A jillion thoughts raced through my mind. Hadn't I been waiting for this moment all my life? So many things I wanted to say. Maybe it was because I was tired. Maybe it was because I was in pain.

Maybe it was because I didn't know what else to say. So I said, "Yeah, I know."

"Allie. You have every right to be mad. I've been an ass."

"Yes," I agreed.

"I saw the star on your palm that day at the store."

I waited a beat before asking, "Did you send me the cell phone?"

"Yes, you needed to know the big picture."

What was I feeling? Anger. Resentment. Joy. Regret. Confusion. I was drowning in a sea of emotion. I needed time to sort it out. Unfortunately, my mouth wasn't willing to wait.

"I just turned fifteen." My voice was choked with tears. "Where have *you* been?"

"I know, I know," he said. "But this thing with the moonstone. It's too big. We have to put the past behind us."

"Easy for you to say."

"What do you want me to do?"

I thought about Faye. How pride had kept her from asking for help.

"Nothing," I said. "We're doing fine."

He sighed. "Just don't shut the door. I'll call you again. Okay?"

I hung up the phone, my righteous indignation quickly turning to regret. He'd been man enough to pick up the phone and apologize. He'd acknowledged my anger and offered help.

Don't shut the door, he'd said.

But I'd slammed it in his face. Mike Purdy wasn't the only ass.

Decision time, Allie. You can be bitter and spiteful like Faye or you can get to know your father.

All right. So tomorrow, I'd call him back.

I pulled the covers up to my chin and looked out the window. The new moon was barely visible in the night sky, an iridescent sliver of light in a field of scattered stars. When I was little, I thought the moon magically changed shape, growing bigger until it was perfectly round, then becoming smaller until it vanished completely. I remembered Faye telling me, "No, Allie. It's always there. We just can't see what's hidden in the dark of the moon."

Like the neophyte moon, I'd stepped from the shadow to begin my journey. I felt like a tiny speck of light dancing across the vastness of earth. Because of the prophecy, my light shone brighter than before, but my future was hidden in the dark of the moon.

I didn't know what tomorrow would bring, but of one thing I was sure:

My name was Alfrieda Carlotta Emerson *Purdy*.

And I was a Star Seeker.

The keeper of the light.

Acknowledgements

Hugs to Deborah S. and Debra D. for your encouragement, kind words and gentle guidance. Thank you for dragging me into the twenty-first century.

About The Author

When she's not vacuuming up enough dog hair to create a whole new dog, Marilee is either reading and completely oblivious to the world around her, or staring at her computer screen, waiting for inspiration to strike. (She calls it writing.) Every now and then, she can be found upside-down. Praying she won't pop a vein in the process, she believes the inverted position increases blood flow to the brain. Sometimes, it just makes her dizzy.

Marilee and her husband, Merl, live in Central Washington State also known as "The Fruit Bowl of the Nation." Unofficial motto: "We never met a fruit we didn't like."

Having survived teaching high school students and raising three sons, Marilee is now working on the next book in the Unbidden Magic series.

Visit her at www.marileebrothers.com

She's just your ordinary, part-demon, teenaged vampire
hunter with a Texas drawl.
And a pet hellhound named Fang.

Bite Me

A Demon Underground Novel
by Parker Blue

Bell Bridge Books
October 2008

Valentine Shapiro got a raw deal in the parent lottery.
Her father was part incubus demon, and her mother's never
quite accepted Val's part-demon nature. Life after high
school is tough enough without having to go fifteen rounds
with your inner succubus. Thrown out of the house by her
mother, Val puts one foot in front of the other and does
the only thing that seems to make any sense—she helps
police battle the local vampires. Those fangbangers are
causing some serious trouble! And, as Val likes to say, "A
stake a day keeps the demon at bay." (But don't call her
Buffy. That makes Lola, her demon, very cranky.)

Soon enough Val finds herself deep in the underbelly
of San Antonio, discovering the secrets of the Demon
Underground and fighting to save those she loves. Whether
they love her back or not.

Great, huh? It gets better. She's the proud new owner
of Fang, a hellhound.

Bite Me

Excerpt

The vampire jumped me again, but this time I was ready for him. We fought furiously, Jason determined to sink his teeth into my neck and rip my throat out, and me just as determined to stop him. Unfortunately, he liked close-in fighting, and I couldn't get enough space to reach the stake I had tucked into my back waistband.

I grabbed his throat and squeezed, but he wrapped me in a vise hold and wouldn't let go. He slammed me up against a brick wall, intent on crushing me. *Trapped.* Worse, the power I tried so hard to keep confined was able to reach him through my energy field in these close quarters and I could feel the lust rise within him as he ground his hips against mine. Pervert.

Though I was able to hold off his slavering overbite and incredibly bad breath with one hand, my other hand was caught between our bodies. He couldn't get to my neck, but I couldn't get to my stake either.

Stalemate.

Time to play dirty. Remembering even vampires had a sensitive side, I kneed him in the crotch.

He screeched and let go of me to bend over and clutch the offended part of his anatomy. That took care of the lust. I hit him with an uppercut so hard that he flew backward, landing flat on his back on the sidewalk. Whipping the stake from its hiding place, I dropped down beside him and stabbed him through the heart in one well-practiced motion.

His body arched for a moment, then he sagged and lay motionless—really and truly dead.

Now that my prey had been vanquished and the demon lust sated, the fizzing in my blood slowed and stopped, leaving me feeling some of the aches and pains I'd inflicted on my body. It was worth it, though.

But adrenaline pumped once more when I heard a car door open down the street. The light was dimmer here between streetlights, but I was still visible—and so was the body I crouched over. "Who's there?" I demanded.

"It . . . it's me."

Damn it, I recognized that voice. Annoyed, I rose to glare at my younger half sister. "Jennifer, what the hell are you doing here?"

She got out of the back seat of the beat-up Camry, white-faced. "I told you I wanted to come along."

"And I told you not to."

She shrugged, displaying defiance and indifference as only a sixteen-year-old could. "That's why I hid in the back of the car."

Stupid. I should have checked. I usually drove my motorcycle—a totally sweet Honda Valkyrie—but on nights when I went hunting, my stepfather let me borrow the old beat-up car since it had a convenient trunk. Unfortunately, it was too easy for my little sister to creep into the back seat and stow away there. Obviously.

And I should have known Jen would try something like this. I'd made the mistake of telling her about my little excursions, even giving her some training on how to defend herself in case she ever encountered one of the undead. She'd been eager to learn everything she could, but Mom had gone off the deep end when she found out, especially when Jen had come home sporting a few bruises.

Mom had forbidden Jen to talk about it again and had

threatened me with bodily harm if I even mentioned vampires around my little sis. Lord knew what Mom would do if she found out about this.

Jen stared down at the dead vamp and grimaced. "I've just never actually seen one of them before."

"A dead vampire?"

"Any kind of vampire."

Was that censure in her voice? "That's what he was," I said defensively. Mom was right—Jen was far too young and innocent for my world. I had to find a way to keep her away from all this. "I don't stake innocents."

"I know. I saw."

"Dammit, Jen, you shouldn't have come. If's dangerous." And if one hair on her pretty little head had been harmed, Mom would have *my* head on a platter.

"Yeah, well, we can't all be big, strong vampire slayers," she said. She tried to make it sound sarcastic, but it came out sounding more wistful than anything.

I sighed, recognizing jealousy when I saw it. I knew Jen envied my abilities—my *specialness*—with all the longing of a teenager who wanted to be something extraordinary herself. Of course, it was the demon inside me that gave me advantages she didn't have. All of my senses were enhanced far beyond normal, including strength, speed, agility, rapid healing, and the ability to read vamps' minds when they tried to control me. Unfortunately, my little sister had no clue as to the price I paid for those advantages.

And she also had no idea how much I envied *her*. Fully human, with All-American blond good looks and plenty of friends, she had everything I had always wanted and could never have—true normalcy, not just the appearance of it. With my Jewish/Catholic, demon/human background and the melting pot that went into my heritage, I felt like a mongrel next to a show dog. My lucky half sister had managed to avoid the bulk of my confusing heritage since we shared only a mother.

But I couldn't say any of that—she wouldn't believe it. "Help me get the body in the trunk," I said tersely.

I usually had to do this part by myself, but why not take advantage of Jen's presence? Besides, participating in the whole dirty business might turn her off for good. I unlocked the trunk and opened it.

She hesitated. "I thought—"

When she broke off, I said, "You thought what? That he'd turn into a neat little pile of dust?"

She shrugged. "Yeah, I guess."

"I wish it were that easy." I took pity on her. "And he'll be dust soon enough—when sunlight hits him. Come dawn, I'll make sure his ass is ash."

Jen grimaced, but I wasn't going to let her off that easily. It was her decision to tag along—she'd have to pay the price. I grabbed the vampire's feet. "Get his head."

She stared down at Jason's fangs and the small amount of blood around the stake in his heart and turned a little green. "Can't you just leave him in the alley?"

I could, but then Jen wouldn't learn her lesson.

Well, damn, I sounded like Mom now. Annoyed at myself, I snapped, "We can't just leave him here for someone to trip over. What's the matter? Too much for you?"

She shrugged, trying to act nonchalant. "No, I just thought Dad might not like it if you got blood in his trunk."

"He's used to it." Besides, the blood would disintegrate along with the rest of the body when sunlight hit it.Jen gulped, but I have to give her credit—she didn't wimp out on me. I'd expected her to blow chunks at the least, but she picked up his shoulders and we wrestled the body into the trunk.

Jen wiped her hands on her jeans and stared uneasily at the casket. "Is he really dead?"

"Mostly," I said, then grinned to myself when Jen took a step back. There was still the remote possibility Jason could heal if the stake was removed from his heart. But for that to happen, his friends would have to rescue him before dawn, tend him carefully for months and feed him lots of blood. Not likely.

I shrugged. "But the morning sun will take care of that." I closed the trunk.

Just as I locked it, the headlights from a car blinded me and a red light from its dashboard strobed the street.

"It's a cop," Jen said in panic.

Not good. But it didn't have to be bad, either. "Relax. Let me handle this."

The plainclothes policeman exited the unmarked car. "Evening, ladies," he said, obviously trying to sound friendly, though he came across as wary and suspicious.

"Evening," I responded.

Though he tried to appear like a guileless rookie, I wasn't fooled. He might only be in his mid-twenties, but he had the watchful alertness of a pro. He hooked the thumb of his right hand in his belt, making it easy to draw a weapon from that bulge under his left arm.

As he came closer, I could make out his features. He was about six feet tall with short brown hair, a straight commanding nose, and a solid bod. Totally hot. I might even be interested if he were a little younger and lost the suspicious attitude.

The demon inside me agreed, wondering what it would be like to enthrall him, get him all hot and bothered, feed on all that lovely sexual energy. That was the problem with being part succubus lust demon—ever since I started noticing boys, the demon part of me had been lying in wait, urging me to get up close and personal, wanting to compel their adoration, suck up all their sexual energy.

I'd given in once, and the poor kid barely survived.

But not this time. Not again. I beat back the urges, which was pretty easy since I'd just satisfied the lust by taking out the vamp.

"What are you doing here?" he asked.

"I'm sorry, Officer . . . ?"

"Sullivan. Detective Sullivan." He flashed his badge at me.

I smiled, trying to look sheepish. "My little sister snuck out of the house to meet her boyfriend, and I was just trying to get her back home before Mom finds out."

"In this part of town?"

"Yeah, well, she doesn't have the best of judgment. That's why she had to sneak out."

Jen gave me a dirty look, but was just smart enough to keep her mouth shut.

He didn't look convinced. "Got any ID?"

"Sure—in the car." I gestured toward the front of the vehicle to ask permission and he nodded. Shifting position so he could watch both of us, he asked Jen for her ID, too.

I retrieved my backpack and handed my driver's license to the detective along with my registration. He glanced at them. "Your last names are different."

"Yeah—we're half sisters. Same mother, different father. We have the same address, see?"

He nodded and took both IDs back to the car to speak to someone on the radio.

"Ohmigod," Jen said in a hoarse whisper. "What if he finds out there's a body in the trunk? We'll go to jail. Mom and Dad will be so pissed."

"Just relax. Everything should come up clean, so there's no reason for him to even look."

Sullivan finished talking on the radio then handed our IDs back.

"Can we go now?" I asked with a smile. "I'd like to get Jen home before Mom finds out she's gone."

"Sure," he said with an answering smile. "Just as soon as you tell me what's in the trunk.".

Oh, shit.

"Nothing," Jen said hastily, the word ending in a squeak as she backed against the trunk and spread her arms as if to protect it. "Just, you know, junk and stuff. Nothing bad."

Oh, great. Like that didn't sound guilty.

Still casual, he asked, "Would you mind opening it for me?"

Yes, I did. Very much. Swiftly, I mentally ran through the options. I couldn't take him out—I didn't hurt innocents. Besides, he'd just called in our names so they'd know we were the last to see him. Taking off wasn't an option, either—he knew who we were and where we lived.

Demon lust fizzed in my blood, the succubus part of me that allowed me to enthrall men, bend them to my will and make them willing slaves. *You could take control of him, force him to let you go,* a small voice whispered inside me.

Heaven help me, for a moment, I was tempted. But I couldn't do that. I couldn't take advantage of humans like that. I'd promised the parents—and myself—that I'd never do it again.

My only choice was to do as he asked and hope he'd give me time to explain. Crap. This was so not going the way I planned.

Gently, I moved Jen aside, unlocked the trunk, and braced for the worst.

He lifted the lid and stared down inside. He didn't even flinch. Good grief, was the man made of stone? Expressionless, he asked, "Vampire?"

This was so surreal. I relaxed a little, hoping I might even be able to come out of this without getting into major trouble. "Uh, yeah. The bloody fangs are a dead giveaway."

He gave me a look. The kind that said I wasn't out of trouble yet and he didn't appreciate smart-ass comments.

"Why did you stake him?"

Why? He was staring down at the dead undead and he wanted to know *why*?

Jen blurted out, "Because he was drinking some guy's blood." She shifted nervously. "I saw it all."

The cop nodded. "So did I."

I gaped at him. "You did?"

"Yeah, I was just calling for backup when you waltzed up and tapped him on the shoulder."

Crap—I'd been so self-involved I hadn't even noticed the unmarked car. Note to self: *pay attention!*

Lightning Source UK Ltd.
Milton Keynes UK
25 November 2010

163472UK00001B/20/P